NOT PART OF THE PLAN

by Clare Lydon

First Edition November 2025
Published by Custard Books
Copyright © 2025 Clare Lydon
ISBN: 978-1-918129-04-5

Cover Design: Sharn Hutton
Editor: Cheyenne Blue
Typesetting: Adrian McLaughlin

Find out more: www.clarelydon.co.uk
Buy direct: clarelydon.shop

Also By Clare Lydon

Other Novels
A Taste Of Love
Before You Say I Do
Change Of Heart
Christmas In Mistletoe
Don't Marry Me At Christmas
Hotshot
It Started With A Kiss
Just Kiss Her
Nothing To Lose: A Lesbian Romance
Once Upon A Princess
One Golden Summer
The Christmas Catch
The Long Weekend
The Princess Match
Twice In A Lifetime
You're My Kind

London Romance Series
London Calling (Book One)
This London Love (Book Two)
A Girl Called London (Book Three)
The London Of Us (Book Four)
London, Actually (Book Five)
Made In London (Book Six)
Hot London Nights (Book Seven)
Big London Dreams (Book Eight)
London Ever After (Book Nine)

All I Want Series
Two novels and four novellas chart the course
of one relationship over two years.

Get great bundle deals and other offers when you
buy direct at clarelydon.shop!

Acknowledgements

The inspiration for this book struck a couple of years ago when I was reading an article about a real-life family and their luxury goods business. Their youngest son was the most successful in the family, yet he'd initially fought against it. I knew there was a germ of a story in there somewhere, so I let it bubble away for a couple of years. That real-life son morphed into family rebel Poppy Voss, and I knew she had to be paired with her nemesis to get the job done. Enter Eliza Carpenter. I wasn't sure where to set the book, but then the Highlands came back into view, as it always does. The fictional hamlet of Goldloch was born, and the rest is herstory.

My deepest gratitude goes to my brilliant bunch of early readers, whose sharp eyes caught a bunch of inconsistencies, typos, and missing words. I rely on these fabulous readers for initial feedback, and their encouragement means everything: I couldn't ask for better champions. That a few pointed to the cream scene as one of their favourites? I hope you love it, too.

As always, I'm indebted to the professionals who polished this book to perfection: Cheyenne for her brilliant editing, Sharn for creating such a cracking cover with my very brief initial notes, and Adrian for his impeccable typesetting. Publishing truly takes a village, and my village always comes through.

All my love to my beautiful wife, Yvonne, who read an early version of this book poolside in Greece. She loved it, which always makes me happy, and she's a tough crowd!

Finally, thank you, dear reader. In these challenging political and economic times, I'm grateful for every purchase and every message. This is my 28th novel, which is still a number that boggles my mind. I hope you enjoy the story of Poppy and Eliza. Next up, it's back to football!

If you fancy getting in touch, you can do so using one of the methods below. I'm most active on Instagram.

Contact: mail@clarelydon.co.uk
Facebook: www.facebook.com/clare.lydon
Instagram: @clarefic
TikTok: @clarelydonauthor
Find out more at: www.clarelydon.co.uk

Thank you so much for reading!

This one is for my siblings.
All seven of them.

Prologue

19 Years Ago

Ipumped my legs harder, and the swing soared higher. Above me the rope creaked, the same sound it had made every summer for as long as I could remember. I glanced up at the fraying strands. If it snapped now, what a way to go. It'd definitely make the local paper.

I had no idea what time it was, but that was the beauty of Highland summers. Daylight stretched endlessly, bedtime became a distant concept, and Mum transformed from her usual stressed London self into someone who actually laughed at my jokes. She was happy here. It made me wonder why we bothered going back to London.

Especially when Eliza travelled up with us, too.

She crouched by the water's edge, searching for the perfect stone. Her long legs had got even longer this summer, and she'd developed this habit of tucking her hair behind her ear when she was concentrating that made my stomach do weird flippy things.

"Right," she said, straightening up. "This is definitely the one that's going to beat your record."

"Good luck with that." I was the reigning stone-skimming

champion, a title I'd held all summer. They should engrave my name on one of the bigger rocks by the lake: Poppy Voss, Undefeated. My older sister Katy had gracefully accepted defeat and was now performing a series of increasingly elaborate cartwheels along the shore, claiming the title of best gymnast instead.

I tried not to think about the fact this was our last night before heading back to London tomorrow. I'd already formulated a plan to convince Mum we should live here permanently. Even every summer would be a start.

She always claimed winters were too brutal, but I quite fancied the idea of snow piling up against the windows and drinking hot chocolate by a roaring fire. When I'd shared this vision with Mum, she'd called me a hopeless romantic. When I told Eliza, she said there was no such thing as being too romantic. I much preferred her answer.

This summer, she'd managed to get a tan too, which was miraculous in Scotland. But we'd had two weeks of sunshine, warm enough to swim in the loch without turning blue. Eliza's tan stretched across her shoulders and down her arms, golden against the white straps of her swimsuit.

"Which type of stone works best again?" She turned to me with a frown, not quite as sure about her stone as she had been moments ago.

"Trade secret." I leapt off the swing with perhaps too much confidence. My ankle twisted on landing, sending a sharp bolt of pain up my leg. I crumpled to the ground with a yelp.

Eliza rushed over, and slipped her arm around my waist to help me up.

I got all lightheaded as heat coursed through me.

"You okay?"

"Perfectly fine," I lied, trying not to wince as I hobbled towards the shoreline. "Though you might need to give me a piggyback home."

"Only if you tell me which stone gives me the best chance of winning."

She looked away from the water. I followed her line of sight to the smoke curling from the chimney of Loch Cottage. Nestled in what looked like an enchanted garden, it was hands down the best house on the water.

"I wonder who actually lives there," Eliza mused. "We always see smoke and lights, but never any people. It's like they're invisible."

"Maybe they're ghosts," I suggested. "Or they've got some kind of magical cloaking device. If they're ghosts, they'll never die, which means they'll never move, and we'll never get to live there." We'd fantasised about living there all summer long.

I couldn't think of anything better in the whole wide world.

Eliza shook her head. "Even ghosts have to move to retirement homes eventually. That's when we'll swoop in." Her eyes lit up with the vision. "Imagine it, Pops. We could drink ice-cold Cokes in the garden, and run straight from the loch to an outdoor shower. Pure genius."

I grinned, following the way she craned her neck to peer at the cottage windows, the elegant line of her throat catching the evening light. At 14, Eliza had started developing curves that made it increasingly difficult to concentrate on stone skimming. Four years felt like a lifetime between us. She was starting Year 10 next month, while I was about to go into Year 6. I was desperate for her to see me as something other than just a kid.

"Should we make a pact to buy the cottage when we're older?" I tried to sound casual. "When we're the ones making decisions instead of having everything decided for us?"

Eliza's face brightened. "Yes! We could start a business selling cold drinks and your gran's scones to tourists. Make a fortune."

"I could set up a Voss Watch stand in the garden, too."

We high-fived just as Katy cartwheeled over. "What did I miss?"

"We're buying Loch Cottage and moving here permanently," Eliza announced.

Katy laughed. "Right. That'll only take about 20 years if you save every penny of pocket money. But hey, good to have goals."

She wasn't wrong. However, as I took in Eliza staring dreamily at our future cottage, I decided 20 years might be worth the wait.

Chapter One

Present Day

The restaurant hummed around me with the polite chaos of the lunch rush, but I barely noticed the clatter of cutlery or the punchy waft of garlic from the neighbouring tables. I stabbed my fork into my chicken salad with unnecessary force, sending a cherry tomato rolling across the white tablecloth.

"He actually said that?" Katy leaned forward, her eyes wide with sisterly indignation. "That your proposal was 'cute'?"

"Cute." My jaw tightened. "Like I'm a four-year-old showing him my finger painting instead of a marketing strategy that could triple our user base." Honestly, my boss could go fuck himself.

"You need to get out of there." Katy reached for her water glass, her wedding ring catching the light. "Which brings me to my brilliant idea."

"No."

"You haven't even heard it yet."

"If it involves Aunt Margot and Voss Watches, then no." I put down my fork. The dull scrape of cutlery against porcelain grated on my nerves. "We've been through this." And we had. A million times. My answer was always the same.

Katy's expression took on that particular brand of impatience she'd perfected since having her twins. "Pops, she needs help. The company needs help. And you need a job where you're actually appreciated."

"I love my job. Today was just a hiccup."

"You do not love your job, you love the work. You love coming up with ideas and problem-solving. There's a difference." Katy tucked a strand of chestnut hair behind her ear, the same shade as mine but cut shorter and more practical these days. If I looked closely, I'd still be able to see the indent from the nose ring she got when she was 19.

She had the energy of someone who'd spent the morning negotiating with toddlers over whether socks were mandatory, which meant my career crisis barely registered on her scale of things worth getting worked up about.

"Look, I know you think Margot likes me better because I pop out babies and remember to call on her birthday, but that's bullshit and you know it."

I winced at her bluntness. "She literally sent you a Hermès scarf for Christmas. I got a gift card."

"Because she doesn't know what to buy you! You're like this enigma to her. Brilliant, independent, always keeping your distance." Katy's tone shifted. "You were a little unhinged for a while, but you've dialled that right back. You've worked things out. You're more stable, and she knows that. I also know she's drowning. I had lunch with her last week, and she was really stressed. She never wanted to run the business, and now she's talking about selling."

The words hit me like a bucket of ice water. My knee jiggled under the table. "Selling? To who?"

"I don't know, but likely a conglomerate. They'd gut it, keep the name for prestige, and move production overseas. The brand and quality would be sold down the river." Katy's eyes searched mine. "Everything our grandma built, everything Mum maintained." She snapped her fingers. "Gone. In an instant."

Something caught in my throat. Voss Watches wasn't just a company. It had paid for our education, our childhood home, every opportunity we'd ever had. But it had also demanded everything in return. Late nights, absent parents, a marriage breakdown, and eventually…

"It killed them, Katy." My voice came out smaller than I intended. "Mum was 56. Grandma was 66. I'm nearly 30. If I take this on, it means I only have a few decades left, give or take."

"Gran got cancer. Mum had an aneurysm. I've watched enough *Grey's* to know they happen all the time. It's just a mix of bad luck, bad habits, and no work-life balance." Katy reached across the table, covering my hand with hers.

"You could do it differently. You don't have to live to work. You could work to live. Promote a different culture in the company. Value your employees, like Mum and Gran did. Make money, give it away, be a force for good. Keep Voss in the family for my girls, maybe, if they want it someday. Or any future children you have."

I turned my hand palm-up, squeezing her fingers. The familiar weight of responsibility settled on my shoulders like a coat I'd avoided trying on, knowing it would fit perfectly.

Maybe it was time to stop running.

"Just meet with her," Katy pressed, sensing the crack in

my armour. "Ask about her plans. You don't have to commit to anything."

I pulled my hand back, wrapping both around my coffee cup. It was barely warm anymore. "And say what? 'Hi, Aunt Margot, I know I've spent the last decade avoiding anything to do with my family and Voss Watches, but I hear you're struggling, so I thought I'd swoop in and save the day'?"

"You could try being honest. Tell her you're thinking about a career change. That you're interested in learning more about the business. That you have some solid business experience to bring, as well as your MBA." Katy glanced at her phone as it buzzed on the table. "She'd probably cry with relief."

"That's what I'm afraid of." I managed a weak smile. "I can handle disappointing my boss. But Margot crying…"

"Would be harder because you actually care about her, despite pretending otherwise." Katy's phone buzzed again, more insistently. She frowned at the screen. "Damn. That's the nursery."

"Everything okay?"

"Probably just Lily refusing to nap again. But I should call them back." She paused. "Promise me you'll think about it?"

I nodded, not trusting my voice. The idea of taking over the company terrified me, but the thought of it being sold to strangers made my chest tight with something that felt dangerously like grief.

Katy glanced over my shoulder, then beamed. "Look who's walking up behind you."

I turned, and saw Sage Morrison making her way towards our table. Her flowing skirt swished around her ankles, and the silver jewellery she always wore caught the light, glinting with each step. We'd known each other since university, though her career had taken some left-field turns since our business school days.

"What a nice surprise to get both sisters in one place." Sage greeted us with a warm smile, her voice carrying that calmness that always made people trust her instantly.

Before I could respond, Katy's phone rang, the vibration loud against the table. She glanced at the screen, and grimaced as she answered. "Yes, I'll be there as soon as I can," she promised, her voice clipped. Hanging up, she sighed and stood, then grabbed her bag. "Lily's thrown up on the teaching assistant. I really have to go."

Katy leaned over to kiss my cheek, then reached for Sage's hand, giving it a quick squeeze.

"Sorry I can't stay to chat, but thank you for last week. Same time next month?" She paused, looking between us. "Take care of my sister, please. She's having an existential crisis. You might be just the right person in this moment."

I rolled my eyes, shaking my head. "I'm really not having that," I started to protest, but Katy was already halfway to the door, her brilliant-white trainers squeaking against the black-and-white tiles as she hurried out.

Sage slid gracefully into the chair Katy had vacated, then flagged down a passing waiter to order a coffee. She turned to me, her dark eyes filled with an unsettling mix of curiosity and understanding. "So. An existential crisis?"

"Career crossroads," I corrected, trying to ignore how her presence made the air feel sharp and charged, like the moment before a thunderstorm. "And why is my sister seeing you again next month?" I hadn't realised Sage and Katy even knew each other that well, let alone that they were meeting regularly.

"We ran into each other at a wellness day I was doing." Sage's tone was casual, but there was something deeper in her words. "You've got quite a distinctive surname, and I think we met once or twice when she visited you at uni. We got chatting about my gift, and I mentioned that I was picking up a lot of… activity around her."

"Activity?" I asked, even though I already had an idea where this was going.

"Spirit activity."

Right.

Along with being a healer and a crystal expert, Sage was also a medium. A good one, apparently, if all my friends were to be believed. I didn't necessarily buy into the idea of a chatty afterlife, but if it brought people comfort, who was I to judge? Until, of course, it involved my sister.

"Katy has been seeing you for your medium service?" I kept my tone as neutral as possible.

Sage took a moment before answering. "You should talk to her, but… yes."

There were so many questions I wanted to ask, but I swallowed them down. Sage wouldn't tell me anything before Katy did. I knew the drill.

Instead, I shifted the subject. "Katy thinks I should join the family business."

"Ah." Sage tilted her head. "And you're resistant."

"It's complicated."

"Family always is. Plus, when you were at university, you

never wanted to join the company. I remember that well. ABV you once told me."

I pulled my gaze from her, shame washing over me. Anywhere But Voss: ABV. That had been my mantra at business school when I was feeling particularly aggrieved with Mum. Now I saw it for what it was: childish and petty. But I couldn't take it back.

The waiter returned with Sage's coffee, and she poured milk from a tiny jug, her rings clinking softly against the white porcelain cup. Then, after a brief pause, she added: "Speaking of family…"

My stomach flipped. I'd run into Sage a few years ago at a conference, and during an unplanned chat at the hotel bar, she'd casually mentioned things about my grandfather. Things she couldn't have possibly known. She'd said he was there with us that night. I hadn't known what to make of it.

"I'm getting some pretty insistent visitors around you." Sage's voice dropped to an ultra-calm tone. "Would you be open to hearing from them?"

A shiver ran down my spine, even though it was a bright April London day. I sat up straighter, glancing around. "Here? Now?"

She nodded.

Before I could think better of it, I found myself nodding too. Maybe it was the weight of the conversation with Katy, or maybe it was Sage's voice, soothing and steady. Either way, my usual scepticism decided to take the afternoon off.

"I've got two women with me. I should tell you I can never see faces clearly." Sage's voice shifted, and I shivered again. "One is carrying a blue pen. The other is quite a bit older."

Her words hit me like a jolt of electricity. Montblanc was my mum's favourite pen brand, and it was pretty fancy. Her favourite pen was blue. The other woman had to be my gran.

Every part of my skin prickled. I'd expected to feel uncomfortable or angry, but instead, a strange, unexpected comfort settled over me like a blanket.

"The woman with the pen…" Sage paused, her brow furrowed. "She wants you to know she's sorry. Deeply sorry for not being there. For all the times work came first."

I swallowed hard, and I took a sip of my now-cold coffee to give myself a moment. I was not going to fall apart here.

"She's showing me a program from a play," Sage continued, eyes closed, and tilting her head as though listening to something. "Something to do with Christmas? Maybe a pantomime? Does that make any sense?"

"It does," I replied. "I was the narrator in the school panto when I was 11. Mum was meant to be there, but she got held up in Switzerland meeting suppliers. Dad came, and he brought the program home for her."

When Mum got home after that, they'd had an almighty row, and the next week, Dad left for good, hardly ever to be seen again. He lived in Thailand now with his new family, and kept in touch sporadically. I was amazed that of all the things Mum had in the afterlife, that program had made it. I would have shredded it by now.

Sage nodded slowly. "She sees it all differently now. The choices she made." Her eyes flicked back to me, sharp and clear. "The other woman." She frowned. "I don't know if this means anything, but she's talking about scones?"

I couldn't help the small smile that tugged at my lips. "Gran made the best scones."

"The recipe," Sage said suddenly. "She says it's in the loft in the big photo box. You've been looking for it?"

My coffee cup rattled against the saucer as I set it down too fast. I'd been looking for that recipe just last month, when I'd cleaned out some old boxes. I hadn't told a soul. I knew it more or less, but wanted my gran's exact measurements.

"They want you to know," Sage continued gently, "that whatever you decide about your future, they support you." She hesitated, her head tilting again, as if catching the last whisper of something. "But they're worried about another woman in your family. They're saying you should support each other."

"I can't." I shook my head. "I don't know how to run the company."

"They're showing me someone." Sage frowned. "Someone from your past who could help. A woman with blonde hair. There's something unfinished there."

My mind raced, trying to piece together who they could mean. A woman from my past? I'd been so wrapped up in my startup life, I'd let most of my old connections fade. Blonde hair. It was a vague description. I knew many blonde women. Some of them might never want to talk to me again.

Sage blinked a few times, her shoulders relaxing, as if releasing a weight. "They're stepping back now," she said quietly, "but they want you to know they're proud of you."

A mix of sadness and elation slipped through me.

"Even though I've been avoiding the family legacy like it's contagious?" I tried to make a joke, but my voice cracked.

"Especially because of that," Sage replied, her gaze steady. "It shows you understand its weight."

She wasn't wrong. I'd spent my whole life learning from my grandmother and Mother. I knew the principles of the business, the suppliers, the factories. Whatever I didn't know, I could learn. I'd just never wanted to consider it before.

But maybe now was the time.

Chapter Two

Sleep had been about as elusive as a straight answer from my startup's investors. Now it was the next morning, and I lay in bed, staring at the ceiling, replaying yesterday's lunch on a continuous loop like some sort of supernatural blooper reel. Had Sage Morrison really channelled my dead relatives over bacon-and-chicken salad?

The thing about mediums is they're either complete charlatans or terrifyingly accurate, and Sage had always occupied an uncomfortable middle ground where I couldn't quite dismiss her. Sure, she could have googled some old *Country Life* interview where Gran waxed poetic about her award-winning scones. But she couldn't have known about my pathetic Sunday afternoon tearing through the loft, covered in dust and decades-old spider webs, desperately searching for a recipe.

Unless Mum and Gran really had pulled up a chair at Carluccio's and decided to play afterlife career counsellors.

I kicked off the covers. The thought of all my relatives, living and dead, tag-teaming me into taking over Voss Watches was like being trapped in one of those cute British supernatural comedies Netflix churned out. Except this was my actual life, and there was nothing charming about it.

The love-hate relationship I'd cultivated with Voss Watches

was a masterpiece of emotional complexity. Yes, it had funded my privileged childhood: private school, gap year, the works. But it had also demanded everything from the women in my family until there was nothing left but sought-after timepieces and yet another black suit.

Still.

Margot couldn't sell.

The thought made my head bulge with a hot mix of panic and possessiveness.

Which meant I was royally screwed.

I rolled out of bed and stumbled into the living room. Amina had left the neon sign blazing again: *Queer & Fabulous!* screamed in electric yellow like a beacon for lost sapphics. My flatmate collected vintage furniture and memorabilia the way other people collected stamps, and this particular piece had pride of place above our second-hand red velvet sofa. I bent to switch it off, watching the words fade from proud declaration to grey glass.

The open-plan kitchen beckoned from the far end of the room. I set the coffee brewing – proper coffee, that dripped into one of those cute American diner jugs – then located my phone on our retro G-Plan sideboard. Amina and I could both afford to live solo, but we liked living together. Plus, I enjoyed living with Amina's good taste.

If I was seriously considering this insanity, Aunt Margot was my first port of call. My phone cheerfully informed me it was April 10th, which meant I hadn't spoken to her since her birthday. Two months of radio silence. In my defence, a lifetime of being the family disappointment had given me excellent avoidance skills.

The thing was, Katy got a free pass. Toddler twins and a husband in banking meant nobody expected her to stride in to play Mrs Fix-It. But me? Single, childless, MBA-wielding? I was supposed to be a slam-dunk. Which is precisely why I'd run in the opposite direction.

I scrolled to Margot's number, thumb hovering over the call button like I was about to detonate something. Part of me hoped she'd be at her place in the Cotswolds, where reception was chronic. She picked up on the fifth ring, slightly breathless.

"Poppy." Not a question, just a statement of mild surprise. Like finding a tenner in an old coat pocket.

"I know. I'm sorry I haven't called sooner."

"Why break the habit of a lifetime."

Ouch. Margot's ability to deliver emotional paper cuts disguised as endearments was unmatched. I probably deserved it.

"I had lunch with Katy yesterday."

Silence. Then, muffled voices and what sounded suspiciously like male laughter. At 9:30am on a Saturday morning. As far as I knew, Aunt Margot was single.

Well, well, well.

"Am I interrupting something?" I tried to keep the grin out of my voice. "I can call back—"

"Don't be ridiculous. I've sent him to make coffee." The dismissive tone didn't quite hide something else in her voice. Warmth? Affection?

"Good for you."

"Sex doesn't stop at 50, Poppy. Despite what the youth think."

I snorted. "Bold of you to assume I'm having any sex to stop."

"That's because you spend all your time at that dreadful office instead of—" She caught herself. Even post-coital Margot knew better than to lecture me. "Why are you calling?"

Deep breath. "I wondered if you were free this weekend. Lunch, dinner, coffee? Whatever works. I'd like to talk about stepping in when it comes to Voss."

The pause stretched, took up a Warrior 2 pose, then stretched a little more.

"I see Katy told you my plans."

"She mentioned something about selling to soulless corporate overlords, yes."

Another pause. In the background, I heard the clink of china. Whoever was making coffee knew their way around Margot's Mayfair kitchen.

"The Mermaid in Soho," she said finally. "The one your mother loved. One o'clock today. Don't be late."

"I'll be there."

The coffee pot gurgled its completion. I poured myself a mug and leaned against the counter, already dreading lunch. The Mermaid had been Mum's favourite restaurant, all pristine white tablecloths and art deco styling. The last time we'd eaten there together, she'd tried to convince me to join the company. Then she'd tried one more time on our last trip to Switzerland. That was six months before her fatal aneurysm.

I took a long sip of coffee and wondered if it was too early to add whisky. Probably. Besides, I'd need all my wits about me for Margot.

Plus, I had to wheedle out of her who the hell was making her coffee.

Chapter Three

Margot strutted towards me on heels that would surely prompt a nosebleed if I tried it. She swept into the restaurant looking like a perfectly mixed martini: ice cold and liable to leave you shaken. The maître d' almost genuflected. Smart man.

She was the human equivalent of a Rolls-Royce: immaculate engineering and prohibitively expensive. Her platinum bob was precise, just like her pearl-grey Armani suit. But I knew she wasn't an ice queen. Margot had a sense of humour, and she loved her family.

At 58, she'd rejected more marriage proposals than I probably knew about. Men circled her like moths to a flame, only to discover she was more blowtorch than candle.

Margot pulled out her chair before a server could assist, and slid into it with grace. She was a society woman who didn't play by the rules. No-nonsense, to the point, just like her sister.

If you wanted something done, you called Margot. Just as long as you didn't want those things done quickly. Margot needed her downtime, and she'd always been honest about that. Running Voss was not her happy place. Her place in Paris had probably developed cobwebs in her absence.

"You're early. Colour me impressed." She flashed me a

wink as a waiter appeared, filled our water glasses, and took our orders for champagne. "A little fizz seems appropriate. How often is it I get to lunch with my youngest niece?"

The question was rhetorical.

"You look good. Fresh-faced. Which means you weren't out face down in a puddle of prosecco last night."

I smiled. "In bed by ten."

My aunt rolled her eyes. "You're one extreme to another, Poppy Voss."

Shame rolled in my stomach as I recalled the stress I'd put my family through in my 'unhinged' period of grieving, as Katy had coined it. I'd partied hard and slept with a fair few women, and the only reason I hadn't ended up in a hospital or a ditch was thanks to my best friend Amina who always had my back. Like everyone always told me, grief hit people differently. For me, the initial period involved a lot of gin and forgettable sex.

"You need to find a happy medium."

Sage flashed into my mind, but I was pretty sure that wasn't what Margot meant.

"Like you have, by the sound of our phone call earlier."

If Margot was blushing, I'd never see it under her perfectly applied makeup. She glossed over my comment.

"Life's treating you well?"

My job is a nightmare and I'm painfully single.

"Can't complain."

The champagne arrived and Margot raised her glass. "To a future as yet unwritten."

"How cryptic." If she was going to play it that way, perhaps I needed to get more specific.

"Katy tells me you're thinking of selling the business." I paused, showing her my intent. "I'm here to ask you not to. I'm ready to step up."

A resigned smile, a small shake of her head. "It's a little late, Poppy. Where were you when I really needed help after your mum passed?"

I bit my lip. "Dealing with my grief."

"As was I."

I winced. I wasn't going to be too hard on myself – my therapist would frown on that after such a trauma – but I knew I could have been there more for my family, full stop. I wasn't the only one who lost someone. We all did. But there was no point raking over old ground. Margot and I had already had that conversation.

"I've apologised for that, but I'm here now. I'm ready to do whatever it takes to keep the business in family hands. I don't want you to sell."

Margot sat back, her immaculate hands stroking the white table cloth.

"This from the woman who told me, in no uncertain terms last year, that she'd 'rather shit in my hands and clap than have anything to do with Voss Watches'."

It sounded like something I might say. "People change. Times change. I've done three years in two different startups, and I know how business works. I want to strike out, and it's either do it at Voss, or start my own company doing something else. If you need help, it makes sense."

"I don't just need help. I want out completely."

I blinked. "Oh."

I hadn't expected that.

"Yes, oh," Margot replied. "This was never my dream, and I think you knew that. My life was going along just fine and then my mum died, then my sister, and I had to be there for my grieving nieces while picking up the company and making every single decision on my own.

"I'm tired, and I don't want to run myself into an early grave. I don't want you to do that, either. Selling is a kindness to everyone. It'll set us all up for life, and then you can open whatever business you want. Voss Watches will carry on, but it won't be a millstone around our necks." She took a sip of her bubbles. "I think after dying of stress, even your mother might agree."

She doesn't, she told me herself.

But that wasn't something I wanted to bring up right now. I wanted Margot to take me seriously, not banish me from the business for being kooky.

"I know I haven't been much use up until now, and I can only apologise. I want to be a better niece, as well as a better support to you business-wise."

"I'm selling, Poppy. You don't have a say until you're 30, which is a year away. As the only other family member who does have a legal say, Katy agreed to stand by whatever I decided. She doesn't want to run the business either, and neither do you really. This is a knee-jerk reaction that you'll regret, given time. I'm saving you the bother. Being a good aunt.

"It's getting harder and harder to sell watches. The competition is fiercer than ever. Go into supplements or be an influencer. Young people don't want watches anymore."

"They don't *think* they do, but they do." I was two-thirds certain that was true. "All my friends want to get away from their phones. We all want to carve out more time for us. We want to buy less, but buy better. A Voss watch answers both those needs. We just need to make them more visible." I'd thought of that in the shower this morning. It wasn't a fully formed idea, but it was a germ of *something*. "I can reach the youth market if you give me a shot."

"I have a buyer lined up."

"Who is it?"

Margot looked down, considering the question.

Was it someone I knew? My mind rattled through my contacts list, but it came up blank.

"Remember Max Carpenter?"

Warmth flooded my system, and I immediately rolled my eyes at my traitor of a body. I remembered Max Carpenter well. Mainly because I'd been best friends with his daughter, Eliza. Until she turned 18, and I was only 14. Then, she dropped me like a hot brick when she went to university, and I was far too young and uncool.

"I do." The last time I saw Eliza was two years ago, on a skiing trip in Les Gets. She'd elbowed ahead of me at the bar, and kissed the woman I'd been working up the courage to say hi to. She was not in my good books, hence neither was her dad.

"Max is interested; he confirmed it this morning."

"On a Saturday?" I frowned. Max might be keen, but I was pretty sure he didn't do business at the weekend. I distinctly remember he made his ex-wife a golf widow at weekends. Between that and sleeping with his numerous assistants, his extra-curricular activities were legendary.

Unless Margot was now one of those activities?

The dots joined right before my eyes, and Margot saw it.

"Did he tell you over coffee?"

She didn't deny it.

"It's best all round if he takes it off our hands. Max is skilled at buying companies and selling them off."

"Not what I heard. Max is a friendly, familiar face, but he's a corporate raider. Buys companies cheap, guts them, makes staff redundant, sells off the properties, and drops the quality. I can't do that to our family business. Not while I'm alive."

She leaned forward and shook her head. "You know, even though Voss is successful, it wasn't always easy. I lived through the ups and downs with my mum and yours. Plus, running a business is very different to working at one. And Max has promised to keep Goldloch as it is. I know your reasons are worthy, but is this really what you want to do?"

She was making me doubt myself now. But still, I nodded. "I want to give it a try. If it's not what I want or if it doesn't work out, I'll accept it. But I have to try. Plus, I'm not going to run it how Mum and Gran did. I won't let it consume my life."

I had to try, if only because of yesterday's weirdest lunch in the world.

"Easy words to say." Margot gave me the saddest smile. "But ones I thought you'd say after our phone call. However, I'm not just going to hand the keys over to you. You don't have big business experience, so I want to bring someone in to help. You'll work with them, and listen to what they say. Put your plans into action, see if it's a job you want to do and if you can see any green shoots of new business. Then we'll come back and see where you are.

"Let's see what you can do in three months initially, six months in all, then we'll reassess and see if this is best for Voss and you. I made a promise to myself that I wouldn't let the business consume any of us. It's a promise I intend to keep."

"Who will I be working with?"

"That's again where Max stepped in. We spoke about it this morning. He suggested someone you know, to make it easier. He came up with Eliza."

My mouth dropped open. "Carpenter?"

Margot shot me a look. "Do you know another Eliza associated with Max?"

"You want me to work with Eliza Carpenter?" Our myriad encounters as adults flashed before my eyes. Stunted words, brushed shoulders, terse nods across the room. As if the previous years of Highland summer trips, London Christmases, the occasional birthday or anniversary counted for nothing. There was no way in hell that was happening every day.

"It's a hard no."

"Then I'm selling the company. Katy has the only other vote right now, and she already told me she's happy with whatever I decide. You're 29: until you turn 30, your mother's will stipulates you don't have a say. This is not an offer, Poppy. Work with Eliza, or we sell. Your call."

"But Eliza is…" I couldn't say the words to Margot.

Stubborn. Opinionated. Disloyal.

Also, blonde.

Sage's words came back to me: *Someone from your past. A woman with blonde hair. There's something unfinished there.*

Holy shit. Maybe Sage *was* the real deal.

"A lovely woman who has agreed to help," Margot finished.

Every hair on my body stood up. I blinked, and tried to get my focus back in the room.

"You arranged all this on a Saturday morning?"

"What can I say? The Carpenters are hard workers. Plus, she's living with her dad, so she was there having coffee with us after I got off the phone with you."

Margot had been at his house? And Eliza was living with her dad following her divorce? Interesting. Last I heard, she didn't think much of her dad and his life choices.

"And she agreed? Doesn't she have a job of her own to do?"

"She was…" Margot picked her next word carefully. "Hesitant. But she works for Max and he can spare her for a couple of months, maybe more." She sighed. "The two of you used to be such good friends. You can get on for a few months, can't you? It's that, or you take Andrew. He knows the business inside out, but I suspect you might want to kill him after a week."

Andrew had been with the company forever. He lived and breathed Voss Watches.

She was right, I would murder him.

I bit my lip. "And what if I want to kill Eliza after a week?"

"Hold your impulses. This company has had enough death to last a lifetime. Tomorrow night, I've booked you into that place all the young people love with the lifts on the outside. Drink tequila, work out your differences." She leaned over and stroked my hand. "And if it's all too much, you know the alternative. Just say the word."

That wasn't going to happen.

I didn't want to be haunted for the rest of my life.

Chapter Four

I made sure I was at least 15 minutes late, because I'd be damned if Eliza thought I was waiting around for her. Yes, it was childish, so sue me. I'd told Margot I was an adult, but then she'd dropped Eliza on me. She wasn't playing fair from the start.

I was aware I needed Eliza for the next few months. She'd trained at the hand of her dad. She knew this world. But that was it. Then we could both go back to our lives that had survived just fine without each other in them for the past decade and a half. Fourteen-year-old me would never have guessed I'd lose Eliza for half a lifetime.

My eyes swept the room, but it didn't take long to spot Eliza. Like the rest of the room, I was drawn to her like a magnet, because Eliza was still *that girl*. You know the one. The type that made heads turn in a room. The one you couldn't go into a queer bar with because every woman wanted to talk to her. Even the ones in relationships.

Shoulder-length blonde hair that was always salon-perfect, crystal blue eyes, and a confident strut and posture that put Margot to the test. She'd obviously had the same idea about timing, because she was only just sliding onto a bar stool that overlooked the glittering city through floor-to-ceiling windows. Apparently, my heart had not progressed past adolescence because it chose this exact moment to perform some sort of gymnastics routine in my chest.

Even though Eliza was gorgeous, it had never been like *that* with us. To me, she was the girl I looked up to. The one I built forts with, laughed with, talked about girls with. When we were kids, we'd decided Barbie didn't need Ken, and that both of our dolls could live together. Eliza was my queer role model when there weren't many others around.

Had I ever thought about kissing her? Of course. She was stunning, and I had been a teenager just realising who I was and who I liked. But I never *really* considered Eliza like that because she was a full-grown woman and I was not. She was out of my league.

Plus, I hadn't wanted to fuck up our friendship. Which just went to show what 14-year-old me knew. As soon as Eliza scored her first serious girlfriend and went to university, she'd barely acknowledged my existence. It still hurt.

Her eyes swept the room and landed on me. She gave me a cool once over, but her face didn't move. No smile, no wave. Normal Eliza. I'd no idea what happened to the girl I grew up with. She couldn't be like this with everyone. I'd seen her laugh in other people's company. Just never in mine. For me, she reserved scowls, sneers, eye rolls, so I gave them right back. It had gone on too long to question now. But maybe one of us needed to do so.

I walked over and pulled out the stool beside her. My bum hadn't even hit the tan leather before she spoke.

"I want you to know, this was not my idea. I'm as enthused about this arrangement as I think you are."

It was such a ludicrous first statement, I almost laughed. "Good evening to you, too." I looked her in the eye. "Great to see you again. How have you been?"

Contrition flickered behind her sapphire-blue eyes, but she didn't respond.

"And no, I'm not exactly pumped about it, but we're here. And if I want to save Voss, I have to make it work. If you could save the attitude for another day, I'd appreciate it."

Something passed across Eliza's face: surprise, maybe even approval. She'd expected the old Poppy, the one who would have shrunk back. This version was unexpected.

"Who rattled your cage?"

She was used to being top dog and getting what she wanted. The only hiccup in her life was her parents splitting up, but at least they were both still in her life. Both alive. A divorce was not a death.

"You," I replied.

The server appeared with two cocktail menus, and I buried my head in it, happy for the distraction. I wasn't sure where my initial bravado had come from, but it was fading fast. My heart-rate, which had kicked up at the first confrontation, had settled.

What cocktail was best for when you felt open, vulnerable?

I scanned the list. My go-to was usually gin-based. All the cocktails had ingredients I hadn't heard of. I settled on something called a Pink Paradox. It described my drink, but also my current situation. Eliza ordered a gin and tonic. Maybe we had more in common as adults than I imagined.

"I was trying to work out, on the way over, when was

the last time we saw each other." She paused. "I mean, IRL. Not on socials. That doesn't count."

"You don't post much."

She shrugged. "I don't have much to say." She extended a graceful finger. "Whereas you, for a while, were almost an influencer the amount you posted." She glanced up. "Lately, you've gone quieter."

"Less drunk."

Our drinks arrived. Mine was bright pink with a slice of grapefruit on the side. I sipped. At least it didn't taste pink.

"Tell me, then," I continued. "If you really didn't want to do this, why did you agree?"

"You're a smart woman. I'm sure you can work that one out."

"Something to do with your dad?"

"Bingo," she said. "My latest project has just gone through, and I happened to be there when Margot got off the phone with you and told him. He jumped to this decision before I'd even blinked. Plus, he's sleeping with your aunt, so he wants to do right by her.

"Also, I need to toe the line, because he's making noises about retiring in the next couple of years. He knows I can take over, but I need to show willing to do whatever he wants." She sighed. "Even though I'm not sure I want to take over, but that's a tale for another day." She gazed off into the distance before her eyes settled back on me.

She didn't want the big job? I'd always pegged Eliza as someone who wanted success at all costs. She had a ruthless streak, and didn't stop until she got what she wanted – in work and in love.

However, staring at her sad face, perhaps that wasn't as true as everyone thought. Or maybe she was already worming her way under my skin. I had to toughen up. I wasn't going to surrender to Eliza's charms the moment she offered them. I was older now. Wiser. I no longer needed Eliza's acceptance and validation.

"But you didn't answer my original question. When was the last time we saw each other?"

"Skiing. You snogged Sophie, who I'd been chatting up all weekend."

She held up a hand. "Sophie?" She shook her head. "You dodged a bullet there. You should be thanking me. She was batshit crazy."

I widened my eyes. Eliza really was a gigantic arse. "If I hadn't already cancelled you, that comment would be grounds for it. I'd laid the groundwork all weekend for her."

"Perhaps your game needs work, as I didn't know that. But like I said, she turned into a bit of a stalker. Thank me later." She smiled then, the first genuine one since we met.

It threw me off guard. Eliza's smile was still like the sun. Warm, dazzling, and even though I knew I should look away, I couldn't stop staring. Even after all these years, she still had this effect on me. But I was going to keep it under control.

"And the same weekend you pranged my car. As if I didn't have enough to deal with."

When I stacked up all the cards against her, even I had to admit it was quite the pile.

Eliza sighed. "That was my fault, and I did apologise. My divorce had just been finalised, and my head was all over the place. But I hope my insurance covered it." She snagged my gaze. "I'm sorry again, Pops."

The nickname hit me like a physical blow. Nobody called me Pops outside my family. Nobody apart from Eliza, back then. I could almost see us at 12 and 16, lying on her bedroom floor, planning our futures. Back when she was the most important person in my world.

"It's Poppy."

Eliza's jaw tensed almost imperceptibly. She'd lost the right to intimacy, and we both knew it.

"Of course it is. All grown up." She gave me a measured look. "But like you said, neither of us are jazzed about this. But we're going to get through it, and who knows, there might even be moments when we don't hate each other."

I sipped my drink. I really hoped that was true, because I couldn't put up with months of pure hell.

"This is just a business arrangement with an end date. A transaction that could benefit us both. I get to put Voss on my CV, and you get to prove to your family that you can actually do this. Three months of full-time me, then after that, we can assess what you need."

It sounded simple when she put it like that.

"Or you recommend that I can't do the job, and the company gets sold out from under me."

"Despite what you think, I'm not your enemy."

I really wanted to believe her.

"I want you to succeed in whatever you do. You've had a rough few years and you deserve a win. If you want to take over Voss, I can help. However, I also think selling is a good call."

She stared at me so hard, I squirmed in my seat. If I didn't know better, I'd swear she could see through me.

Maybe once.

Not anymore.

"When I was told you wanted to take over, I was surprised. When you were a kid, you always said you could think of nothing worse than running Voss Watches. That you never wanted to end up like your mum. I remember being up in Scotland one summer, your mum working all the hours, and you swore to me then you would never turn into her."

Her words winded me. Eighteen months on, I thought I'd dealt with my mum's death. But sometimes, when someone from the past who truly knew her spoke about her, it made me realise how much I missed her. That I'd never see her again.

"I stand by 10-year-old me," I told her, my voice steady. "I don't want to run this business like my mum. But I do want to run it. There's a difference."

She looked like she wanted to reach across the table, the way she would have years ago. Instead, her fingers tightened around her gin and tonic.

"If that's what you want, then let me help you. Even though we're not close anymore, I still know what makes you tick."

"You know nothing about my life."

But no matter how much I'd changed over the years, I was still that scared 14-year-old Eliza knew well. Did people change that much from their younger selves? The older I got, the more I thought the answer was no.

Eliza's gaze softened. "I know enough."

Chapter Five

"It's honestly my worst nightmare come true."

London's Victoria Park was showing off this April: tulips blooming in violent pinks along the pathways, a group of young men putting on batting pads for their cricket game, and the morning sun painting the lake with a glittering sheen.

Even at half-past nine, the place hummed with joggers like us, dog walkers with their overexcited charges, and cyclists who clearly thought they owned the tarmac. I dodged a particularly determined golden retriever who seemed convinced I had treats hidden in my running shorts.

Amina flicked her long black hair over her shoulder with the kind of dramatic flair that made her lethal in courtrooms. Even while jogging, she managed to look effortlessly put-together in her matching navy running gear. "Seriously? Your worst nightmare? There's a cost-of-living crisis, climate change, a reality TV star running a country, but this tops your list?"

I scowled at her, then nearly tripped over a tree root that jutted up through the path. I stumbled, but managed to get back on track. A metaphor for life.

"Your aunt could've stuck you with some 50-year-old mansplainer who'd critique your breathing technique. Or someone who eats apples all day and crunches in your ear 24/7.

But Eliza Carpenter – successful business operator by your own admission – and someone you actually know? What a bitch."

"At least with Captain Mansplain, I wouldn't have my teenage humiliations thrown back at me every five minutes."

Amina slowed to an on-the-spot jog beside a cluster of cherry trees that were spilling over with pink blossoms. A gentle breeze sent a few petals spiralling like confetti. "Eliza makes you feel like a failure?"

"She's been showing me up since we were kids."

"You mean you've been letting her live rent-free in your head since then."

The truth in that statement made my toes curl. "You didn't watch her ace everything while I tripped over my own shoelaces. She got too cool for me years ago, and now when we do cross paths, she's still the same. You'd think shared queerness would create some solidarity, but apparently not."

We started off again, and rounded the corner past the ornamental gardens where an elderly man was already setting up his easel to paint the fountain. Morning joggers streamed past us in both directions: some grim-faced and determined, others chatting easily. A woman with a pushchair jogged by, her toddler giggling at something only he could see.

"Maybe you need to buck up, because it's an ultimatum. Prove it or lose it. Plus, maybe Eliza actually wants to help? And perhaps, *just perhaps*, spending time with someone with more experience than you is something you can learn from." Amina raised an eyebrow, her breathing still perfectly controlled despite our pace. "When's the dreaded second meeting?"

"Next week."

"What about your job?"

"I told them to go fuck themselves and walked out."

Amina snorted. "About time."

"There was no time to be polite and work my notice. Margot wants us both up to speed as soon as possible, and acquainted with the main production facility in the Highlands. We're taking the overnight sleeper to Goldloch to meet all the staff properly. The people who make Voss Watches tick. Literally."

"Wait." Amina sidestepped a particularly aggressive cyclist, who rang his bell like he was announcing the apocalypse. "Your watches are made here? I thought your mum was always jetting off to Switzerland, where all luxury watches come from?"

"That's the problem. Everyone assumes we're just another European brand. But we're British: have been since Great-Gran started the company. Mum used to visit Europe to keep tabs on competitors, and some of our parts came from there, but our actual production is in the Highlands. Offices in London, but they're made in Goldloch. Mum always said Scotland was her spiritual home, but she needed to be in London for business."

We'd reached the part of the path that curved around the lake, where ducks paddled importantly between the reeds and a heron stood motionless like a grey statue.

The reality of it all hit me suddenly. This was it, the start of something big. There were no second-chances, this was make or break. I had to do this right for me, Katy, Aunt Margot, and my nieces, Lily and Vivien.

I slowed down and put my hands on my thighs, gasping. Somewhere across the park a dog barked frantically.

Two days. A full 48 hours trapped with Eliza Carpenter. And it *had* to work.

"Maybe you could go instead?" I straightened up, watching Amina stretch her calf against a nearby bench. "Be my corporate stand-in? You're brilliant at arguing, and you could definitely match her word for word. When she starts showing off, you could shut her down properly."

"Or you could realise her cleverness might actually help you. Plus, last I checked, you're pretty smart yourself. If she needs to be brought down a peg or two, bring up something embarrassing from her childhood." She grinned at me, her dark skin glowing with the faintest sheen of sweat.

"That cuts both ways."

Amina smacked my arm and picked up the pace again. We were approaching the home stretch now, where the path wound back towards the main entrance through an avenue of plane trees.

"Use this as time to prove you can handle the job. Think of it as a working interview. If you keep bitching and moaning, she might tell her dad you're not up to the job. It's time to put your game face on and try to get along with her. I know you can do it. Stop treating Eliza like the enemy and start being charming. You need to win her over, remember? Especially after that Sage situation you mentioned. Your mum wants you running this company, and the path to that goal goes straight through Eliza Carpenter."

She flicked her hair out of her eyes with lawyer-like precision.

"You think you can handle that, my little Pop Tart?"

Amina was definitely the only one of my friends who got to call me that.

"I guess we'll find out."

Chapter Six

There was an issue with Eliza's room on the sleeper train. The sort that involved meaningful glances between staff and the kind of customer-service smile that screamed damage control.

"If you'd like to visit the club car, your first drink is complimentary while we resolve this," one attendant chirped, shepherding us away from whatever cock-up they were covering.

At least their crisis management was top-notch.

"Do you still run?" I squeezed through corridors so narrow I had to almost deflate my ribcage to make progress.

Eliza turned, shaking her head. "Injury in my mid-twenties. These days it's yoga and the occasional guilt-driven gym session." She shrugged. "I was only ever fast because Roger was fast. But sibling rivalry makes terrible motivation long-term."

Roger was Eliza's older brother, who'd gone to the Olympics and represented Great Britain in middle-distance running.

"Is he still in the US?"

Eliza nodded. "Married, two kids, coaching at Stanford, seems happy."

"Does he get back much?"

"Not nearly enough for Mum's liking, though she's taken to stalking him via transatlantic visits."

A door swung open ahead of us. Eliza stopped dead, and I promptly walked straight into her back like some sort of human domino.

"Sorry, I—"

But the apology died on my lips as her scent hit me. Clean soap and something indefinably warm that sent my memory careening back to stolen moments in the school library. I'd told myself I was studying, but really I was watching Eliza with her friends across the room, cataloguing the way she laughed at their jokes, how she bit her lip when she concentrated. I'd convinced myself it was admiration, maybe a touch of hero worship.

But standing here now, breathing her in, that same flutter of awareness I'd dismissed as teenage confusion swept through me. Maybe I'd been lying to myself about what those feelings really were.

An elderly couple emerged from their room, mercifully breaking the spell. We followed them to the club car and waited to be seated.

We slid into seats opposite each other, on a table for four. I studied her face in the fading evening light filtering through the windows. I doubt she remembered those library afternoons the way I suddenly did. I doubt she'd even known I was there.

"How are Katy's twins? Mum mentioned they're at nursery now?"

I couldn't help the smile that spread across my face. Our family had experienced its fair share of death in the last few years, but Katy having the twins a few months before Mum died had been a bright spot. Without having to get up for the girls, Katy told me she may have laid in bed for months. They might never know it, but Lily and Vivien helped us all through the fog of grief just by existing. They would always be our miracle, healing babies.

"The twins are incredible. A shit-ton of work that would put you off having kids for life, but you know what Katy's like. She was born responsible, and she and Bryce are doing well as parents. I go over every few weeks so they can go out to the pub and have a meal together.

"I remember my mum telling me you spend the first five years of your child's life trying to stop them injuring themselves. I understand that description now."

"It's nice that you're close, though," Eliza replied. "Roger lives thousands of miles away, so his kids don't know me."

The conversation felt surreal: like picking up a book I'd abandoned mid-chapter years ago, and finding the plot surprisingly familiar. I glanced at Eliza as she read the menu, wondering if the feeling was mutual.

"Wonder who our dinner companions will be," I mused. "Fingers crossed for two humans on the right side of the political divide. Could be awkward otherwise."

Eliza's eyes sparkled with mischief. "If they're properly horrified by lesbians, we could always put on a show. Full sapphic passion before they've even delivered the bread rolls."

She followed up that statement with her trademark laugh: that slow, deliberate sound that seemed to have its own gravitational pull. It was unchanged since we were kids, but now it carried 33 years of knowing the effect it had on people.

The kind of laugh that made nearby conversations pause. I hadn't realised how much I'd missed it.

Our chat was interrupted by a couple who looked to be in their 60s approaching the table with our dining car hostess. She introduced us to Cindy and John, and the couple sat down. They radiated *A Place in the Sun* energy: like they'd both just retired and decided to blow their nest egg on a two-bed flat in Mallorca. I hoped it didn't have a leaky roof. Cindy wore a floral-print shirt, while John was a walking monument to the power of beige.

"How thrilling!" Cindy declared before introductions were fully complete. "We never take trains, but sleeping on one feels positively Victorian, doesn't it? We're touring Britain. We just did the south coast, now we're heading as far north as possible. Retirement's marvellous for spontaneous adventures!"

She barely paused for breath. "This is part of our ruby anniversary celebrations. Forty years married, can you believe it?"

"You get less for murder," John joked with a broad Yorkshire twang. "Are you two married?"

I blinked. "We're not."

"Old friends," Eliza added smoothly.

Cindy's face lit up. "Old friends, that's what I'm picking up. You have lovely energy together. Our niece just married a woman who looks exactly like you," she pointed at Eliza, "doesn't she, John?"

John nodded obediently. "Spitting image."

"You'd make a lovely couple if you ever changed your mind," Cindy added. "Very photogenic."

I bit down a smile. No show needed. Was I right to feel a little sad?

"Are you on holiday?" Cindy continued, clearly viewing conversation as a competitive sport.

"Work trip," Eliza replied. "Though I'm hoping to explore a bit. Poppy and I grew up in London, but we used to come up to Scotland the occasional summer in our childhoods. It'll be nice to revisit some of our old haunts, and find some new ones." She gave me a shy smile.

Was Eliza actually looking forward to this?

Interesting.

Chapter Seven

It turned out, Eliza's room was double-booked, so I had to squeeze her bag into my room and share my bunk beds. Something I hadn't done since the last time Eliza and I were together as kids in Scotland.

This was not how I'd expected tonight to go. Having Cindy's constant chatter over dinner had been a blessing as buried feelings about Eliza crashed through the careful barriers I'd built around those memories.

The truth was, I had liked Eliza back then. *Really* liked her. But every cold interaction, every eye roll, every moment she'd treated me like an inconvenience in the interim had helped rewrite our history. I'd told myself I'd simply admired her, looked up to her as someone to emulate. That when she smiled at me, the butterflies in my stomach had been about wanting her approval, nothing more.

But now, trapped in this tiny train compartment with nowhere to hide, those old feelings flooded back with uncomfortable clarity. That summer at the lake and her white swimsuit. The way I used to find excuses to sit near her during family dinners. How I'd memorised which books she read so I could casually bring them up in conversation. The devastation I'd felt when she got her first serious girlfriend and suddenly had no time for me.

I'd buried it all so deep that I'd almost believed my own revisionist history.

Almost.

However, even if I was starting to reconsider whether or not Eliza was a totally terrible person, nothing would ever happen. First, because my aunt and her dad were knocking boots, and I didn't want to keep things in the family too much. Second, because the next six months were really important, and I couldn't afford to be sidetracked by a pretty face.

She'd told me she wanted to help, and she seemed sincere. But it had been 15 years of avoidance. Of slights and knocks. And now? I was lying on the top bunk listening to her pee in our teeny-tiny toilet.

My plan, post dinner, had been to decompress and give Amina a call. Now, I had Eliza in my face. Not part of the plan. However, lately my life hadn't gone fully to plan, had it? Was this my mother and Gran meddling, getting me to trust Eliza again? If I believed in the afterlife – *which I clearly didn't* – I wouldn't put it past them.

Eliza eased herself out of the toilet which also served as the shower. She gave me a pained smile, then disappeared from view onto the bottom bunk with a sigh.

"Are you okay up there? You always used to sleep on the bottom when we were kids."

I blushed, despite myself, then leaned over the top.

"I've got more versatile as I've got older."

She grinned. "Good to know." She held up a card. "Have you seen there's a gin menu and you can order to the room?

What do you say we order in and get comfortable? They've got Pringles, too. Sour cream and chives, or salt and vinegar?"

"So long as it's not barbecue, I don't mind."

An attendant named Carlos brought us gin and green Pringles. Eliza told me to come to the bottom bunk, and we both sat with our backs to the wall, the motion of the train making us sway constantly, shoulders and thighs pressing together. It wasn't entirely unwelcome.

"Is this weird how this doesn't feel weird?" Eliza rolled her neck.

I smiled. It was like she could read my mind. "I was thinking the same thing at dinner."

"I guess we're not starting from scratch."

"Margot threatened Andrew might shadow me instead of you. He's been with Voss for life. I'm glad I'm sharing this carriage with you, not him. That could have been a little trickier."

The thought of that made us both laugh.

"Sitting side by side like this reminds me of sitting up in our old tree house that my granddad built. You remember that?" It had been one of the best birthday presents I'd ever received. My granddad loved building things, and my tree house was a place just for me. Often, just for me and Eliza.

She bumped my shoulder with hers, and when I turned my head, she had a wide grin on her face. I could tell she was picturing being up there, too. The smell of freshly cut grass, the heat of the sun, the annoying midges that always managed to find their way in and never their way out.

"I remember your tree house. It was one of the single greatest things that happened in my childhood. A place to get away from adults. Your tree house is still the holy grail.

No internet. No TV. Just a place to sit and talk. This train carriage is copying that vibe."

For a moment, I glimpsed the Eliza I used to know beneath all the years of careful distance.

"Is Loch Cottage still there?"

I nodded. "I think so. I don't go that way often when I visit." There were too many memories in Goldloch, so I'd tied them up and stored them away.

"Maybe we can take a look when we're there." Eliza's face was hopeful.

"Maybe."

"But also, I was hoping we could get to know each other as who we are now on this trip," Eliza continued, not looking directly at me. "If we're going to work together, I want to look forward, not back. It'll help when we do business."

I nodded. That made sense. She'd started off saying it was professional, but it was never going to be. Not with our history. "Okay. Tell me about your life. What did you do at the weekend?"

Eliza considered my question. Was she deciding whether to edit for a better story? "Saturday was tile shopping in Islington with my mum. Sunday, we hit an outlet village hunting for dining chairs." She held up a hand before I could comment. "In my defence, I'm doing up a house, and that requires surrendering all recreational time to really boring things."

"You moved from where you were?"

Eliza nodded. "Bought a doer-upper. I regret it most days. Especially because I'm back at my dad's while contractors destroy my sanity and bank balance in equal measure."

I raised an eyebrow. "I was surprised when Margot told

me you moved in with your dad. You never saw eye to eye when we were growing up. A little like me and Mum."

She nodded. "That's true, but needs must. He's got a big house, and I needed somewhere to live."

"How's that working out for your social life?"

Something flickered across her face. Amusement, maybe embarrassment. "I've become a nun since I broke up with Michelle, so it's not really an issue." She leaned forward slightly. "What about you?"

I knew all about people letting you down and leaving. I wrote the book on it.

I held out a hand. "Sister Poppy here, also doing the lord's work."

She shook my hand with a laugh that I was thrilled to be the architect of. I don't know if it was that or her touch, but as she wrapped her fingers around mine, an electric current ran through me with a force I was unprepared for.

When I risked a look at her, I was sure I caught a hint of surprise behind her eyes, too.

She dropped my gaze and cleared her throat. "Lesbian nuns is a thing now, right?" She shook her head softly. "Honestly, after Michelle, I thought about becoming a nun. I wondered if it was really all worth it. We bought a house, we got married, then she buggered off to New York."

"Ouch. I heard you broke up, but I wasn't sure of the details."

Eliza caught my gaze, blushed, then looked away. "It was a classic case of me not paying enough attention. I put work first and didn't prioritise her enough. Which she told me in no uncertain terms when she walked out."

"Are you still in touch?"

Her cheeks blushed red. "We see each other when I go to New York on business." She took a sip of her drink and avoided my gaze. "Anyway, enough of my sad life. Tell me tales of your wild convent years."

When we were growing up, she used to make me laugh all the time, just like now. I'd never forgotten that.

"There's not much to tell." I suddenly wished there was, because Eliza was older and had been *married*. She was always ahead of me, in every aspect of life.

"You're not seeing anyone?"

I shook my head. "I'm not a nun, I've had dates, but then my job got busy, and it kinda fell by the wayside."

"Aren't we a pair?" she replied. "Things have changed for you since the Playgirl Poppy era."

My whole body stilled. I knew exactly the era she meant. It was the era I was always trying to flee from. "Playgirl Poppy? Is that what you called me?"

Eliza winced. "And there's me running my big gob off again, just when things were going so well." She held up an apologetic hand. "Sorry. Forget I said it." She grimaced a little more, a Pringle held in front of her mouth.

"Who called me Playgirl Poppy?"

She shook her head as she crunched, then swallowed.

"Not me. It was something I heard the last time I was in Les Gets." She dropped her head. "In that gay club we all go to."

My stomach churned. I couldn't quite believe that time in my life had earned me a nickname. "Right after my mum died? That trip?" I couldn't look at her. "I was never Playgirl Poppy. I was sad, angry, vulnerable Poppy. And yes, I partied hard. But if I took any women home, I probably passed out before much happened. That time of my life was anything but playful."

Eliza took a deep breath, then leaned over and put her gin on the bedside table. She sat up, and took my hand in hers.

I didn't shake her off.

"Look, I'm really sorry. We said we wanted to get to know each other now, and I brought up the past. I know it was a difficult time for you. It just slipped out."

A barrage of the past and present ricocheted through me. All at once, I wanted to be enveloped by Eliza, but I also wanted to punch her. I wasn't sure I'd ever be able to smooth out my emotions into something more palatable. Our childhood had been easy. Our adult relationship had been anything but.

"Can you forgive me? Otherwise, it's going to be a really long trip."

I blew out a long breath and shook my head. "You hit a nerve, you know? I wasn't in a great place then."

"I get that. Even bringing that up was a stupid move. But you must remember from our childhood that I can be impressively stupid?"

Despite myself, I smiled. "I do remember that."

"Let's circle back to you working too hard."

"Yeah. After Playgirl Poppy was put away, Work Boss Poppy emerged. I needed something to put my energy into, and work won the prize. But it did mean that everything else suffered. Relationships, friendships, family. Aunt Margot wasn't best pleased with me. Neither was Katy." I shrugged. "I wasn't best pleased with me either, but I had no idea how to make a change. Until I really started to deal with Mum's death and went to therapy."

"Let me guess: Margot wanted you to come and work in the company?"

I nodded. "She was going to give me Mum's office. The place where her brain popped and she died on the floor. It was the last place in the world I wanted to be."

The devastation still rattled through me most days, but its after-effects were getting calmer.

Eliza stroked my arm, and a multitude of fireworks went off under my skin where she touched me. Her fingertips blazed hot, and I leaned into her touch without thinking. When had someone last offered me comfort like this? When had I let them?

"But something's changed now?"

Something had. "Now she wants to sell, yes. Plus, more time has passed, and I've had therapy." I paused. "Which clearly means I'm an over-sharer now, too."

She looked at me, and something in her eyes blazed.

"Let me join in with the oversharing. When your mum died, I wanted to be there for you. But we hadn't spoken properly for ages and I couldn't just drop you a message. Then I bumped your car, and you were super angry with me. I used it as an excuse to stay away. I should have done more. You went through a horrible loss, and it was less than a decade after your gran. I was a shit friend, even though we weren't officially friends. I'm sorry for that, too."

I picked up my glass and stared into it. "If we're anything to go by, it's true what they say about gin making you maudlin."

That got a smile at least.

"But honestly?" I added. "I don't blame you for not coming near me. I was in a bad place, and we weren't close then."

"I could have tried. Yes, I was going through my divorce and things were messy, but your *mum* died. That trumps everything."

I shook my head. "I wouldn't have let you. I'd have shut you down." I hadn't let many people in since. It was something I was working on.

"I could have tried even when your mum was still alive. Our mums were friends, just like us when we were kids. But after I went to university and we stopped talking, it became the norm. It always saddened me. Then when we did talk, it was weird and edgy. Not like this."

She shook her head with a smile. "Let's just agree that we both could have been better to each other over the years. But this trip? We're going to soak up everything Voss Watches, and we're going to be nice to each other. I know we can do it. I can't wait to go to Goldloch again. I haven't been back since that last two weeks we spent there as kids. I think we were 10 and 14 then?" She smiled at me, then. A pure, genuine smile. The same one that always lit up every room she was in.

I remembered the vibe of that summer like it was yesterday. It had been idyllic. Me, Katy, and Eliza. The three of us running free, with no cares. They were far simpler days.

"You know, I often thought you had the work-life balance thing all sorted. I've still to master it," Eliza said.

I snorted. "Let me tell you, I didn't. First, I was too much play. Then I crashed. Now I'm too much work."

"So we're both workaholics with no relationship?"

"That's about the size of it."

"At least it means we might work for the next few months."

"Not if you call me Playgirl Poppy again."

Eliza bit down a smile. "I promise those words will never pass my lips again. Cross my heart." She drew a line from her right shoulder to the left-hand side of her waist, then did the same on the opposite side.

"Maybe we both have things to learn. You have to learn to play more. And I'm learning that if I want to take over at Voss, work has to come first. Which is why it's my priority for the next six months. I have big plans, and they all start here."

Eliza ran her tongue along her top teeth before she replied. "Six months? I thought the deal was three to start, and then we see where we are. Whether we stick or twist."

"Is that what Margot told you?"

A slight wince crossed her face, and I could see her deciding what to tell me and what not. In the end, she gave me a slow nod. "And Dad."

A dark shadow fell on me. I had to remember that as nice as Eliza was, she also had interest in the other side of the deal, too. "We agreed it was three to make my mark. Six to fully convince. I plan to make my mark. If you're reporting back to Margot or your dad, make sure they know that." I paused. "I haven't come to play. I mean business."

Chapter Eight

Voss Watch's main production plant still sat on one of the most picturesque industrial parks I'd ever seen. Set on the outskirts of Goldloch, the modern estate somehow managed to blend seamlessly with the Highland landscape. The old Victorian red brick building had been lovingly maintained, its tall windows gleaming in the spring morning light. Beside it, newer extensions had been sensitively added to accommodate the growing business, the living gardens on their roofs showing a shock of green.

From the car park, the River Ness wound its way towards the loch. To the left of the main entrance was the tourist pier where the old Ferris wheel sat dormant, waiting for the season to begin. Katy and I had begged to ride it every summer, spinning slowly above the dark waters while scanning for any sign of Nessie, the Loch Ness monster who was supposed to live below.

When I stepped through Voss's door, it was like being transported back in time. The reception area was exactly as I remembered it: polished wooden floors that creaked in all the familiar places, tartan upholstery on the waiting area chairs, and the same framed photographs of Highland landscapes lining cream walls. There was also the one of Mum and

Gran, arm in arm just after Mum took over as CEO, with the caption: Petula Voss with her daughter, Felicity, the future of Voss Watches.

The smell of the machinery drifted through from the factory floor beyond. The noise. The focus. And there, laughing about something with our receptionist, Leah, was Voss's heartbeat and Chief Operating Officer, Fiona. A little older, a little greyer, but still there. Watching over the company like a guardian angel.

I hadn't seen her since Mum's funeral, when I'd collapsed into her. Today, I was stronger, but it still tugged at something inside when she crushed me in a hug. With Fiona, I'd always be eight years old, no matter what time passed.

"My goodness, look at you, all grown up!" She held me at arm's length and shook her head. "A bonnie wee lassie if ever I saw one."

Fiona had used the same line every time she saw me my entire life, but it always made me smile. I'd woken up to a message from Katy this morning to tell her hi. She loved her, too. Fiona was our Scottish mother.

"And tartan trousers." She beamed at my clothing choice. "Your Grannie would be proud."

"When in Goldloch," I beamed back. "You're looking great, as always. Katy says hi. Do you remember Eliza?"

Eliza held out a hand, but Fiona wouldn't have a bar of it. She hugged her right away.

"Of course I remember Eliza. Your mum showed me some photos of you when she and Felicity came up here together about five years ago. All grown up, too. It's great to see you."

She turned back to me. "Margot was on the blower over

the weekend, telling me you'd be here to show Eliza around. Who'd have thought the two wee girls from all those summers ago would be in charge some day?"

"I guess it's always what Mum and Gran intended." I swallowed down the lump in my throat.

Fiona grasped my arm. She radiated warmth and kindness, but she was equally no-nonsense and business savvy. Her laugh lines spoke of decades spent finding joy in small moments, and when she smiled, her whole face transformed into something that felt like home.

"They'd be so proud you're here, carrying on the family name. In their absence, I'm proud."

A tingle went down my spine as Fiona hugged me again, and I swear, for a minute, I got a waft of something familiar. Something floral. Was it Mum's favourite perfume?

I glanced around over her shoulder, but there was nothing there. Or maybe there was, but I couldn't see it. If Sage were here, she might. Sweat broke out on the back of my neck and my palms. I clenched my fists to regain control. I couldn't spend the few days here looking out for actual ghosts. There were enough hiding around every corner as it was.

"Shall we give you the tour, then we can look at the books? I've asked Andrew to have everything ready, and he's arranged passwords with Simona, so you have it all at your fingertips. Ronnie is joining us just after lunch, too. Got a dentist appointment this morning. Dicky tooth."

Ronnie was Fiona and her husband Harvey's second son, and also a key in Voss's success here.

She rested her fingers on my arm. "I know Margot is keen to sell, and I understand why. But this business? It's not ailing. It could do better, but there's a solid foundation to make that happen. If you can do anything to keep it in the family, this whole factory would be grateful. There's a lot of rumours and understandable nervousness ever since Margot started touring with potential buyers."

I glanced at Eliza. "Your Dad's already been here?"

A bitter pill of reality fizzed through my system. After sharing a room last night and listening to Eliza's gentle snores, it was easy to forget she worked primarily for her dad, not for Voss.

She gave me a pained look. "I don't know. He's been absent for a few weekends, but he didn't tell me if he did come here, I promise. He and Margot have been away a lot, I lose track of where they've been and where they're going."

I could just imagine the romantic weekend he and Margot had, followed by promises of the company. I pulled back my shoulders and took a deep breath. Eliza was compromised by her present. I was compromised by our past. Could this relationship ever work?

"Before we do anything else, shall we get a coffee?" Fiona asked.

* * *

It was after 5pm when we left the factory. Without a word, we both headed for the loch, just as we always used to as kids. The path down was exactly as I remembered. A dusty track worn smooth by decades of workers' boots and summer visitors, winding between gorse bushes that caught at my tartan kecks with every step.

"Careful," Eliza called from behind me. "That bush has

it in for your left leg, even if it is cosplaying as a Scottish limb dressed in tartan."

I turned and gave her a look. "I'm fully Scottish, as is my leg."

Eliza snorted. "Your trousers definitely are."

Our shoes kicked up small clouds of dirt with each step, the fine dust settling on everything. The air smelled of heather and something indefinably Scottish: peat, maybe, or just the particular sweetness that clung to spring afternoons in the Highlands. As we descended, the sound of the factory faded until all I could hear was our footsteps crunching on the gravelly path and the distant lap of water against the shore.

"It's like stepping back in time." I paused to catch my breath and take in the view. The loch stretched out before us, mirror-still except for the occasional ripple from a fish rising to the surface. Rolling hills carpeted in purple heather swept down to the water's edge, and beyond that, mountains peaks were topped with wisps of cloud. The whole scene looked like something from a postcard, all impossible greens, and blues that seemed too vivid to be real.

"Even that old jetty's still there." Eliza pointed to the weathered wooden platform jutting into the water. "Remember when your gran dared us to jump off it that summer? Then she did it, and we couldn't believe it?"

"We were both still too terrified to do it until the last day." I smiled at the memory, brushing dust from my trouser leg. "Then we spent the entire afternoon launching ourselves off like tiny cannonballs."

"Speak for yourself. I was extremely graceful." But Eliza grinned as she said it, and for a moment she looked exactly like the 14-year-old who'd spent that magical summer convinced she could teach herself to dive.

The closer we got to the water's edge, the more the years seemed to peel away. Nothing had changed. Not the stony part of the shore, not the fallen log we'd claimed as our private bench, not even the rope swing that still hung from the old oak tree. Somebody still used it, because the rope looked far stronger and newer than I remembered.

Without discussion, both of us started scanning the shoreline for the perfect stones. It was automatic, muscle memory from our childhood summers. I crouched down, running my fingers through the smooth pebbles until I found what I was looking for: flat, round, just the right weight in my palm.

"Still going for the tiny ones, I see." Eliza hefted a stone twice the size of mine.

"Size isn't everything." I brushed grit from my knees, enjoying the familiar weight of the stone in my hand. I hoped I remembered how to do it.

A light breeze rippled across the loch's surface, carrying the distant bleating of sheep from the hills beyond.

"Ladies first," Eliza said with exaggerated gallantry.

"Who you calling a lady?" But I stepped forward anyway. I drew my arm back, snapped my wrist forward, and my stone kissed the surface once, twice, three times, before disappearing with a soft plop. Not bad.

"Beat that." I rolled my shoulders back and turned triumphantly, wiping my damp fingers on my trousers.

Eliza stepped up beside me, her shoulder almost brushing mine. I caught a whiff of her perfume mixed with the dusty heat from our walk down. She wound up like she was playing a different sport entirely, hurling her stone with more force than finesse. It hit the water with a loud splash and sank immediately.

"Technique, Eliza. It's all about technique. I thought you of all people would know that." I couldn't hide my grin as I selected another stone. This one was even better: perfectly smooth under my thumb, the right thickness, the right weight distribution.

"Shut up and throw," she replied, but she was smiling, too.

"I don't throw," I told her with a wink. "I finesse."

The second stone flew from my hand in a low arc, hitting the water at exactly the right angle. One, two, three, four perfect skips before it sank.

"Show off," Eliza said, but there was warmth in her voice.

In the old days, the prize had been bragging rights to our parents. I wasn't sure what the rules were today. I wasn't sure of anything where Eliza was concerned. From being sure she was a robot who hated me, I'd flip-flopped to the fact I'd carried a crush on her half my life, to then thinking she was a spy working for her dad, out to get me.

However now, skimming stones by the loch, we'd relaxed. Her next two shots sunk without trace. Whereas mine skimmed the surface with fluid precision. She tried a couple more times, then sunk onto our familiar log, a frown on her face.

"Turns out, I'm not always good with my hands."

I grinned. "Not what the graffiti in the club toilets claims."

Her laugh echoed around the loch.

"Dammit, I thought I rubbed that off."

We sat in silence for a few minutes, letting the breeze caress our faces.

"This is so different from our usual lives. Less hustle. No bustle." Eliza leaned back, spreading her hands on the log behind her. "I used to think that as a kid, and I always thought it was strange. Now, as an adult, I'm wondering if it's the key to a good life."

I snorted. "You'd never hack it. You thrive on corporate life, and what would you do without your Pret coffee? Jetting off places, doing deals." I swept an arm. "Trust me, the only deal happening around here is Marcus – Fiona's eldest who runs our pub – negotiating with his wife Val for a lads' weekend in exchange for her getting a girls' trip next month. Pure negotiation genius."

Eliza stretched out her long legs and stared at her chunky green loafers. She tucked her hair behind her right shoulder, then turned her gaze to me.

"You're probably right," she said. "I'm too far into the game to drop out now. But imagine living here? What a different life we'd lead. Did you see Fiona's skin? I couldn't believe it when she told us she just turned 65. And not a hint of retiring."

The thought had crossed my mind when she told us her age. "I hope not." She couldn't: Fiona was eternal.

"Whatever they put in the water clearly agrees with her."

I knew what she meant. As soon as I got off the train at Goldloch, it was like we'd stepped into another universe. Life here moved at a different pace.

Eliza dug both hands into her trousers. "It hasn't changed since we were kids, has it?"

I shook my head. Every time I came here, I was painfully aware of that. It was something my mum had always loved about the place. Same went for my gran.

"Untouched by the ravages of time," I replied. "Although the inn we're at does have flavoured gin and the internet now."

"Flavoured gin is never progress," Eliza told me. She stretched her arms over her head and leaned her head back, revealing the elegant line of her throat. Her golden hair fell away from her face, and I stared for longer than I should have, until I caught myself.

At 33, Eliza had perfected the art of looking beautiful sat on a damp log in the middle of nowhere. It was almost irritating how good she was at it.

"You're probably right, though," Eliza continued. "About this being a place to come for a visit, not to live. Isn't it ironic that we run off to all these far-flung exotic places to get away, when really, we should just come to the Highlands as a balm for the soul."

"What are you running from?"

But she shook her head instantly. "Nothing in particular. I'm just…" She frowned, searching for the right word. "Questioning what I'm doing with my life. Wondering if Michelle was right, and I might wake up one day and realise I've wasted it on people and things that didn't really matter."

I laughed. "She didn't mince her words, your ex-wife."

"Not known for it." Eliza smiled. "Plus, do I want to work for my dad forever? I'm at a crossroads if he wants to stop and hand over the keys. Roger's not interested. He always assumed I was. Am I?"

She didn't wait for an answer. "It's probably just cold feet. Plus, we're a little on top of each other. Living together isn't helping." Eliza paused. "It's nice to have a bit of a break from him. The irony is that it's with you." She winced. "And that came out wrong."

She gave me an apologetic smile. "You know what I mean.

We used to be friends. There's been a lot of water under the bridge since then. You've been through unimaginable pain, I've had a horrendous breakup, but we're still here, and beneath it all, we're still friends. I guess what I'm trying to say is, I'm glad my dad put me on this project in the end. It's good that this is not just work. It's good that we're friends again."

Chapter Nine

We wandered back along the loch's edge towards the town centre, our earlier formality abandoned for loose limbs and the occasional shoulder bump.

We passed the cottage that we'd both dreamed about owning when we were young. It was a lot more run-down and overgrown, but it still had the perfect view across the water. The sign outside told the world its name: Loch Cottage. Outside, there was a For Sale sign.

Eliza nodded towards it. "Remember we always said we'd love to live there?"

I smiled. "I do. Someone else is going to get that chance now. It's still got the world's best view."

"The loch never changes."

She stopped and stared for a moment, then we pressed on.

"So," I said, kicking at a loose stone, "what did you think of the factory on the surface? You've got way more experience with this sort of operation than I do."

Until she died, my mum always kept me up to date with Eliza's job, whether I wanted to hear it or not. I knew it included touring factories and assessing what they needed to work better. I used to scoff at her job. Now, it was her expertise I was looking for.

My eyes saw the business built by my family, laden with nostalgia and memories. Hers would see how the business ran, what we could do better, and how we could make it more efficient. One thing I knew: I wanted to do so without denting headcount or morale.

Eliza was quiet for a moment, her eyes fixed on the water. "Honestly? I was impressed. Fiona and Ronnie run a tight ship. Everyone we met knew their stuff and cared about what they were doing. You can't fake that kind of investment."

That was good to hear, but I also detected a hesitation in her voice.

"What's the 'but'?"

She glanced at me sideways, and her sapphire-blue gaze pierced my defences. I gulped as my pulse raced, willing myself to think business only.

"But if we're serious about expanding sales, we're going to need a bigger premises. That's my main concern. The business is chugging along fine as Fiona said, but it's already running at capacity. We either build, or we go elsewhere."

I stopped walking. "You're not suggesting we move production completely?"

Because if she was, it was a big fat no.

A no so fat, you could see it from space.

I couldn't do that. We'd shaken hands with the staff, looked them in the eye, assured them we were on their side. That I was one of them, and not simply a nepo baby who didn't care at all. I'd put a couple of grand behind the bar for a Friday night pint after work as a thank you for the latest launch and whatever came next.

"I'm just saying—"

"Because we can build. Extend. The council would approve it in a heartbeat. They're desperate to keep businesses here." The words came out sharper than I'd intended, but the thought of uprooting everything made my stomach clench. Voss Watches was started here, and it needed to stay here.

"We're not there yet, so don't panic. We need to prove there's demand for growth before we act." Eliza's voice was gentle but firm. "If the company ends up being sold, new owners might decide it's more profitable to rip the whole operation out of Goldloch and move it somewhere more accessible and cheaper."

Of course a new owner would do that. They didn't have the ties that our family did. Fresh dread ran through me. Was my mum shaking her head somewhere on a cloud above me? Was she tutting and giving her a disappointed face, the one I knew only too well?

I resumed walking, this time at a quicker pace. "What if I have a plan to ensure the company stays put?"

Eliza raised a single eyebrow. It was perfectly arched, almost balletic. How was it possible that even her facial expressions looked like they belonged on stage? I ignored it, along with the heat that shot straight through my chest and settled somewhere considerably lower. I felt her curiosity like a physical thing, felt the way she watched me from the corner of her eye.

"Do you? Have a killer idea? Because if you do, I'd love to hear it."

She sounded like she didn't believe me. I could see her point, but I was sure this would work.

It *had* to work.

Because it was the only plan I had.

"Our designers already have a new watch that we're launching soon. What if we get a big pop star on board? Someone young, relevant. Repackage the launch with them in mind. Make Voss Watches not about a piece of jewellery you put on your wrist. Instead, we'll sell them a statement of intent, that if you wear a Voss Watch, you're performing an act of self-care. Making time for yourself. Valuing who you are. Getting yourself away from digital pressures, returning to analogue, to offline. You don't need a pomodoro timer or a sprint to see how productive you can be. What you need is a moment to yourself. To stare at beauty. To be mindful. To take time for you. Also, to wear the same watch that your favourite pop star is wearing."

When I looked down, my fist was clenched against my chest, my knuckles white. I was shocked by the belief I had in this idea. I'd done a presentation for Margot, but I hadn't sold it like I meant it. Not like I was now.

Being here, where the dream began, made this essential. It was about more than money, about being a success. This was about living up to expectations. Ones I'd never managed while Mum and Gran were alive. Now that I knew they were watching, I wasn't about to let everyone down again.

My heart-on-my-sleeve moment definitely had Eliza's attention.

"We sell them a dream: a luxury you can't afford to be without." I sucked on my top lip as I stared at Eliza, waiting for her reaction. I didn't have to wait long.

"Your conviction is great. It's a huge change from where you were. But the clock's already ticking."

I shook my head. "I have an in. Someone I know is friends with Roka's manager. I already have a meeting booked in. If we get Roka on board, sell her the dream, the sales bounce would be instant. Then we get a marketing agency to flood social influencers."

It sounded easy. I knew it wouldn't be.

Eliza started walking again, hopefully chewing over my ideas.

"Is this like when we were kids, and you wanted to launch your own brand of watch for teenagers?"

I stopped walking again. "I clean forgot about that." I had. "I wanted to topple Swatch, didn't I?"

"And your mum and gran wouldn't listen." Eliza bumped my shoulder. "For what it's worth, I thought that idea was gold. If you can get this one to work, it could be the same. She's about to launch her new album, and it's called 23. We could name the new watch Roka 23."

My eyes went wide. "I love that!"

"But it's a big if. When's the meeting?"

There was excitement in her voice, but also scepticism. She still saw me as Playgirl Poppy. I was going to change her mind.

"Next week. She's in New York at the moment, so it might involve a trip there. But it's a shot worth taking." I bit my bottom lip. "Are you up for a trip to the Big Apple?"

Eliza stopped walking. "I've had worse offers."

"If I had more time, I might try to work up more ideas. But I don't. All my eggs are in the Roka basket. But she's all about female empowerment and supporting other women in business. Especially queer women." I paused. "Plus, I'm going to offer her an enormous wedge of cash."

Eliza's laugh wrapped itself around me, and my pulse took

detailed notes. It was a laugh I didn't want to give up anytime soon.

"You're going to sway Roka with the sisterhood and a big cheque, and you're going to sway me with a trip to New York? The first might work. The second, you forget Michelle is there. And every time I go there, we always hook up, sleep together, and I take two giant steps backward."

Something sharp and unexpected flared through me at her casual admission. I pushed it down before it could fully form into anything recognisable. Like, say, for instance, the fact I definitely didn't want Eliza sleeping with her ex.

Instead, I gave her a look that told her I had the answer. "You keep falling back into Michelle's bed? That's easy. We go out in New York and you pull someone else. If Michelle is in the same bar and sees it, all the better.

"Because here's the thing, Eliza. You need to remember that you're the prize asset here. You keep repeating the same shit, you'll get the same outcomes. Change it up, get a Voss Watch, take time for yourself and make sure you're a priority?"

Eliza put a hand on her hip. "When did you get so fucking wise?"

Apparently sometime in the last 48 hours when I developed opinions about who she should sleep with, but that seemed like the kind of revelation best kept under wraps.

"I had a lot of therapy post Playgirl Poppy. I read a lot of books. These things merge into personal and professional." I shrugged. "Aren't you glad you took on this job now? You're going to have a professional win to put on your CV, and you're going to get out of your relationship slump. You can thank me later."

Chapter Ten

The one thing I hadn't accounted for in going away to New York was the fact that it was the twins' second birthday next week. Katy and Bryce were having a big party, and Katy was going to be pissed with me. I called to deliver the news as soon as I got the flight and hotel confirmed by my new Voss PA.

"But you're their godmother, Pops!"

She and Margot were the only people in the world allowed to call me that. "And as their godmother, I will bring them back the best gifts from New York." How could I sweeten the deal? "Plus, I'll babysit so you and Bryce can have a night out, too." Surely that would do it.

There was a pause on the end of the line. "I guess that would work. So long as you throw in a gift for me from New York, too."

I laughed. Maybe I should hire my sister to work with me. She was a skilled negotiator.

"Done deal."

"But let's circle back to the facts of this. You're going to New York with Eliza?" Katy's tone was sharp, surprised. "I'm pretty sure the last time you said her name, it was laced with venom."

I waved a hand even though she couldn't see it. "Water under the bridge."

Katy didn't need to know my fears about Eliza, because neither of us could do anything about them. I had to trust Eliza, or this was never going to work.

"As long as you mean that. But even with Eliza's help, this is a tall order. Give it your best shot, and whatever happens, at least you tried. You don't owe me and the girls anything. Our family is way more than Voss Watches."

Sometimes, Katy channelled so much of our dead grandma, it made me forget to breathe. That's exactly what she would have said. Mum, on the other hand, would have told me to go in all guns blazing and not to leave until the deal was done.

"I know that."

Another pause. "For the record, Eliza has never been the villain you made her out to be. You needed someone to blame for everything, and she was a convenient stooge. She went off to college and you were 14. She's allowed to ignore you for a bit. It was never the crime of the century."

"Whatever. We're friends again now."

"Right." Katy cleared her throat. "She broke up with her wife, right?"

But she's still sleeping with her. "She did."

"Sad for her. Interesting for you."

I frowned. "Why?"

"Oh come on. Isn't there a reason you had beef with her all this time? If you hate someone that much, there's usually some underlying reason. Like, maybe, that you like them?"

I hated when she was that perceptive.

"Not everything comes down to sex. You've been watching too much *Grey's Anatomy*."

"True. But certain things do." I could almost hear her grin down the phone. "Plus, wouldn't it be nice to meet someone?"

"Not this someone. I have issues with her, remember? Plus, no distractions. I'm not even starting anything new on Netflix. I'm following everything that Roka does on her socials. I'm watching all our competitors and influencers. I've got spreadsheets coming out of my ears."

"I seem to recall you telling me that you weren't going to become obsessive and block out everything else in your life for the sake of the business like Mum did. You're missing the twins' birthday, and you're cutting off parts of your life. This sounds precisely the opposite."

It wasn't the same at all. This was short-term pain for long-term gain.

"I'm not going down the same path. As soon as I've secured the company, I'll take my foot off the gas. But for now, nothing can distract me."

I changed the subject before she could respond.

"But before I go to New York, can you tell me about your meetings with Sage?"

"What do you want to know?"

"How long you've been chatting to Mum without telling me?"

She paused before she replied. "Why would I mention it? You'd just tell me I'm throwing money down the drain."

I cringed. That is what I might have said.

"What does Bryce think?"

There was a longer pause. "He doesn't know. He thinks

I'm at yoga. I know he'd have the same tone as you. But I don't care. She's told me things she had no way of knowing."

"She has the internet."

Katy growled down the phone. "Thanks for illustrating my point. I know she has the internet, but there are things the internet doesn't know – *couldn't know* – that Sage has told me."

I thought about Gran's scone recipe, and Mum telling Sage about missing my school pantomime. I knew she was telling the truth. But I wasn't ready to share or believe it quite yet. I needed a little more hard evidence.

"Like what?"

"Sage said Gran kept calling me 'her little piglet' and laughing about how I used to snort when I was a baby. Nobody outside the family ever knew Gran called me that. It wasn't something we ever talked about with friends or posted anywhere."

I swallowed that one down. "Even I don't remember Gran calling you that."

"It was before you were born, and luckily I grew out of the snorting thing. She also said Mum was really proud of how good a mother I was. Better than she was."

"Successful businesswoman isn't the best mother, shocker. Even I could have magicked that one up."

"Yes, but she also said that Mum was tapping her Montblanc pen."

Something cold settled in my stomach. Sage had brought up the Montblanc pen when we'd spoken. I'd forgotten how much Mum loved that thing. She'd carried it everywhere, claimed it was her lucky charm, never signed anything important with anything else.

"It could be a lucky guess." But that wasn't what my stomach said. "Successful people often have favourite pens, it's not that unusual."

But even as I spoke, I could hear how thin it sounded. A Montblanc, specifically?

"I thought that. But then she mentioned about the red chair in Mum's office. The one she loved to sit in." Katy's voice was gentle but pointed. "Come on, Pops. What are the odds she'd pick that exact detail?"

I rubbed my temples, feeling the beginnings of a headache. Because Katy was right: what were the odds? However, acknowledging that meant accepting something I'd spent my entire adult life dismissing. It also meant I might need to listen to what Sage and Mum were saying. Could Sage help me stop Margot selling the company? Could she tell me what Mum thought about it all?

"I have to meet with her again," I blurted.

"Sage?"

"Yeah. Mum might have some advice that I haven't thought about yet. Some words of wisdom." I paused. "And I need to buy a Montblanc pen."

"You can have Mum's."

"I said I'd do things my way, which means I need my own pen."

"It's just sitting in my drawer, but suit yourself." Katy paused. "I really do think Sage is telling the truth, because how could she not be? Plus, we hadn't seen each other in literally years when we ran into each other again and she told me so many things about Mum. She couldn't possibly have researched our family beforehand."

"Like when I ran into her with you."

"Exactly." She cleared her throat. "Did she sit with you? Say anything that day?"

"Not much. Just a couple of things."

I was going to have to give her something.

"She told me about Gran's scone recipe which I'd been searching for the week before. Gran told me where to find it." A shiver ran through me again. "She also told me about a time Mum missed a show I was in." I stroked my face. "It was… a lot. But also, kind of comforting?"

Katy sucked in a breath. "You've been in your own world over the past few years, pulling your life back together. I'm proud of you for that. But I miss Mum and Gran. Sage was an opportunity to get back in touch with them. I wasn't going to pass that up."

And now I saw that Sage might be the key to knowing what to do.

"Do you have her number?"

"It won't work if you're a sceptic."

"I promise, I'll go with an open mind."

"That goes for everything in your life, by the way. Including Eliza." She paused. "And don't forget the presents."

Chapter Eleven

The executive car's punnet of penny sweets lasted exactly five minutes before I caved. Despite leaving with plenty of time, I was still wolfing down Flying Saucers and Fruit Salads in lieu of actual breakfast, determined to beat Eliza to the airport and avoid that look. The one that made me feel I was already failing before I'd even started.

My phone chimed as I extracted half a Fruit Salad from my molars.

> En route, hope you are too and not still sleeping.

The assumption stung.

> Race you there.
> Loser buys coffee.

I was trying to sound breezy.

She replied with a runner emoji.

Typical Eliza: economical even with her emojis.

I grinned at the empty motorway flying past, feeling genuinely competitive for the first time in months. Maybe it was pathetic, but I wanted to prove something to her. That I wasn't the chaotic mess she still partly thought I was.

Five miles to the airport, confidence coursing through me, I made the mistake of scrolling through Eliza's Instagram. It was a sterile wasteland of professional shots that revealed absolutely nothing personal. There was private, then there was this. Like she'd surgically removed any trace of humanity from her online presence.

I found a three-year-old post of her and Michelle at some Highgate gallery opening, both polished and radiating the kind of effortless sophistication I'd never master. They looked perfect together. Michelle's arm draped casually around Eliza's waist, both of them smiling with practiced ease. Eighteen months later they were divorced, so clearly that perfection was an illusion. Had Eliza been performing even then?

I zoomed in on their faces, searching for hairline cracks in their facade, when the car lurched with a violent bang.

"What was that?" Panic shot through me immediately.

"Not sure," the driver replied, his tone tense. "But something is dragging."

Not now.

I bet Michelle was always on time.

We limped onto the hard shoulder beside an SOS phone. Cars thundered past, making our Peugeot rock in their wake. If Eliza wanted evidence I was unreliable, here it was.

Half an hour later, still stranded, my competitive spirit had curdled into a custard of dread. I could already hear Eliza's internal monologue: *She says she's serious, but is she really?*

I texted my sister first.

> Find my body in New York
> if Eliza kills me.

Then, swallowing what remained of my pride, I messaged her.

> Car died. Going to be late.
> Please don't murder me.

Her reply was swift.

> It only happens to you,
> Poppy.

An hour later, rescued by a tow truck, I rushed through the terminal with my heart slamming into my sternum. I found Eliza at Pret, and even scowling she was beautiful. Her hair was perfectly styled despite the early hour, and her posture oozed controlled irritation. The realisation hit me: I actually wanted her to like me. Not just professionally, but as a person. I wanted her approval.

"I'm so sorry." I hated how flustered I sounded. "The car literally broke down. I was stuck on the hard shoulder with lorries flying past at full speed. It was pretty hairy."

"I know it wasn't your fault." However, her tone suggested she thought the universe conspired differently around me. "But shit happens in business. You have to be early, be prepared, have contingency plans."

Heat flashed through me, born of embarrassment and

frustration. "I don't need a punctuality lecture like you're head girl and I'm some hopeless first-year."

"I was head girl."

I rolled my eyes. "I know. I was there, remember?"

I recalled how she'd commanded respect even then, how she'd always been kind when she didn't have to be. How she'd made everyone feel like they mattered.

Somewhere along the way, I'd forgotten all of that.

* * *

I'd fallen asleep on the flight as I always did, and woke with my head on Eliza's shoulder. I'd also dribbled on her jumper, much to my horror. But when I lifted my face, bracing for the scowl I deserved, her mouth had a slight upturn and her eyes sparkled with actual humour. Relief flooded through me like warm honey.

Our cab driver from LaGuardia was the essence of New York, grunting responses and scowling when we wanted to pay by card instead of cash.

At least our Tribeca hotel looked decent; my PA had done a bang-up job. The lobby was all exposed brick, slate and Edison bulbs, industrial chic to the max. After a shower and fresh clothes, it was almost as if my body clock hadn't been brutally assaulted by a five-hour time difference.

The hotel bar was dimly lit with copper fixtures and too many succulents, buzzing amid a sea of designer trainers. I was simultaneously underdressed and overdressed, which seemed to be my default state around Eliza.

"I'm sorry about being shitty earlier," Eliza said once we'd claimed two velvet bar stools that spun delightfully.

"Punctuality is a bugbear of mine. But I know some things can't be helped."

I shook my head. "No problem. Shall we get a cocktail and drink to this trip's success?"

Mine arrived first, a Pink Gin Spritz that looked like liquid confidence in a glass. Eliza's Old Fashioned followed, amber and serious, which seemed fitting.

Eliza was twitchy, not her usual composed self. She kept scanning the room like she was expecting an ambush, her fingers drumming against her glass. I had a hunch I knew why.

"Does Michelle live anywhere near here?"

At her ex's name, Eliza flinched, spine straightening like someone had yanked a cord. She glanced at me without quite meeting my eyes.

"Not directly, no. But she works in SoHo. There are some cool places around here. It's not impossible she might turn up."

"Here? In this overpriced hipster paradise?" My tone made it clear I thought that was bollocks.

She gave me a tight smile. "You'd be surprised. Michelle always knew the right places." There was something wistful in her voice that irritated me. "I guess I'm just nervous. This is the first time I've been here without telling her or arranging to meet. Is it weird I feel like I'm somehow betraying her?"

"A little, when you've been divorced as long as you have. Plus, unless she's stalking hotel bars, you're probably safe."

"This place is full of New Yorkers, believe me." She gestured at a table of impossibly cool women in vintage leather jackets who looked like they'd stepped out of a magazine.

"The more important thing is why you're feeling like this.

Why you never made a clean break. Why you're sleeping together. Are you still in love with her?"

Eliza frowned, then shook her head. "Definitely not. But she was my person for a good few years, you know? I guess I miss that." She took a slug of her drink. "Plus, you know what lesbians are like. We all stay friends with our exes."

I smiled. "I don't."

"That doesn't surprise me. You don't even stay friends with your friends."

I widened my eyes. Eliza was hurt by the time we'd spent apart, too? It was good to know it wasn't just me. She was opening up to me, being vulnerable. Perhaps I could do it with her, too.

Maybe.

Sometime in the future.

"You're not still pining for your ex?" I had to be sure.

She shook her head again. "I'm not that pathetic."

"Is sleeping with her every time you're here doing you any good?" I already knew the answer, but I wanted her to realise it.

"Of course not." She took a large gulp of her drink, wincing slightly. "But we were still attracted to each other even after everything fell apart. We kept hooking up because it was easier than actually dealing with the mess we'd made. And yes, I know how pathetic that sounds. But we still worked in bed. It seemed a shame to let that go just because everything else had dwindled."

"Did you cheat on her?"

"Not with a person. With my work. I was never there. I prioritised every client meeting, every late night at the office, every family crisis over her. She used to joke she was married to a ghost."

The pain in her voice was raw, unguarded. I felt an unexpected urge to reach across and cover her hand with mine.

"Did she cheat on you?"

She shook her head, but there was hesitation. "Not really. I mean, I think she slept with other people towards the end, but I'd already emotionally abandoned ship by then."

"You were still married, though." She was being a little too forgiving for my liking.

"In name. Nothing else. We were like polite strangers sharing a mortgage. And now, we're not."

The rawness in her voice made me want to know everything. How they'd met, when it had started going wrong, whether she'd fought for it or just let it slip away.

"How long were you together in total?"

"Five years. Two years of happiness, one year planning a wedding that felt sort of forced, then nearly two years of stubborn denial we could fix it."

"Was it just work that killed it?"

Eliza twisted her mouth like she was tasting something bitter. "Work was the symptom, not the disease. It was family values. Michelle thought getting married meant creating this insular little bubble, just the two of us against the world. She couldn't understand that my family was part of the package."

"That must have been lonely."

"Incredibly. I mean, my dad winds me up at times, but I still want to see him. I felt like I was constantly choosing between the people I loved, and my mum got upset by it. Michelle always made it feel like choosing her meant abandoning everyone else."

"But you still miss her?"

"I miss the idea of her. The version of us that existed before we became so bloody toxic." She stared into her drink like it might hold answers. "But coming here without telling her feels like cutting the last thread, and that's terrifying and liberating in equal measure."

Something in her vulnerability made me brave. "What's the lesbian equivalent of cock-blocking? Because I'll be that for you."

She laughed for the first time all day. The sound was a relief.

"Clam-jamming?" she offered.

I made the face that deserved. "Whatever it is, I'm on it."

She stared at me for longer than was strictly allowed, and the corners of her mouth turned upwards. "Thanks. I appreciate that. But enough of my romantic disasters. How are you feeling about meeting Roka tomorrow?"

"I'm bricking it," I admitted, grateful for the subject change. "It's mad we're doing this at all. Three months ago, I was still working in my old job. Now, I'm meeting a pop star in Central Park like I'm in an episode of *Friends*. Hopefully not the one where everything goes wrong. I keep running through my pitch, but I think it all comes down to chemistry. Whether she actually likes us."

"We're all queer. That's got to count for something."

"True, though she's fresh off a very public breakup with that supermodel. I can't imagine having your heart splattered across every gossip site in the world."

Eliza winced. "Just don't mention the ex. Or any exes, including mine. Let's keep it professional."

"Obviously."

I thought about my chat with Margot before I flew. Her patronising looks and pats on my arm.

"Margot thinks I'm completely delusional, you know. She hasn't said it outright, but I can tell. She thinks this is some elaborate fangirl moment disguised as a business strategy."

Eliza rolled her eyes. "Dad's the same, and I'm not used to that. He normally trusts me, but I can tell he thinks this whole project is ridiculous. He gets this look: like he's watching me play with toy cars while the house burns down. He thinks we're idiots for flying across the Atlantic on what he calls 'a whim'."

"Maybe we are idiots." I raised my glass, feeling reckless. "But we're idiots with a plan. And sometimes the biggest risks pay off the most spectacularly."

"Or they go down in flames."

"Either way, it'll make a good story." The alcohol was making me philosophical. "Here's to tomorrow, and to proving everyone wrong."

Chapter Twelve

The morning light streaming through the hotel curtains did nothing to improve my mood as footsteps approached in the hallway outside my door. Eliza was probably coming to lecture me about being late. We were supposed to meet in the lobby 15 minutes ago, and this was possibly the most important meeting of our professional lives. I braced myself for the knock, then heard nothing.

The silence was somehow worse than yelling would have been. I pulled one of my favourite blue tops over my just-dried hair, then yanked the door open before she could decide whether to murder me in the hallway, or wait until we were somewhere more private. Her face spelt the word 'sour'.

"I know, I know, I'm late."

I beckoned her in, but Eliza shook her head and leaned against the door frame.

I ducked back into my room to grab my phone and bag, did a last check in the mirror, then gave Eliza a grin that I hoped papered over my embarrassment.

"I went for a quick run this morning, just around the block a couple of times, I swear, and then my key card wouldn't work when I got back. I had to go all the way down to the front desk, and the guy was new and—"

"It's fine," Eliza cut me off. "We still have time. I built in a buffer. We'll call an uber when we're downstairs."

I blinked. "Really? No lecture about punctuality and professionalism?"

"Not today." She turned and headed towards the elevator. "Not after the morning I've already had dealing with my dad."

I shot her a glance. "What's wrong with your dad? Has he got something to say about what we're doing today?"

She walked at speed down the hotel hallway, her linen blazer somehow managing to look crisp and irritated, just like her. Even when she was pissed off though, Eliza had this effortless way of putting herself together: dark jeans that fit perfectly, simple white (and expensive) trainers, and that blazer thrown over a soft grey T-shirt like she'd just grabbed whatever was closest. Except I already knew she hadn't. Eliza didn't do 'whatever was closest.' She did 'carefully curated casual that looks accidental but definitely isn't.'

"He had plenty to say, and don't even get me started on the fact that he called me at 5am, so I am beyond tired."

"That's thoughtful."

She rolled her eyes. "I know."

"What's his issue?"

She went to say something, then seemed to think better of it. "Don't worry about it, he's not your problem." Her jaw tightened again, before she painted on a semi-smile. I wasn't fooled. What had her dad said, and why was she so agitated by it?

However, we didn't have time to focus on that. We had a pop star to charm.

Eliza appeared to be thinking the same as she snapped her

fingers at me. "Remember, I'm doing the talking initially. I'll warm her up, then you can bring the personal story and really grab her. But please, don't make any promises we can't keep."

"I won't. Although I have told you before, people respond to openness and honesty."

"Honesty is not always the best policy."

It sounded like she was talking from personal experience.

She was silent in the car on the way there, the only sound the sole of her trainer tapping in the footwell as she furiously typed messages on her phone, a perpetual frown on her face every time I looked over.

I had a bad feeling, but couldn't decide if it was to do with Eliza and her dad, or that today simply *had* to go right, and there was no real way I could prepare for it more than I already had. What did I know about talking to an international pop star? What if she was insufferable, as some reports said? What if she hated us on sight? What if she couldn't stand our watches?

My heart scrambled in my chest as all the possibilities of what could go wrong today whirled through my head like a tickertape parade of doom.

I had to pull it together, and inject a little positivity into my day. All those negative things? They're what Margot and Max thought was going to happen. That Playgirl Poppy was going to bugger this up. I had to focus on the positives, so the negatives didn't come true. I wasn't going to fall into their trap. I was going to be Positive Poppy. Playgirl could jog on. I patted the watch box I'd brought in my bag.

The Uber dropped us by Central Park. We dodged through a stream of runners as we made our way to the meeting place.

We found Roka exactly where she said she'd be, sitting on a bench near the Bethesda Fountain with a baseball cap pulled low, and glitzy oversized sunglasses that did little to make her less conspicuous. Or maybe pop stars liked to be a little out there, whatever the situation. It was weird to me that she wanted to meet up in public in the first place.

In person, she was shorter than expected, but there was something magnetic about her up close, even in her semi-disguise. People who didn't get near enough to her orbit walked past without a second glance, not knowing that one of the most famous people on the planet was right in front of them.

She'd shot to fame in the past year with an insanely catchy song about getting over a breakup that had gone global. Showing she was no one-hit wonder, she'd followed it up with two more smash hits. How much longer would she be able to get away with a baseball cap and sunglasses as a disguise? Her hair – a modern mullet with skin at the sides, bouffant on top – was normally on show, so perhaps the hat was what threw people off.

"You must be the watch people." Roka stood and extended a hand. Her nails were bitten to the quick, but her smile had charm and serious wattage: the type that filled stadiums, and made fans forget their names. "Thanks for accommodating my need for fresh air. I've been in the studio all week, and if I have to sit in another room with fluorescent lighting, I might actually lose it."

"No problem at all." Eliza slipped into her professional mode that made her voice go up half an octave. "We're just happy you took the time to meet us, aren't we, Poppy?"

Stunned she'd included me already, I made a honking noise to tell Roka that yes, we were thrilled.

Roka gave me a stare that I fully deserved.

"I'm Eliza, this is Poppy," Eliza added.

Roka shook our hands, and introduced herself too, like we didn't know who she was. I liked that.

"Great. I was thinking we could walk? Or maybe rent one of those boats?" Roka gestured towards the lake, where a handful of rowers yanked oars through the water with varying degrees of success. "I haven't done anything spontaneous in weeks. Unless you count a bottle of Patron on my rooftop in the middle of the night with my producer. Which I don't."

Eliza's face didn't show her panic. Even though I knew she didn't much care for rowing boats, having been tipped out of one when she was little. "A boat? I'm not sure that's the best environment—"

"It's perfect," I jumped in. "Plus, it sells into our brand of taking time for yourself, right, Eliza?"

The look she gave me could have melted the Statue of Liberty.

I walked up beside her. "If she wants to go on a boat, we should do it," I whispered.

"I know," Eliza hissed back.

"You could stay on the bench. I'll go with her."

But she gave me a very firm shake of the head. "It's fine."

It wasn't.

Twenty minutes later, I took a deep breath on the jetty as the young attendant held out his hand to help us in. I asked if he could look after our bags, just in case a freak storm capsized us.

The only person looking thrilled about this was Roka.

But if she was thrilled, I was, too. "Business is all about making people like you." I was heeding my mum's words.

Roka climbed in, ignoring the attendant's offered hand. "We can take it from here." She slipped the young guy a note which must have been more than normal judging from his grin.

"If you're sure."

Once the guy was gone, she carried on talking.

"You should probably know, I don't usually do big-brand partnerships. My manager, Beth, screens out most of the corporate stuff." She held out her hand to help Eliza down. "But you're different. Family business, right? Plus, Beth mentioned you're both queer, which honestly makes everything easier. I'm so tired of working with straight men who think they need to explain my own demographic to me."

The boat wobbled as Eliza picked her way to the far seat, clearly wishing she could levitate and not rock the boat. I swear she was also holding her breath, just in case that helped.

Roka turned to me, but I somehow missed her hand and stumbled into the boat.

"You good?" She grabbed my arm to steady me. It did the trick.

"Like I'm on solid ground," I replied, trying not to show how rattled I was. I sat before I dared speak again. "Your manager researched our personal lives?"

"Honey, my manager researches everyone's personal lives. It's her job. I don't want to get into a boat with a couple of stalkers, do I?"

Roka settled onto the rowing bench and grabbed the oars with the confidence of someone who'd done this many times before. "Now, tell me why I want to wear your watches. I got the photos you sent and they look great, but I want to know the real reason I can't wait to strap one on."

Interesting choice of words.

Eliza opened her mouth to launch into her pitch, just as Roka steered us away from the dock with smooth, powerful strokes that made it look effortless. The boat cut through the water like an Olympic duck.

"Voss Watches has been family-owned for generations," Eliza began, trying to find her rhythm while the boat rocked gently. "We specialise in timepieces that combine traditional craftsmanship with modern innovation—"

"Hold up," Roka interrupted. "That's the corporate speak. What's the real story?"

I licked my lips, and glanced at Eliza. When she hesitated, I jumped in.

"The real story is I spent 15 years running away from this company because I thought it robbed me of my family, and because I thought watches were old news. But after my mum and gran died, I realised I want to keep the company going. But to do that, I need to make it appeal to a new, fresh, younger audience. I want to reinvent the brand. I want to make watches cool again."

"Poppy." That was Eliza's warning shot.

I ignored it.

"We make these incredible pieces that people keep forever, and hand down through generations." My hands moved as I talked, and the boat rocked a little more. "I want to push the brand to the forefront in the biggest way, while also honouring the legacy of my family. I also want this company to flourish, and with you on-board, I believe it could."

Roka's rowing never faltered, but I caught her smile. "Tell me more."

"We want to seriously collaborate: not just lip service. We want your ideas," I told her. "I brought our latest watch to show you. If you join with us, I'd like to bring out a special edition called Roka 23, to match your new album. We're not messing about here. Ads, photoshoots, product placement, the works. Maybe we could do a special release box of your album plus our watch."

"The details of what can and can't be delivered haven't yet been worked out," Eliza added, shooting me daggers.

Roka laughed. "I like her," she said, pointing a finger at me. "She's got no filter." She caught Eliza's expression and added, "Don't worry, I'm not going to hold you to whatever she says in the middle of the lake. But I want to know who you really are if we're going to work together. Both of you."

Roka stopped rowing, and all three of us glanced towards the morning sun, just breaking through the clouds. On the far side of the lake, somebody let out a gigantic belly laugh.

I grinned at Roka, thanking the universe she was a normal person and not an idiot. "Do you row a lot? You're pretty good at it." Her toned, tanned arms suggested she did. Although if she was in the studio as much as she said, perhaps the tan was from a bottle.

"I work out regularly, need to for my tour. Good core strength and endurance is what you need for touring and rowing." She lifted an oar. "Wanna try?"

I shook my head. "I'd probably sink us."

"Believe her when she says this," Eliza said.

But Roka simply shrugged.

Before Eliza could draw another breath to object, I nodded, and Roka talked me through the switch. "Take it easy," she warned as I started to rise. "Don't stand, just slide over—"

Of course, I stood anyway.

The boat lurched to one side like it had taken personal offense to my very existence, and my eyes went wide as gravity decided to make an example of me. I windmilled my arms, probably looking like an inflatable tube man at a car dealership during a particularly aggressive windstorm. Meanwhile, my legs forgot the basic principle of staying upright.

For one brief, glorious moment, I thought I might defy physics and recover my balance. The universe was having none of it. I crashed into the lake sideways with all the grace of a fridge being pushed off a cliff.

The water was shockingly cold, and tasted like algae and a thousand nights out. I tried not to think about it too hard as I spat it out. I surfaced, gasping and probably looking like a half-drowned cat, just in time to see Eliza shoot to her feet.

"Poppy!"

But her standing only made the boat rock a little more. I watched in slow motion as she yelped, lost her balance seconds later, her face cycling through surprise, resignation, then acceptance of her fate. She fell backwards into the water with a splash that somehow managed to be both graceful and wholly undignified.

My amusement vanished in an instant. Eliza hated boats for this precise reason.

I kicked towards her, my waterlogged clothes making every movement feel like I was swimming through molasses. "Eliza!"

She surfaced nearby, her hair plastered to her face as panic flickered across her features. "Oh my fucking god, whose idea was it to get a bloody boat?" She winced as she spat out the stale water.

"I've got you," I told Eliza, swimming close. "You're okay. Hold on to me."

She threw her arms around my shoulders, and we both caught our breath. To my right, three swans started to swim towards us. I decided not to alert Eliza to that.

Roka leaned over the side of the boat, which was somehow still upright despite our dramatic exit. "Are you guys okay? Want to try to get back up?"

I shook my head. "We'll live," I replied. "But I don't think trying to clamber back up is the answer." My teeth started to chatter. "Can you get hold of the boat attendant to come and get us?"

However, when I glanced in his direction, his motorised dinghy was already on its way.

"The cavalry is coming," Roka said, waving her arms.

"This is your fault for agreeing to get into the boat in the first place," Eliza huffed into my ear.

"My fault?" I turned my head. "You're the one who jumped in after me."

"Don't flatter yourself, I fell. Besides, I have to keep you alive. It's the minimum I can do, especially now Margot practically lives with me."

I smiled that she was still combative, even up to her neck in algae. Thankfully, the swans had changed course, maybe put off by Eliza's scowl.

"Can we agree to disagree, just this once?"

Eliza shook her head, but there was a ghost of a smile on her lips. "Never once in any previous business trip have I ended up in the middle of a lake."

I spluttered out a laugh. "Didn't I tell you working with me would be fun?"

Chapter Thirteen

Roka's apartment turned out to be a Brooklyn Heights penthouse with the kind of stone steps and huge windows that screamed 'movie set', complete with a kitchen island that sparkled like it'd been dipped in glitter.

She let us in, then disappeared briefly and returned with tracksuit bottoms for us both and two Roka tour T-shirts. I seriously could have kissed her. Getting out of these lake-drenched clothes was my top priority. Of all the things I'd imagined might go wrong, mutual drowning hadn't made the list.

Meanwhile, Roka's top priority had been making sure the lake bloke didn't spread the story. She'd promised him two tickets to her upcoming intimate Manhattan show plus a tip that made his eyes go cartoon-wide, all in exchange for pretending we were competent humans who hadn't just provided the afternoon's entertainment for half the lake.

"Use my guest rooms to get ready." She indicated two doors next to each other. "They both have their own bathrooms with everything you could need, but take your time. When you're ready, I'll be on the roof with fresh coffee."

When she disappeared, I glanced at Eliza. "Even though this isn't going exactly to plan, I feel like we've made an impression."

She rolled her eyes, but laughed all the same. "You always make an impression, Poppy Voss." She stared at me for a beat too long, stroked my arm, and then bolted through one of the doors like she'd been scalded.

I had no idea what to make of that.

Having intended to have the quickest shower of my life, I ended up spending more time marvelling at what pop stars have in their guest bathrooms. Acres of stylish tiles and enough plants to supply a garden centre was the answer, along with hotel-soft towels.

When I eventually made it outside, Roka was on the sofa chatting to Eliza, in a rooftop garden that offered a picture-postcard view of Manhattan's skyline. Fairy lights were strung between potted olive trees, and comfortable seating areas were scattered around like someone had actually thought about how people might want to relax rather than just pose for Instagram.

Roka had changed into jeans and a vintage Fleetwood Mac T-shirt, and without the baseball cap, her famous sculpted fair hair caught the afternoon light.

"You made it!" she said when she spotted me. She jumped up, poured me a coffee from the pot on a side table, then we all settled down amid a mammoth pile of cushions I would not want to fluff up on a daily basis.

She held out her wrist, the latest Voss watch strapped snugly to it.

"What do you think?" Roka asked. "Eliza gave me your latest."

"I think it suits you," I told her, then flashed Eliza a grateful smile.

Roka studied the watch, then nodded. "Me, too." She

paused. "Eliza was just telling me her ex-wife lives in the city. Do you have any skeletons in Manhattan?"

That was news. I thought Eliza was all about holding back, keeping things professional, but apparently she'd changed her mind.

"I'm squeaky clean where New York is concerned. London's a different matter, though."

"I'm in the UK next month for a festival. Maybe you could tell me the best places to get into trouble?" Roka smiled. "But tell me more about Voss Watches. We were up to the bit where you hated the company but then you didn't, before you took a dip in the lake."

I stood, and gazed out at Manhattan, trying to channel every business documentary I'd ever watched. "Are you a born and bred New Yorker?"

Roka nodded. "Born in Brooklyn, raised in Queens, moved to Manhattan, hated it. Finally back where I belong."

"Then you understand the love of a city. I'm the same with London, but also with the Highlands. It's where my family are from." I gestured to Eliza. "It's where we spent idyllic summers in our childhood, too, so Eliza understands."

Eliza gave me an encouraging smile that made my stomach do something acrobatic.

"Voss Watches straddles both locations. My great-grandmother started the company with nothing but determination and a talent for annoying men who thought women couldn't understand engineering. It's in my heart and my blood, even though I tried to deny it."

Roka blinked. "You two know each other from way back?" She sounded surprised.

I nodded. "Our parents were friends, so we've always been in each other's orbit."

She licked her lips thoughtfully. "Old friends. It makes more sense now."

I frowned. "What does?"

"The chemistry I feel between you." She paused, studying us both with the kind of interest that made me want to hide behind a cushion. "Just friends? Nothing more?"

Eliza shook her head perhaps a bit too quickly. "No. We're old friends, but we haven't actually spent much time together in the past decade. Our paths haven't crossed much since university."

I could already tell this was piquing Roka's interest, so I let it roll.

"But I've got six months to prove I have what it takes to run this company, otherwise my aunt is going to sell the business to some corporate vultures who'll probably turn it into smart watches that count your steps and judge your life choices. I don't want that to happen. Eliza is here to help me get the job done. But it would give us a huge boost if you'd agree to help us."

"Poppy has the vision and the energy. But truly great things only happen in collaboration."

Eliza raised her gaze to me as she said that, and a lightning bolt of realisation slammed through me. Not your budget lightning bolt, either. A full-body slam that almost knocked me off my feet.

Oh.

Oh, bloody hell.

This wasn't just nostalgia or gratitude or the general

confusion of being in New York with someone I'd always admired. Was what Katy said right? Did I really like Eliza in *that* way? And if I did, how had it taken me until I was 29 to realise it?

I wanted to kiss her. Right here, right now, in front of a global pop superstar on a rooftop in Brooklyn. And it wasn't purely because she'd just said something nice about me.

Great timing, Pops.

Christ, I was an idiot.

Roka studied me, then Eliza, then stood with a knowing smile. "I like you two, and doing business with two women who understand me and my music makes sense. Also, I have a new song called 'It's About Time'. Maybe we could do something with that?"

"That would be incredible," I replied.

"Plus, I love the idea of my own watch. Nobody's ever offered me that before. I like your ethos. It'll all come down to timing, but I hope it can work. Shoot my manager some dates and a contract, and let's see what we can do." She paused. "What are you doing tonight?"

I shrugged, trying to look casual while internally having a complete meltdown about my feelings and Roka's agreement. "It's our final night, we're going to see where it takes us and soak up the city."

"I've got a friend who runs a bar in Bushwick. She's having a sapphic night if you want to go along? I'm going to try to make it, but her nights are always brilliant. Lots of queer women, good music, bad dancing, the works."

I glanced at Eliza, whose cheeks had gone slightly pink. "Sounds good to me."

Chapter Fourteen

It'd rained in the afternoon, and the burnt orange evening sky was reflected in the puddles on the cracked pavement. The bar in Bushwick reminded me of the bars I sometimes ended up at in Dalston or Stoke Newington. Small, exposed brick walls covered in queer art, and more undercuts per capita than most cities.

"We're friends of Roka's," I told the woman behind the bar, a statuesque blonde with sleeve tattoos and the kind of confident smile that suggested she could handle anything from drunk tourists to minor apocalypses.

Her face lit up. "Any friend of Roka's is a friend of mine."

I ordered two gin and tonics, but before she made those, she lined up two shot glasses and filled them with something that looked suspiciously like it could strip paint.

"These are on the house. Fair warning: they're strong enough to make you confess your deepest secrets. Or start a fight with a street lamp."

I grinned, then knocked mine back, making an immediate face. Was it, in fact, paint stripper?

Eliza threw hers back and did similar. "Blimey, that is lethal. But if it makes you confess your secrets, here's mine. I'm impressed with myself because I've been in New York for more than 24 hours and I haven't contacted or shagged Michelle. This is genuine progress."

I nodded. "I was surprised you brought Michelle up with Roka. What happened to keeping it professional?"

"Normal rules went out the window with a pop star. Also, after you gave us both an early bath. Which I still haven't forgiven you for."

"You have," I told her with a grin. "And I'm proud of you for not contacting Michelle." I framed my face like I was in the Vogue video. "Clearly, all you really needed was this gorgeous face to distract you."

Eliza's smile died midway to fruition.

I didn't think my boast was *that* out of bounds.

"You're like a reformed addict, but instead of avoiding drugs, you're avoiding your ex-wife's—"

"Don't finish that sentence." The colour drained from Eliza's face. "Oh, fuck. Fuck, fuck, fuck. Whose idea was it to come to a sapphic night where Michelle might also turn up, too?"

My mouth dropped open as I swivelled on my bar stool. "She's here?"

I followed Eliza's gaze to the entrance and saw the woman I'd only ever viewed via Instagram. Tall, dark-haired, wearing a highly styled jeans-and-cardigan combo. Like Eliza, Michelle was the kind of woman who turned heads. She'd just turned both of ours, but not for the right reasons.

Michelle scanned the room, and I turned back to the bar, slapping Eliza's leg in an effort to make her do the same. She complied.

The bartender delivered our gins.

"I can't deal with this," Eliza said. "Not tonight. Not when I was finally feeling like I might be getting my life together. I don't want to speak to her. I don't want to be weak again."

This was panic stations. But Eliza had helped me out. I had to return the favour.

Then it struck me what we needed to do.

"Right," I said, my brain kicking into gear. "We're together. As of right now, we're madly in love and have been for a few months."

"What?" Eliza looked at me like I'd suggested we rob a bank. However, when she looked over my shoulder, she swore, then ducked her head.

"Shit, I think she saw me. She might be walking this way."

"This is not the world's biggest bar. You can't avoid her unless you do something drastic."

Eliza winced and threw me a panicked stare.

"She needs to see that you've moved on. That you're happy. But we need to sell it properly before she walks up."

"What do you mean?"

"I mean…" I took a deep breath, hardly believing what I was about to suggest. "Lean in and kiss me. Like you mean it. Just for show."

I knew it sounded ridiculous. I also knew that my heart was beating overtime at the thought that it might just happen.

Eliza stared at me for a moment, her eyes wide. Then she glanced over my shoulder, and something decisive flickered across her face.

Without another word, she cupped my face in her hands, looked me straight in the eyes, licked her lips, then pressed them to mine.

Even though I'd suggested it, nothing could have prepared me for this.

Because this wasn't a tentative, awkward kiss. Not by a long shot. It was soft and urgent, making every nerve ending in my body wake up and pay attention as if they'd been sleepwalking for years. Her lips were warm and tasted faintly of that lethal shot, and when she deepened the kiss, her tongue sliding against mine with a confidence that made my knees forget their job, I forgot entirely why we were doing this.

I forgot about Michelle, about the bar, about everything except the way Eliza's fingers gripped my face, and the small sound she made against my mouth that went straight through me like a live wire.

On the rooftop earlier, I'd wanted to kiss her. But this? This was something else entirely. What I'd suggested as a simple distraction was rewriting something fundamental inside me, as if my brain was frantically scribbling corrections in the margins of everything I thought I knew about myself. About us.

The trouble was, I had no idea if she was just that good at pretending, or if the ground was shifting under her feet, too.

When we finally broke apart, the absence of her lips was like a physical ache. My mind scrambled to reassemble the pieces of reality, but it was like trying to solve a puzzle after someone had shaken the box. It was as if I'd been struck by lightning, and then immediately hit by a bus for good measure.

Eliza no longer looked over my shoulder. Instead, she stared at me with something like the same freaked-out wonder that must be written all over my face.

She opened her mouth, closed it, then shook her head like

she was trying to clear it. When she finally did glance over my shoulder, her eyes widened.

"She's leaving. I think it did the trick." Eliza ran her fingers through her hair, then sat looking at them, as if she'd forgotten they were attached to her body. When she glanced up at me, her gaze went to my lips, but she dragged it away almost immediately.

She stared at the door. "Should I run out after her?"

I reached out and ran a hand up her arm. Which only caused more shockwaves to echo through my body. I tried to control my nerves which were beyond frayed, but it wasn't easy. I took deep breaths and tried to pretend I snogged my former friend-turned-nemesis-turned-mentor every day of the week.

"Why would you do that? You wanted to avoid talking to her, right?"

She nodded. "But now I feel a bit mean." She stared at her drink, then back at me.

Her eyes had changed from their usual crystal blue to something darker: storm-cloud blue in the dim bar lighting. I wanted to chart the way her cheekbones caught the shadows, how her mouth was still slightly parted from our kiss. When had I started noticing these things about Eliza? When had the sharp angles of her face become something I wanted to trace with my fingertips?

We sat there for another moment, the weight of what had just happened settling between us like an uninvited guest. The kiss was fake, a performance, but it had felt 100% real to me. What if it never happened again? I couldn't let that be one and done.

Before I could even think about what I was doing, I leaned in and pressed my lips back to Eliza's. When she responded, my entire body sparked back to life.

This time, there was no pretence, no audience to perform for: just the soft press of her mouth against mine and the way she tasted of something that was purely her. Her hand found the back of my neck, fingers threading through my short hair, and right then, I didn't care about how this complicated *everything*. Tomorrow was a different story. Right here, in this moment, she was perfect.

"You two!"

A familiar voice cut through the bar noise beside us.

I jerked away from Eliza like I'd been caught doing something illegal, my heart rate immediately switching from post-kiss flutter to full panic mode.

Roka slid onto the bar stool next to us, still in her Fleetwood Mac T-shirt, hair a little more slicked back. "I thought I picked up a vibe, but you were both being so coy about it."

"We're not—" I started.

"Actually, we're really not..." Eliza said at the same time.

Roka waved us both away with a grin. "Please. You were just sucking face so hard at this bar, people were pulling up stools to stare in wonder. You want me to believe you just fell into each other?"

My face burned with the kind of heat that meant I'd turned an alarming shade of crimson, and my hand shook as I reached for my drink. The adrenaline from kissing Eliza coursed through my system, making everything feel too bright and too much. The last thing I wanted was to make conversation with a pop star. But I had no choice.

Roka signalled to the bartender, who greeted her with a fist bump, and lined up three shots of the liquid that got us into this mess in the first place.

"Believe it or not, that was our first kiss. Ever." I stared at Eliza. I still couldn't believe what had just happened.

"You've been wasting a lot of time if that was the first. I suspect there might be more to come." Roka grinned, then raised her glass. "To you two, and to our future collaborations."

I took a large gulp to cover my embarrassment.

"I've been thinking about what you said earlier about collaboration and taking risks. I'm doing a festival next month in Suffolk. Why don't you come as my guests? VIP backstage passes, stay in one of our fancy glamping tents."

Eliza glanced at me, then back at Roka, her eyes wild. "One question: is there a lake?"

Roka laughed. "I'll put it on my rider: no lakes. How's that?"

I grinned, thankful that the spotlight had turned 90 degrees.

"Are you serious about the festival?" I was already thinking about what might happen in the glamping tent. The thought of being in such close quarters with Eliza, away from our normal every day, sent a thrill through me that had nothing to do with business partnerships. Look what had happened when we came to New York. Would we kiss again in Suffolk? Would the festival vibe make things escalate?

"Completely. It'll be fun, and you get to see me in action. I did just witness you two in action, so fair's fair."

Eliza's cheeks turned purple, but she gave me a slight nod and a shy smile.

I looked at her, then at Roka, and gave her a nod.
"We'd love to."
Was Eliza thinking what might happen in the tent, too?

Chapter Fifteen

The next morning arrived, and my brain was on a go-slow, the result of last night's evil shots, along with a kaleidoscope of weird emotions pacing around it. I shuffled into the hotel's dining room and found Eliza staring into her coffee. In front of her was a bowl of fruit and yoghurt, along with a pain au chocolat. She hadn't touched either.

I wasn't sure what to say. We'd skilfully avoided talking about the kiss last night and gone straight to our rooms when we got back to the hotel. Should I get my own table? No, that would be weird. I had to confront this head-on. I couldn't afford any fuckups. I got myself a coffee plus scrambled eggs on toast, squirted some ketchup on the side, then slid into the seat opposite.

"Morning," I croaked.

She glanced up and gave me a slow smile.

I tried so hard not to focus on her lips, but I'm pretty sure I failed.

"Apparently it is," she replied. "You sleep okay?"

I nodded. "Like the dead. Which is what I look like this morning, too."

Her smile got a fraction wider. "You look great. Just like always."

Then she winced and lowered her gaze.

We sat in silence for several seconds, both of us finding our breakfast fascinating enough to warrant intense study. I swore my scrambled eggs rolled their eyes at me.

"So," I said eventually, because someone had to break the silence and it clearly wasn't going to be her. "Our flight's tonight. We've got the whole day to see the city."

"Mmm." Eliza took a careful sip of coffee, like she was afraid any sudden movements might cause her head to fall off.

"What do you fancy doing? I mean, we've both done the touristy bits before."

She sucked on her cheek before she answered. "The High Line, then some lunch? Not too energetic, but we'll feel like we've achieved something."

"Perfect. Low-key sightseeing for the walking dead."

As we made our way through the city later, the fresh air and gentle movement seemed to revive us both. The High Line was busy but not overwhelming, and there was something soothing about walking among the plants and art installations while Manhattan buzzed below us.

When we paused to look out over the Hudson, Eliza glanced my way. "Michelle messaged this morning."

My stomach clenched and I tensed. I had no hold over Eliza. We weren't together. She could do whatever she wanted. Including getting back together with her ex.

"What did she say?"

"That she's glad I've moved on; that what we had was unhealthy." Eliza's voice was carefully neutral. "But also, did I have to come to her city to rub it in her face?" She gave a small shrug. "Anyway, she's seeing someone new. A doctor, apparently."

My fists scrunched in triumph.

"That's good, right?" I was going for supportive. "She's got someone. And you've got… me."

Eliza frowned.

I had no idea why I'd said that. I blundered on. "It's been a while since you split. It's good she's moving on. And you did what you set out to do. Break the chain."

"It is good." Eliza blew out a heavy breath, making both her cheeks billow. "It stung a little when I got her message, but then, I realised you helped me. Made me change my patterns, get out of that destructive cycle I was stuck in." She turned to look at me properly. "Thank you for that."

Warmth spread through my chest that had nothing to do with the lunchtime sun.

"You're thanking me for kissing you?"

Eliza's cheeks went bubble-gum pink. She fidgeted with the strap of her handbag, then tucked a strand of hair behind her ear with the kind of nervous energy that suggested she was reliving every second of last night just as intensely as I was.

Second by second.

A click-worthy montage.

"Let's just say it was a necessary evil." She still hadn't met my eyes.

"Wow." I tried to inject some levity into the moment before the tension flattened us. "I must have really lost my touch if you're now describing my kissing as evil."

Her blush deepened, and she gripped the railing like it might save her from this conversation. She bit her lower lip:

the same lip I'd briefly sucked into my mouth last night. My pulse quickened at the memory.

"You know what I mean," she said quietly. "It finally put a full stop on my story with Michelle. Which is bittersweet, but a good thing. The divorce should have done that, but it didn't. Not fully."

I paused, trying to shake the kiss from my brain. The shape of it. The taste of it. How our lips slotted together perfectly. How her hands had tangled in my hair, how she'd made that small sound against my mouth, how for those few minutes the rest of the world had completely ceased to exist. It wasn't an easy task.

"For what it's worth," Eliza said, finally snagging my gaze with her own. "You weren't a terrible kisser. Quite the opposite, in fact. You sold it like you meant it."

Her gaze bore into me. I wanted to tell her I had meant it, but I couldn't. We had a job to do, and if we started kissing each other all the time, the work wouldn't get done. That was not part of the plan.

"As did you."

We looked at each other then, and the air between us shimmered with possibility. I could see the exact moment she remembered how it had felt. Her eyes darkened slightly as she dropped her gaze to my mouth.

"But I don't want things to be awkward," she said quickly, like she was trying to convince herself as much as me, "so we have to shelve it. Pretend it never happened."

"Obviously," I agreed, because I did. Even though every cell in my body screamed in protest.

"Which will be easy in the interim because I'm working

from home a lot next week as I have to be on top of my build, and then I'm away with my mum for ten days in the Caribbean for my cousin's wedding. Roger, Ellen and the kids are flying in, too. Remember I told you about that?" She snagged my gaze. "But I will work a couple of days and keep on top of everything I have to do. I've been in touch with Ronnie and he's helping me out."

She had told me, and I'd forgotten.

But this was good news. A couple of weeks break, and then when she got back, we could go to Roka's festival as friends. Which was far better than the enemies we'd started out as.

Back in my hotel room later, I sat on the bed surrounded by my half-packed belongings and let myself think properly about yesterday. What a completely mad, hilarious, and wonderful day it'd been. Capsizing in Central Park, meeting Roka, spending the afternoon on her rooftop talking about dreams and ambitions. And then last night: the bar, the shots, Michelle, and that kiss.

Damn, that kiss.

It had been so easy in that moment, in this city, far from home and real life and all the complications that waited for us back in London. Here, we could be anyone. We could be two women who kissed in queer bars and made pop stars think we were madly in love.

But tomorrow, it would be back to reality and back to work. Hopefully with Roka on board, and with a real chance of saving the company. That kiss had been a moment in time, nothing more. A necessary performance that had got slightly out of hand.

I shook my head and shoved my knickers in my case. There was no point dwelling on it. We'd agreed to pretend it never happened, and that was for the best.

Chapter Sixteen

The Lamb and Flag was heaving as it always was on quiz night. Fifty quid for the winning team had a way of drawing people in. Plus, Barney the quizmaster took his job very seriously. The way he handled hecklers and dealt with put-downs with aplomb told me he was also a frustrated comedian.

The first round had been about sport, and he'd kicked out a punter who'd booed when there was a question about women's football.

"Right then." Barney's enthusiasm was infectious. "Round two is all about New York City."

Amina let out a little squeal and punched my arm. "We're going to ace this, you were there a few weeks ago."

I rubbed my arm and frowned. "So long as the questions are about queer bars and lethal shots, we're golden."

Barney pushed his round wire glasses up his face. "Question one: What's the most visited tourist attraction in New York City?"

"Times Square," I whispered.

"You sure?"

"Either that or the Empire State or Statue of Liberty, but say Times Square. It's more accessible. No boats or lifts required."

Amina scribbled down the answer. "Did you go there?"

"Are you mad? Too many tourists."

"Question two: The High Line in Manhattan was originally what type of infrastructure?"

I leaned into Amina and whispered: "Railway." I could feel the ghost of that day's hangover, along with the memory of standing on that very walkway with Eliza, both of us tiptoeing around what happened the night before.

"I like this Poppy who memorised the guidebook."

I shrugged like it was nothing. "We went to the Highline. It was…" I was stumped for words. "Memorable."

Amina frowned. "You have a weird look on your face right now. Like there's something you're not telling me. The same look you had when you pretended you definitely hadn't eaten my leftover Thai food last month."

"I always tell you everything."

"A blatant lie," she replied.

"Question three: Which borough of New York is home to the neighbourhood of Bushwick?"

"Brooklyn," I told her, the question immediately transporting me back to the queer bar and *that kiss*.

"Poppy Voss." Amina pointed her pen at me like a weapon. "You can shake your head all you want, but there is something, and I will get it out of you."

I stared at my bottle of Heineken, then gave her a smile that made her roll her eyes. Of the next seven questions, we knew five and guessed the other two. When Barney called a break in proceedings, Amina drained her beer and went to the bar.

I got my phone out and stared at the string of messages

Eliza had sent me over the past few days. The first lot were work-related: questions about the Roka campaign timeline, feedback on the latest agencies we were dealing with, updates on the influencers we'd approached and their fees (in my next life, I was coming back as an influencer). But the last few were a masterclass in plausible deniability.

They included a photo of her flat stomach glistening by the pool, our latest watch glinting on her wrist. The message read:

> Testing how it looks in natural light.
> Very important for the optics, and for
> Roka when she gets her special edition.

Another of her legs stretched out on a lounge chair, a pina colada balanced on her thigh.

> Making sure it photographs well from
> every angle. Plus, the cocktails here
> are a notch up on Bushwick. The
> company's not, though. ;0)

Another of her in a white bikini, her mouth turned up in a smile I knew well, with the watch beside it.

> Goes well with my smile. If Roka
> falls through, I'll be the new model
> for half the cost.

Each message was technically about the watch and work-related. Technically keeping within the boundaries we'd agreed on after that kiss that definitely couldn't happen again.

But I'd already spent enough time wondering what her stomach might look like. Now I knew, and it was better than I'd imagined. The fact she was sending these while supposedly having quality family time made it even worse.

Or better.

I couldn't decide.

Amina put a fresh bottle of beer in front of me, then sat opposite me with renewed purpose.

I quickly clicked off my phone lest she see the photos, and turned my attention back to her.

"Don't get your phone out, they'll think you're cheating!" Amina tested a new pen she'd picked up at the bar because "that last one was getting on my nerves", nodded, then put the lid back on it.

"Right. You're telling me everything, and I mean *everything*. What happened in New York that is making you give this face?" She waved her fingers around my jaw.

If I voiced it, I knew it became more real. I'd vowed to bury it. However, I wanted to talk about it. To try to make sense of it. And Amina was my best friend...

"If I tell you, you have to swear on your mother's grave you won't tell anyone."

"My mother's not dead."

"Details. Fine, swear on her life, then."

"That seems worse somehow. Like I'm wishing her dead. You wouldn't like her to be dead. You love her samosas, remember?" She rolled her eyes. "Okay, I swear on my mother's continued existence that I won't tell anyone your New York secrets."

I took a large gulp of beer for courage. It was icy cold. "I kissed Eliza."

Amina blinked at me. "You did what now?"

"I kissed Eliza. Or she kissed me. There was definitely mutual kissing happening."

"Hang on, back the fuck up." Amina held up her right hand like she was trying to stop traffic. "Eliza as in 'nothing's going to happen, we work together, it's strictly business' Eliza?"

"That's the one."

"I knew you were hiding something! I stalked her a little on Instagram when you were away, and she is easy on the eye. She doesn't give much of herself away online though, which is admirable or suspicious. I had to see what she looked like as I was picturing someone vaguely businessy with sensible shoes."

"She doesn't wear sensible shoes."

"Clearly not if she's kissing you in bars. Right, I need details. Start from the beginning and don't leave anything out." She checked her Voss watch. The one Mum had been so excited about before her death, and never got to see its success. I'd gifted one to Amina for Christmas.

A chill ran through me, and I instinctively looked around. Was Mum here now? I thought about her every day since her death, but since meeting Sage, now I wondered if she was here and reading my thoughts. I really hoped not, for her sake. There are some things that should be sacred between a mother and daughter.

"You've got five minutes until the quiz restarts."

So I told her. About Central Park and getting soaked and meeting Roka, about the queer bar in Bushwick and the free shots, about Michelle appearing like some sort of perfectly dressed harbinger of doom.

"And then what happened?" Amina leaned forward.

"We needed a plan to make Michelle leave, and I told Eliza we should pretend to be together to ward her off. That we should kiss. She looked weirded out at first, but then she kissed me."

Amina's eyes widened. "Just like that? No persuasion or preamble?"

I shook my head. "It was spontaneous."

"What kind of kiss are we talking about here? Peck on the lips? Friendly smooch? Or full-on tonsil hockey?"

Blood rushed to my cheeks. "It was... comprehensive."

"Comprehensive?"

"There was tongue involved."

"Poppy!"

I knew I was blushing. "And her hands might have been in my hair, and I may have made some sort of noise that was definitely audible over the music."

Amina's grin was wide. "Well, well. Isn't this quite the story."

"It's a disaster because the kiss was good. *More* than good. But Eliza was my enemy but now is my sort-of friend. Plus, I have to work with her, so this can't go anywhere. The business depends on us being able to function together professionally."

Amina gave me a look that told me she understood that, but also knew it wasn't what I was feeling.

"But you like her."

It wasn't a question. I dropped her gaze and stared at the floor.

Did I like Eliza?

Of course I bloody did.

"Yes, I like her. I *really* like her. But that's exactly the problem."

Amina put her chin in the palm of her hand, and leaned her elbow on the table. "How good was the kiss, on a scale of one to ten?"

I closed my eyes and was transported back. Suddenly, I could smell Eliza's perfume, feel the weight of her pressing into me.

I could already feel myself getting wet.

"Twenty-two," I replied.

She let out a low whistle. "Oh my. That is a very big number. Did you fuck?"

I shook my head. "We just kissed."

"But you wanted to fuck her?"

Amina had always been blunt. I shook my head, but then changed it to a nod, then back to a shake.

Amina grinned a little wider. "How is liking someone you kissed a problem?"

"Because…" I struggled to put into words the complicated mess of feelings that had been churning around in my head since we got back from New York. "Because kissing often leads to more, which leads to feelings, which leads to everything going wrong, and ultimately, them leaving and me never seeing them again."

I was on a roll now. "Plus, what if we try something and it spirals and then we can't even be in the same room together? I have to focus right now, you know that."

Amina was quiet for a moment. "I know you've had a rough few years, but not everything ends in people leaving, for whatever reason. I know your mum and dad both did, but it's not the default."

I sighed. "I know that. I've spent enough money on therapy."

"Money well spent, by the way," Amina replied. "My question is: you know it, but do you believe it? Because until you do, nothing is going to stick. You have to be open to things changing, otherwise they won't."

"Opening up right now is not an option. I have work to do. Besides, Eliza has kept it very professional since New York, because we both agreed that's how it should be."

Apart from those photos.

"I haven't seen her much, she's been away. I've tried to work it out of my system."

"I can see that's going really well." Amina raised a single eyebrow. "She hasn't been in touch at all?"

Blood rushed to my cheeks as I recalled her cocktail and poolside messages. I shook my head. Amina didn't need to know everything.

"Just work stuff."

She seemed to buy it. Or else, she knew time was running out because we needed to swap quiz sheets with the next table to mark them.

"When are you seeing her next?"

"Next weekend, start of June. We're going to a festival in Suffolk. Roka's playing and she's given us VIP passes and we're glamping for a night on the Saturday."

Amina's eyes went wide. "A weekend away? Just the two of you? When the last time you were away together, you ended up sucking face?"

I bristled. "Not a weekend away. It's one night. And it's work."

"Dress it up however you want. This is a romantic weekend in the countryside with someone you've just discovered you have serious chemistry with, and you really think nothing's going to happen?"

I stared at her. I'd convinced myself that by the time we got to the festival, the kiss would be very much in the rear-view mirror. But now I knew Amina was right. The last couple of weeks, Eliza hadn't been far from my mind. Absence had definitely made my heart grow fonder.

Lust and panic fizzed through me like an Alka Seltzer. "What am I going to do?"

"You're going to go to Suffolk and see what happens. And if something does happen, you're going to call me immediately with all the details."

"That's your advice? See what happens?" I'd expected more. Amina had been in a relationship with her girlfriend, Noelle, for over five years. She was my romance role model.

"Poppy, you've been single forever. You either shag women or work constantly, and the last time you tried to date, it went very wrong." Amina reached across the table and grabbed my hand. "For once in your life, if it feels right, just go with the flow. The worst that can happen is it's awkward for a bit, and then you both move on."

"The worst that can happen is we can't work together, and then Margot sells the company."

"Or," Amina said with a grin, "the best that can happen is you have great sex and you figure shit out as you go along.

Not everything has to be extremes. You're both grown adults. Sex doesn't have to be complicated."

But even I knew that it normally was.

Chapter Seventeen

The incense was so thick I could taste it, which wasn't great as it was some sort of patchouli-sandalwood hybrid that reminded me of Amina's flat at university. She'd got the flat cheap because there was no kitchen, just a kettle and a camping ring on top of a chest of drawers. Food hadn't been a focus of her life back then.

Sage was clearly doing well with her business, as she now lived on a very fancy road where everyone had renovated their Victorian properties with the kind of aggressive enthusiasm that suggested they were competing to see who could cram the most skylights into one building. The room we were in looked out over a beautifully manicured back garden. Crystals of all shapes and sizes littered every surface, and there were enough candles to pose a serious fire risk.

"How have you been since I last saw you?" Sage asked. "You had a lot of decisions to make. Did you make them?" We both sat on her very squishy sofas.

I nodded. "I did. And you were right. A woman with blonde hair from my past did come back to help me."

She shook her head. "I had nothing to do with it. I'm just the mouthpiece." She gave a measured smile, but her gaze penetrated me.

I gulped.

Then, just as quickly as we sat, she jumped up. "You want tea or coffee? I'm going to make a strong pot if you're interested?" She nodded towards the door. "Follow me to the kitchen?"

I did as I was told.

Where the room we'd just left had been what I expected from a medium's home, her kitchen-diner was anything but. This room was all sleek marble worktops, shiny chrome appliances and her fridge had a TV in the door. Light streamed in through the bifold doors, and a deck stretched out to the lawn I'd seen from upstairs.

She saw me looking and smiled. "I don't normally bring clients in here, but you're not just any client. Katy loves this room, so we do all our sessions in here." She pointed at her art-deco cabinet handles. "She even copied my handles for her kitchen."

Now I looked closer, I could see that was true.

"Somehow, people think mediums drink kombucha, or that mushroom stuff that pretends to be coffee. But I like the strong stuff just like the next person." With that, she filled her machine and set a pot to brew, before putting a hand on her hip and staring at me. "I take it you're back at Voss since I last saw you?"

I nodded. I didn't want to tell her too much, because I didn't trust she wasn't pumping me for information. However, it wasn't Sage who'd arranged this meeting.

"I am. Aunt Margot gave me six months to prove myself. And Eliza Carpenter is along for the ride."

Recognition flooded Sage's face. "Last I heard, she was busy doing her dad's dirty work."

Something tightened in my chest. However, all Eliza had done so far was encourage my instincts. She was on my side.

"She's good." Especially when she's kissing me. "She's being really helpful, which is great."

Sage nodded. "I always liked Eliza. She had good energy."

What did she think about my energy?

Sage hadn't been lying about her coffee preferences. The cup she poured me made my eyeballs ache, but in a good way. We walked back to the first room, and settled onto the sofas.

"I take it this isn't a social call. What can I do for you?"

I blew out a long breath. "I know I can't ask specific questions, but I want to know if I'm going about things the right way."

Like, is kissing my business partner a smart move?

However, I didn't ask that, because I was pretty sure I already knew the answer.

"Is my current promotional idea going to work out? Should I trust Margot?" After what Sage had just said, I also wanted to ask if I should trust Eliza. But I couldn't get the words out of my mouth.

"You know I can't tell you that." Sage took a sip of her coffee, then put it back on her wooden coffee table. "Also, you're a bundle of frenetic nerves, so you're probably blocking any activity. You need to relax."

Easier said than done. I rolled my shoulders, a familiar mixture of scepticism and hope coursing through me. I had to have faith, that's what she was telling me. Just like Amina had told me in the pub last week. I had more belief in myself since I started therapy, but believing and trusting other people was still a flaw I needed to fix. That included Sage, my family, my friends, and even my dead family.

Also, Eliza. But for now, I put her to the back of my mind.

"Have you heard from my family recently? Has anyone told you anything?"

Sage gave me a slow smile. "When people speak to me, they don't exactly turn up with bullet-pointed advice lists."

She got up and pulled something from the shelves. A pack of tarot cards. She held them up. "How about we do a reading to help you focus?" Sage set the cards down, her gaze never leaving my face.

When she studied a spot behind me, I turned and jumped, half-expecting to see my mother materialising between the crystals, probably with her arms crossed and about to give me a lecture about the importance of inbox zero.

"Try to calm down. Take some deep breaths for me."

Sage demonstrated, and I followed. I was tightly wound, but who could blame me? I was just about to share a tent with Eliza, and I didn't know if, when it came to it, Roka would actually sign on the dotted line. Everything was balanced on a knife's edge, and I had no idea which way it would all go.

Sage shuffled the deck, then handed the cards over. "Pick three for me, and lay them face down."

As I did so, nostalgia swept through me. We'd done this exact thing at uni parties, tarot being Sage's party trick. Then, I thought it was just a fun thing to do. I don't think even she thought she could work it up into a business.

"Remember doing this at Faye Hartley's party?" I asked.

Sage glanced up, then nodded. "I do. That party freaked me out. We did a Ouija board afterwards, and I had so many spirits talking to me, I thought I was going mad. I stepped away from it afterwards, but then I realised, it's a gift, not a curse. But it took me a fair few years before I acknowledged that."

I nodded. I guessed it would be weird.

She flipped the first card, which showed a figure hanging upside down from a tree, looking oddly peaceful despite their precarious position. I had a vague memory of this card from our uni sessions, though I could never quite grasp what any of them were supposed to mean back then either.

The second card made my stomach clench. A figure lay beneath ten swords, blood pooling around them under a dark sky. It looked like a medieval massacre.

The third card was slightly less apocalyptic. It showed a woman in flowing robes pouring water between two cups, mountains rising behind her in the distance.

"Okay." Sage tapped the first card with a silver-ringed finger. "The Hanged Man. This is about suspension, waiting, seeing things from a different perspective. Something you want might require you to let go of control."

"Could you be more specific? That could apply to anything in my life."

But Sage simply moved to the second card. "Ten of Swords. This looks dramatic, but it's actually about endings that lead to new beginnings. Betrayal, yes, but also the kind of rock-bottom that forces you to rebuild something better."

Was I there already, or was this in my future?

"And the last one?"

"Temperance," Sage replied. "Balance, patience, the blending of opposing forces into something harmonious. But it requires careful timing and a willingness to trust the process."

I stared at the cards, feeling like they were mocking me with their cryptic symbolism. "What does that actually mean for my life? You used to be much more specific at university."

"That was different. Those were party tricks with cheap wine." Sage's expression grew more serious. "This depends on what questions you were really asking when you laid them out. But only you know that. The cards give guidance, but they can't control how you act."

I drained my coffee, and sat back, feeling even more confused than when I'd arrived. I knew my questions were fuzzy, which is why the answers mirrored that.

"Do you think I can trust Eliza?"

I couldn't quite believe I'd said that out loud. But I couldn't take the words back.

Sage didn't flinch. "It doesn't matter what I think. It's what you think that counts."

But then her eyes got wider, and her movements slowed. She held up a hand. "Hang on, I'm getting something."

Cold washed over me, and every hair on my body stood to attention. I looked around again, but knew I wasn't going to see anything. However, I swear the temperature went up a notch as a weird energy wrapped its arms around me.

"Are they here?" My voice was hardly audible.

Sage didn't look at me, but gave a slight nod.

"An older lady is here. She's wearing a blue coat."

My gran. She loved that coat. My throat went dry and I couldn't speak.

"She's saying to trust your instincts. But you should also trust others, too. She's telling me that people are generally good in the world."

My gran was always optimistic. My mum, on the other hand, would probably tell me the opposite.

I sat forward, my heart thumping against my chest wall. "Anything else?" I looked around, desperate for a physical sign. The window opposite was open, and right at that moment, a feather blew in.

My mum loved feathers. All her cushions and pillows were feather. Was that clutching at straws? Maybe, but it felt like something.

"She says Voss Watches is in good hands."

"With me or with Margot?" I needed specifics.

But then, just as quickly as they'd arrived, they went away again. I could see it in Sage's movements as her shoulders relaxed, and she leaned back on the sofa.

"I know you have trouble believing. Unlike Katy. But if you try, you'll get more back. If you don't believe, you block the pathways. Resistance isn't good here. Try to be a bit more open." She looked me direct in the eye. "That's a good motto for life. Go after what you want, trust your gut. The spirits aren't here to tell you what to do. They're here to shine a light on something you already knew."

"Apart from the scone recipe."

Sage blew out a sharp breath, then grinned. "Apart from that."

I checked my watch. "I should go. I'm off to a festival with Eliza this weekend. We've got a big deal we're hoping to close on."

I wasn't sure exactly which big deal I was referring to.

"But I'll come and see you again soon."

"I know you will," Sage told me.

Chapter Eighteen

The morning sun was already fierce despite the early hour, and sweat gathered on the back of my neck. I'd worried all the way here that we wouldn't be on the list, because communication with Roka's people hadn't been stellar. However, there were no hiccups, we got our VIP lanyards, and our luggage was being stored at Roka's base until our glamping tent was ready.

Now, as we strolled through the rapidly filling grounds of the festival, I tried to act normal, as if New York hadn't happened. We hadn't spoken about it since, had spent hardly any time outside work with each other since, but being with Eliza again brought it all back into full focus. Every time our arms came into contact, an electric volt shot through me.

"So," I said, trying for casual. "Did you give your dad a full debrief on the New York trip?"

Eliza adjusted her tortoiseshell sunglasses, and her tongue snaked along her top lip.

I was *really* glad she didn't know what that did to me. I tensed my jaw and let the reverberations rattle through me.

"Only what he needed to know. Business stuff. Same with Margot?"

I didn't think she was going to tell him we snogged.

"Same." I kicked at a discarded paper cup, sending it skittering across the dusty ground. "Margot's still treating it as if we're playing at business. Has she been around much lately? At yours, I mean?"

The way Eliza's shoulders tensed told me everything I needed to know. "She has." Her tone was clipped. "She makes very good fried eggs in the morning."

My spine went stiff. Margot had never made me fried eggs at any time of day. Why was she mothering Eliza? She had a mother. If anybody needed mothering, it was me and Katy. Plus, since when was Margot a domestic goddess? I had so many questions, but they weren't for now. Instead, I changed the subject.

"How's the renovation going? Still a building site?"

"Totally. Honestly, I can't see progress, even though my builder keeps telling me it's being made." She glanced my way. "It's why I've not been in as much this week. I kept having to go round to make decisions on radiators and plumbing." She paused. "But it's preferable to hearing Dad and Margot going at it. I walked past their room the other night, and I'm not sure I'll forget the sounds coming from it in a hurry."

I nearly choked on my bottled water. "Christ, Eliza."

"I know! It's traumatic. I was grumpy with my builder this week, but I just want to get it done and be able to get back to my life. Living with my dad is complicated. Especially when he keeps trying to advise on this project."

My ears pricked up. "He does? In what way?"

Eliza blushed, then shook her head. "Nothing. He always thinks he knows best; you know how it is. He's the experienced head, even though he trusts me."

Our chat stopped when we stumbled into the fairground part of the festival, with a dodgems track right in front of us.

Eliza put a hand to her mouth. "Remember we used to go on these every summer in London at that terrible funfair? You were so little, you nearly got strangled by the seat belts?"

I grinned. "You don't forget something like that." The painted cars here were just as battered as the ones from our youth, the same tinny music playing, the same smell of hot rubber and electrical sparks filled the air.

"You think we should ride again?"

Eliza nodded. "Obviously." Within moments, she bought tickets from a booth to her left, and then we jumped onto the circuit, a bloke with a straggly ginger beard pointing us to a vacant car.

"Last one if you're happy to ride together. Otherwise, you have to wait for the next trip."

I glanced at Eliza, who shrugged. "So long as I can drive."

The moment the electricity kicked in and we lurched forward, I was transported back to being 10 years old, screaming with laughter as we careened around the small track. Every collision sent us slamming into each other, my shoulder against hers, her thigh pressed against mine as we braced for impact. A guy in a red car seemed determined to target us specifically, and each hit sent us into fresh fits of giggles and closer together in the confined space of our tiny vehicle.

"What's his fucking problem?" Eliza shrieked as the red car slammed into us again, sending me almost into her lap.

"Get him back!" I yelled, and she spun the wheel hard, sending us careening across the track in pursuit. When we slammed into the side of his car, he grinned at us as he spun, and we both threw our heads back laughing. Ever since Eliza and I had come back into each other's lives, I'd been holding my breath. Being in this car in this moment, my guard dropped. I was glad it had.

When the ride ended and we climbed out, breathless and dishevelled, there was a moment where we looked at each other, still riding the adrenaline high.

The dodgems had given an excuse for contact we couldn't justify elsewhere: my whole body pressed to her as we span round a corner, her thigh crushing mine, the way I'd grabbed her knee when that bloke slammed us from behind. All perfectly innocent. All completely necessary for the ride.

But now, standing on solid ground with the flashing lights painting her face in alternating shades of pink and gold, the air between us was charged, like the static electricity from the ride had somehow transferred to us.

Something dangerously close to that moment just before we'd kissed in the New York bar passed between us. Only this time, there was no reason to kiss. Nothing to hide behind.

The only reason to do it was because we wanted to.

We walked towards a cinnamon doughnut stand that was doing a roaring trade, the smell of sugar and spice immediately transporting me back to countless festivals and fairs from my childhood.

"We should get some." I pointed with my finger.

Eliza stopped dead in her tracks.

"What's wrong?"

"It's just... they're Michelle's favourite. I haven't had one since we split."

I rolled my eyes. "Cinnamon doughnuts are everybody's

thing. You can't walk through life avoiding everything Michelle liked. Take control, take back some agency. Especially when it comes to cinnamon doughnuts."

For a moment, I thought she might argue, but then her shoulders squared in that way they did when she'd made a decision. "You're right. Fuck it. Let's get doughnuts."

We ordered two each, and when she took the first bite, Eliza's face lit up as she chewed, sugar dusting her lips.

Her very perfect, inviting lips.

Not now, Poppy.

"Damn, these are perfect," she grinned. "You're a good influence on me, you know that?"

I nearly choked on my doughnut. "I'll remind you of that later."

She stared at me for a beat too long, and I swear her eyes sparkled. But that could be the sugar rush that was almost instant, making everything that bit brighter.

We found a patch of grass near a large tent that was pumping out old-school 90s tunes, and settled down with a couple of ciders that tasted like crisp summer sunshine. The alcohol loosened my tongue, and before I realised what I was doing, I was telling her about Sage.

"She did a tarot reading. Said Gran was in the room with us, which was either comforting or mental, depending on your perspective." I was comforted, on reflection.

"Mum sees her, too," Eliza said quietly. "Your gran, I mean. Says she pops around for tea sometimes."

My brain exploded inside my skull. Did everyone have chats with my dead Gran apart from me? "Next you'll be telling me she brings scones."

Eliza smiled. "My mum loved your gran. She was the mother she never knew. She enjoys her visits from beyond the grave."

I blinked hard. This was difficult to take in.

"She talks to her?"

But Eliza shook her head. "No, she just says she feels her." Eliza took a long sip of her cider. "I made the mistake of telling Margot one morning after seeing Mum, thinking she might be pleased. She dismissed it as hippy-dippy mumbo-jumbo."

"I can just imagine her tone, too."

I'd always connected to Margot the most, but we'd drifted since my mum died, which was mainly my fault. We were similar. Perhaps too much at times. She'd always been the fun aunt who let me stay up late and watch inappropriate movies. But that relationship felt tainted now, scorched around the edges by everything that was happening.

"I can't quite decide what I believe. Sage seems genuine, and she won't take my money. She's got no skin in the game." I turned to Eliza. "Do you think it's possible we get visited from beyond the grave?"

Eliza licked her lips. "It's not that I don't believe. I just trust myself more, I suppose. I'd rather look forward than back, you know? Though I can see why it brings people comfort. Sage is providing a service. But it's not for Margot."

"She was always my favourite," I said. "It's why I don't want this business to ruin that."

"It doesn't have to." Eliza's voice was gentle. "When she's not having sex too loudly with my dad, I like her. She's good for him. But I've watched Dad go through women since he and Mum split. I don't want him to do the same thing to Margot."

"Margot can look after herself."

"A bit like her niece?"

The way she said it, the way she looked at me made something hot flare inside me. "Something like that."

We stared at each other for what seemed like many long moments, before I checked my watch, and jolted. Sitting in the sun and staring at Eliza was not going to get any deal done, was it?

***

When we arrived at the VIP courtyard, Roka was smoking what looked like a joint with another woman who had a buzzcut and striking green eyes. Roka's hair was freshly shaved at the sides, and sculpted upwards on top.

When she saw us, she waved, then walked over with a sure swagger, embracing us with both arms. The end of her joint snagged on my arm, but I didn't flinch. If Roka wanted to brand me with her joint, she could. Anything to get this deal over the line.

"You made it! I was just going to send out a search party. How are my two favourite totally-not-together humans?"

I stuttered, and Eliza cleared her throat.

But before either of us could reply, Roka jumped in. "I gave you one of the best glamping tents with a nice big king-size bed. If you're together, it works. If you're not, you can easily avoid touching each other."

She winked, and I wanted to die on the spot. Heat flooded my cheeks and my stomach dropped to somewhere around my ankles. I didn't dare risk a look over at Eliza, terrified of what I might see in her face.

Horror, embarrassment, or worse, nothing at all.

One of Roka's staff, a girl with intricate braids called Amber, led us through a break in the trees to a gorgeous space with around ten glamping tents, each with their own wooden deck, easy chairs, fairy lights, and hot tub.

"Wow," was all I could say, though my voice came out slightly strangled.

"Exactly my thoughts," Eliza replied.

"You're in tent six," Amber told us, a hand planted firmly in her jean pocket. "I'll leave you to get acquainted, but come back and join us in the courtyard when you're ready. We'll have some drinks and I'll give you your backstage passes. Roka wants you to have a night to remember."

The words 'get acquainted' seemed to echo in the space between us as we followed the wooden pathway through the trees. I was suddenly very thirsty, and also hyper-aware of each step Eliza took, the way her arm occasionally brushed mine as we walked.

When we got into the tent, our luggage was there already, along with a bottle of champagne on ice, a tube of Pringles, and some expensive-looking chocolates.

The space was beautiful: rich fabrics draped everywhere, soft lighting, the kind of romantic setup that would have been perfect if we'd actually been the couple everyone seemed to think we were.

Also looking back at us was our king-size bed, its crisp white sheets housing far too many implications.

"I forgot she thinks we're together." A blatant lie, but I had tried to forget.

"I had, too."

We stood there for a moment, the weight of everything unsaid hanging between us like a physical presence. The air felt thick, charged with something that made my skin prickle.

"But we can cope for one weekend, right?" Eliza's question was rhetorical, but there was something underneath it, a tremor that made me look at her properly. She normally looked assured. Here, she looked anything but.

"We don't want to rock the boat until she's signed the contract."

"I think you already did that in New York," Eliza replied, one eyebrow raised.

"That we did." I was pretty sure my cheeks were bright red. "But if she likes us together, we should be together when we're around her." But my throat constricted as I spoke.

"Agreed. We can be adults about this." But now Eliza's voice had gone husky. When she spoke the word 'adults', her gaze flicked to the bed, before snapping back to my face.

I nodded. "Absolutely. Sensible. Mature."

But when I turned my head, I could see the same fire behind Eliza's eyes that I felt in my very soul.

One weekend.

One bed.

One increasingly flimsy excuse to maintain the careful distance we'd been keeping since New York.

Chapter Nineteen

The pre-show hospitality was way more full-on than I'd imagined. Roka had commandeered a chunk of backstage and turned it into her own personal cocktail party, with a proper bar and queer energy pulsing in the air.

"I thought she wasn't high maintenance, but she's got her own cocktail for her show," I whispered to Eliza as a bartender mixed another Roka Rebellion which was apparently made of gin, vermouth, and something a horrible shade of lime green.

"Does it matter when it's free?" Eliza accepted a glass from the bartender, who gave her a wink so sultry, I felt the force of it. And then, I wanted to jump the bar and scratch the woman's eyes out.

Okay, interesting reaction.

Roka walked up to us wearing a black leather catsuit that practically purred. If I'd have tried the same outfit, I would have looked ridiculous. She swigged from a bottle of water, no lime-green concoction anywhere to be seen.

"You've got a cocktail, great." She leaned in. "Just to be clear, the festival came up with the cocktails for all the headline acts, not me. I'm not that extra, and I never drink before a gig." She squeezed my shoulder. Roka was very tactile this time around. "One thing: don't get too wasted before my set because I might call you up on stage."

I shook my head. "You don't need to do that." Panic took every stitch of its clothing off and streaked through me, screaming.

But she just grinned. "I know. But I might want to."

Holy fucking shit.

When she winked and walked off, I turned to Eliza.

"We might need another drink."

The act prior to Roka was an all-female guitar band who had great energy and songs to match. The crowd responded with gusto, and from our elevated position to the side of the stage, we saw Roka high-five them all as they came off.

I drank in the view as my eyes wandered the sea of people stretching far back, all watching the stage, waiting for the breakout star of the year. Roka's music was the soundtrack to many adverts and film montages, as well as being great songs in their own right. She'd done so well, and I still couldn't quite believe we were here as her guests. Flags fluttered in the warm evening breeze, and the crowd noise swelled every time a technician took to the stage.

"Look at all those people," I said. "How is Roka not absolutely bricking it?" Because after what she said to us, I was.

Below, Roka was doing an elaborate stretching routine.

"Some people thrive on it. I don't mind giving presentations, but getting up in front of this crowd is another level." Eliza's expression spelt freaked.

Twenty minutes later, a woman with a clipboard positioned us by the side of the stage. "Don't move, because I'm not sure when she wants you. My guess is she'll do three songs, then get you on." She turned up her grin. "Try to enjoy it, ladies. This is a once in a lifetime moment."

From our new vantage point, we could see everything from stage level. The crowd flexed and swayed, the lighting rig creaked overhead, and Roka paced behind the backdrop like the coolest lioness imaginable.

When she finally walked out, the noise was deafening. I'd been to plenty of gigs, but this was something else entirely: the kind of roar that seemed to come from the earth itself.

Roka owned that stage like she'd been born on it, prowling from one end to the other, stoking the crowd and giving them exactly what they wanted: hit after hit. Her voice cut through the festival noise, her guitarists were slick, and her drummer hit her drums like she meant it. By the third song, she had the crowd in the palm of her hand.

Sure enough, after song three, she quietened the crowd.

"I want to tell you about some great women I met recently," she said into her microphone, chatting like she was in my kitchen and not speaking to 10,000 people. "Have you heard of Voss Watches? Because if you haven't, you soon will. They're so pretty and cool, and I'm hoping to collaborate with them. Their owners are queer and we're releasing a special edition watch to go along with my album, which is sick. Get out your best queer cheers for Poppy and Eliza!"

Holy fucking shitbags. Even though she'd told us, I was not prepared for this moment.

"I think I might vomit." Eliza gripped my arm so hard I was pretty sure she'd left permanent marks.

"On the plus side, I guess this means we've got the deal," I whispered in her ear.

She turned, dropped her eyes to my lips, then dragged them back up to me. "Smile like you mean it," she told me, then took my hand and pulled me out on stage as the spotlight swung towards us.

***

The afterparty migrated back to the VIP courtyard, where our favourite bartender was still wielding cocktails like weapons, with a side of that dangerous smile. My head buzzed with post-stage static: I was fairly certain sleep was now a foreign concept.

How did Roka survive nearly two hours under those lights without combusting? No wonder pop stars developed pharmaceutical habits. Standing in front of that crowd was like mainlining pure voltage. Great as a one-off, but I wasn't born for the spotlight.

But despite commanding a festival stage like she was born to it, Roka moved through the afterparty with zero ego. She worked the crowd of 50-odd people like she was hosting a dinner party, and when she drifted our way, she'd collected the stunning green-eyed woman en route.

"This is Sasha," she said, making introductions. "Old friend, happened to be in the country, so I persuaded her to come see me."

The way Roka looked at Sasha, I wondered if she was more than an old friend. Or perhaps she wanted her to be? It reminded me of the way I'd been looking at Eliza of late.

"I am *obsessed* with your English festivals," Sasha announced in pure Manhattan vowels and consonants. "I had two pints of cider earlier, and I'm ready to apply for citizenship. You simply don't get drinks like that in the US." She paused to sip something alarmingly purple. "Also, when Roka mentioned your collaboration, I nearly died. I've loved your watches since I could suddenly afford shit when my modelling career took off. Plus, your whole female-dynasty thing? Pure genius. Your family are absolute legends."

Dead legends, but still.

"How was the stage thing?" Sasha continued. "I watched from the VIP area thinking I'd literally murder Roka if she ambushed me like that."

We didn't really have a choice.

Roka's grin was unrepentant. "Everyone wonders what it's like behind the microphone, right? Besides, I'm genuinely excited about this partnership. We could build something extraordinary: for both of us, and for the planet. If you agree to my terms, which include giving a percentage of our profits to charity, then we're on."

I raised my lime-green cocktail, which was currently rewiring my nervous system. "To our success, and to saving the planet on the way there."

* * *

We stumbled the few steps to our glamping tent, drunk on the day and the buzz of Roka's commitment to us. Up above, the sky was scattered with diamonds, impossibly bright away from the city's glow. The smell of baked earth filled my airwaves, along with the taste of potential. Like the first sip of wine you've been saving for the right moment: complex, promising, with notes you can't quite identify yet, but you want to explore further.

We'd left when the party was in full flow, having had enough green drinks and socialising for one day. Plus, Roka had spent the last half hour snogging the face off Sasha. When they slipped away, it gave us permission to do so, too.

However, other non-green drinks were still fair game, so we raided the minibar with the dedication of people who weren't quite ready for the night to end, settling on the deck with tiny bottles of tequila.

"I haven't had a moment like this in forever." Eliza's voice caught as she stared upwards. "Just completely removed from everything, yet somehow more present than I've felt in months. Living with dad and juggling the renovation hasn't been easy. But being away from it all, and being with you? I can breathe again."

I wasn't sure being with Eliza was easy, but I knew what she meant. She had this way of making the world feel manageable, of softening the edges.

"It's all down to you. This whole weekend, New York and shedding Michelle, feeling lighter than I have in months. I'm really grateful Margot and Dad picked me for this job."

Her profile in the moonlight was magical. "I'm really grateful they picked you, too." I gulped. I knew I was going to say it.

I couldn't stop myself.

I didn't want to.

"And after what happened in New York? I know we said we'd bury it and carry on, but I haven't thought of much else since. Especially when I'm just about to fall asleep."

The stars wheeled overhead, indifferent to our tiny human dramas.

She nodded, staring at them, before catching my gaze.

Everything inside me clenched. The trees around us held their breath.

Eliza cleared her throat. "Same. I've tried really hard, but I knew this weekend would alter things again."

I stared at her in the fairy-light glow, and something shifted in the air between us. The space contracted to just this moment, suspended like a question neither of us had dared to ask.

Maybe somebody had to be brave.

Before I could second guess myself, I reached out a hand, and my fingers traced her knuckle. Even that slight touch ripped a low moan from my throat. I felt it *everywhere*. In my heart, in my veins, in my very soul.

What were we doing? I didn't care anymore. Because if this was wrong, then why did it feel so right?

It seemed like we had the same thought at around the same time, because soon, our drinks were abandoned, and we reached for each other, the cool summer air pressing us together. Before either of us could think too hard about it, we were kissing.

Last time, it'd started out soft, tentative. This time, there was none of that. Our mouths came together hard, aggressive, with purpose, like this is what we'd been craving forever.

Heat spilled down my body and I knew right then that if this was what the kissing was like, the sex was going to be off the scale. Was I ready for that? I didn't have a choice. As Eliza's tongue slipped into my mouth and her hand found the back of my neck, fingers threading through my hair, the outcome of tonight was writ large.

She groaned into my mouth, which only made my pussy tighten. Everything intensified that fraction more. She tasted like tequila and something sweeter, like the promise of things I'd been afraid to want.

The kiss deepened more. I wasn't sure how, but she made it happen, urgent and desperate, like we were trying to capture every unspoken thing that had been building between us since time began. Eliza's hand found my breast, then my nipple, and squeezed. My hand slid between her legs and pressed.

She gasped.

Both our eyes sprang open at the same time.

Her pupils were blown wide.

I grabbed her hand and hauled her up. Then I unzipped the tent, and pulled her inside.

Chapter Twenty

The glamping tent glowed like a lantern, fairy lights strung along the canvas ceiling casting a warm, flickering haze over the plush bed.

I'd thought about what sex with Eliza would be like. I'd seen the swell of her breasts beneath her clothes, and I'd imagined what it might be like to suck her nipple into my mouth, then suck everywhere else on her body.

But now we were inside the tent, with Eliza in front of me, every rational thought I'd ever had was quietly showing itself the exit. She was my business partner. My former crush, and my former nemesis. The person I'd sworn I could never let my guard down with: a promise that was currently crumbling faster than my resolve. Here I was, guard not just lowered but apparently setting itself on fire while I watched.

Before I could form a coherent thought, she pushed me down on the faux fur throw on top of the bed, then ever-so-slowly undid my shirt buttons one by one, looking up to make sure I was paying attention. (What else would I be doing?) Then she took my hand in hers, and moved it inside her top, until I found her breast.

She smiled, fixed me with a stare that held me in place,

then grabbed me round the neck and sucked my mouth so hard, she almost inhaled me.

Hot Eliza was a different beast to the calm, manicured, reasoned version that I encountered daily. Between the sheets, Eliza was masc. Which made me want to punch the air, but I didn't, because my fingers were too busy holding Eliza's breast. It was the perfect handful.

"Fuck, you're sexy," she whispered in my ear, all husk and no finesse. That, along with the weight of her thigh on top of mine, made me melt. I went to unbuckle my belt, but she grabbed my hand, then licked my ear lobe.

"No need to rush," she said, going against everything her recent actions had shown me. Her breath was still hot in my ear. "Why don't you let me do it?"

She reached down, pulled the leather of my belt, and simultaneously sucked my bottom lip into her mouth.

I closed my eyes as my mind swam. Eliza had surprised me from the moment we started working together. It looked like she wasn't about to stop any time soon. I'd known Eliza forever, but in this moment, she was a sexy stranger, someone I'd just met. Which only made this that bit sweeter. Forbidden.

She pressed her hand to my arse, gluing me to her. Then she shimmied down my jeans, and I didn't utter a word in protest. Every part of me was a mess as Eliza's fingertips skated across my bum cheeks, dipping in the middle to let me know what was to come. When she slipped inside my white knickers, and touched me right at my core, I gasped.

"Just a little taster," she whispered.

I wasn't sure I was ready, but I had to be.

Then she slid down my body, kissing me hungrily. She

peeled back my bra, exposing all my skin, flushed under the tent's golden light. When her tongue found my breasts, then my nipples, my mind blanked and a slow, sensual buzz began in my head, before working its way down my body and ending in my cunt.

I spread my legs wider to show what I wanted, and felt the upturn of Eliza's lips as she snagged my nipple between her teeth. Pleasure and pain rattled through me like a pinball.

I groaned, and Eliza grinned. "I know what you want, but I'm going to make you wait a little longer."

I groaned again. "Tease."

She snagged my gaze, then licked her lips. "I'm a pro at it."

Her tongue was a blur all over my skin as she worked me up into a frenzy. Then her fingers slid down my body, and finally arrived where I needed them most. She slipped two fingers inside my pants, nudging the cotton aside.

I spread my legs wider: I was practically begging.

I didn't care. I wanted Eliza inside me. But she wouldn't comply, instead slipping around my clit, causing small explosions all over my body. My heart thudded so hard in my chest, I was surprised the whole festival didn't feel the tremors. Perhaps they could.

Outside, someone laughed, and I smelt woodfire.

"I thought we did well not fucking in New York," Eliza told me, sliding two fingers around me.

I closed my eyes as my own internal firepit caught alight, a warmth rumbling through me. When Eliza's fingertips slipped inside, I gasped, and so did she.

"You're so wet," Eliza whispered, her voice brittle as she trailed kisses down my neck, nipping at my pulse point. My hands trembled as I fisted the cotton sheets, but she didn't pull away. This was surrender, raw and real. If I'd been scared about opening up and being vulnerable with her, this was one surefire way to break the dam.

We'd been friends, rivals, sworn enemies, always circling, always clashing. But tonight, after days of tension, we were crossing the line. There was no coming back. From the look in Eliza's eyes, she knew that, too. She curled her fingers inside me, then dropped down until her breath was over me.

I sent up a prayer to the goddess of love as Eliza's tongue began a slalom course over my clit and her fingers slid slowly in and out.

I crushed my head into the plush pillows as the fire inside truly took hold.

Outside, the leaves rustled in the wind; inside, Eliza picked up a rhythm, checking in with me that it was okay, before she took over completely, ramping up the intensity until I teetered on the edge. Then she was on top of me, her mouth rough against mine, her fingers a blur of activity as she took me over the top, before opening my parachute for a safe landing.

As I came, the wind chimes outside applauded. I stared up into Eliza's deep-blue eyes and marvelled at this woman who was somebody completely different in the bedroom. She was wild. Untamed. Which suited the setting, and oddly, suited her in the sheets.

Now I'd sampled a hint of it, I only wanted more.

The only problem was, I wasn't sure I'd ever be able to articulate that, because I could never imagine speaking again. This was me now. Mute, but happy.

Eliza seemed to understand what I was feeling through

the medium of eyelash flickers. She kissed both my cheeks with a tenderness that made my insides ache, then she gathered me into her arms as if I was the most precious cargo in the whole world.

Being cared for in this way was my weak spot, because my parents had never done it, and neither had any partner. Nobody had ever figured it out before. It had to be Eliza who made the connection on the first night.

A flash of uncertainty passed through me, as I remembered who I was with and where I was. But I brushed it aside. I didn't want to spoil this moment.

"That was incredible. You're incredible." She stared at me like she was snapping the moment for later. "I know we said nothing could happen, but after we kissed, it felt inevitable, didn't it?" Her gaze didn't falter.

I could hardly breathe. "It feels like I've finally come up for air after a month underwater."

So many times in the past few years I wanted to throttle Eliza. Had it all been because I secretly wanted to jump her, as Amina said? Perhaps. But now, looking into her beautiful face, I had to trust her.

An orgasm aftershock rattled through me and I shivered, closed my eyes, then climbed on top of Eliza, still high on the sex sugar rush.

"Now I've got my breath back, how about I make you breathless?" I said.

Eliza grinned wide. "I really want your mouth on me. After kissing you, I've thought about that all week."

I pulled her top off, then straddled her. "I'll see what I can do."

Chapter Twenty-One

The following morning, my head felt like it had been used as a percussion instrument by Roka's overly enthusiastic drummer. It took me several moments of squinting at unfamiliar fabric walls to work out where I was, and then it all came flooding back with the subtlety of a brick through a window.

I turned my head 90 degrees to see Eliza next to me, her blonde hair splayed across the pillow.

I smiled before I could stop myself.

Then, the thought, *Oh, fuck* crashed into my consciousness.

Last night had been... well, calling it immense seemed inadequate. It had been expected in the way that watching someone play with fire expects eventual burning, but also completely unimaginable in terms of actual execution.

In the heat of passion (and yes, I was well aware I sounded like a 1970s romance novel), I'd pushed aside all my doubts about Eliza's intentions and just focused on the moment. On the all-consuming pleasure she'd given me.

Now though, those doubts had formed an orderly British queue at the edge of my brain, each one politely waiting its turn to explain exactly how sleeping with Eliza was an error.

Actually, scrap that: the sleeping had been fairly minimal. What we'd done was have sex. Repeatedly. Enthusiastically.

In positions that probably violated several health and safety regulations.

I put both hands over my face and tried to steady my breathing, which was becoming slightly erratic as memories from the night before decided to replay themselves in vivid Technicolor.

This was going to be fine. We were both adults. We could absolutely work together after this. It would not be awkward. Maybe if I repeated that enough times, I might eventually believe it.

I stared at Eliza's sleeping face, and my fingers twitched with the urge to reach out and smooth that wayward strand of hair away from her cheek. The want was so strong it was almost physical.

Get a bloody grip!

Even if we managed to navigate this passion bomb that had exploded between us without completely destroying our professional partnership, I couldn't go around stroking her face like some lovesick teenager.

I had to work with Eliza. I had to forget how absolutely incredible she was in bed. Forget the way she'd made me come so hard I nearly pulled a muscle. I had to focus on maintaining some semblance of professionalism. Which was going to be challenging considering my entire body felt like it had been thoroughly and expertly ravaged. I'd forgotten it was possible to have that many orgasms in one night. It had been a while since anyone had wrung that kind of response from me. Nice to know I was still capable.

But waking here, tangled in sheets that smelled like sex and her, I needed air. I needed coffee. I needed to think.

I checked my watch: 7:30. The coffee stand in the courtyard had been advertising breakfast from early morning. Worth a try.

I slipped out of bed, trying to be quiet, then spent an undignified few minutes hopping around trying to get my jeans on without falling arse-first onto the floor. Every movement reminded me of how Eliza had taken those same jeans off me the night before, peeling them away with a surefire confidence that made me putty in her hands.

The memory sent a fresh wave of desire straight through me, which was not helpful given my current mission to pretend last night had been a momentary lapse in judgment rather than the best sex I'd had in years.

I pulled on my red sweatshirt, grabbed my trainers, and headed for the door.

"Morning!" chirped a woman from the neighbouring tent who I vaguely remembered meeting last night. Her tent, while separate from ours, wasn't a million miles away.

"Morning," I managed, heat flooding my cheeks as I shoved my hands deep into my pockets – *how much had she heard?* – and made a beeline for the copse of trees.

The courtyard was blissfully quiet compared to the previous night's chaos. In fact, there was only one other person visible as I approached the coffee truck, chatting to the barista.

"Morning, Roka," I said, attempting to sound casual as I approached.

She jumped, letting out a shriek that probably woke half the festival.

"Jesus fucking Christ!" She clutched her chest. "Don't sneak up on me before I've had caffeine."

"Sorry. I didn't think I was being particularly stealthy."

"What are you having?" she asked.

This early in the morning, I was impressed her hair still looked show-ready. Maybe she had so much product on it, she woke up like that.

"Long black for me, flat white for Eliza." Saying her name aloud made me blush again, probably because Roka had practically predicted last night before we'd even admitted it to ourselves.

"Same as me." A definite flush crept up her neck.

"Went well with Sasha, then?"

This time the blush was unmistakable. "It did. I've been wanting it to for ages, but the timing was always shit, me being in the studio, then touring, then more studio. Sasha's industry isn't nine-to-five either, so she gets it, but still. Anyway, I sent her a ticket and she came. I figured everyone likes a romantic gesture, right?"

I nodded. "Can't think of many people who don't."

"Yeah, well, I just hope she still thinks it's romantic in the harsh light of day and not completely out there." She held up her coffee cups. "Thought I'd hedge my bets with caffeine. Nobody can resist a woman who comes bearing morning coffee, right?"

It was oddly comforting to discover that even international pop stars had morning-after anxiety.

The barista finished Eliza's flat white with an elaborate leaf design that seemed far too cheerful for my current emotional state.

"Tell me," Roka continued, "why were you so cagey about being together when we first met? I mean, you know I'm queer, I wasn't going to judge."

I considered telling her the truth for approximately two seconds before my self-preservation instincts kicked in. We were in business together, not having a therapy session.

"It's complicated." Which wasn't a lie. "There's history. I wasn't sure where we stood."

"Fair enough." She paused. "For what it's worth, you look good together. Plus, you inspired me. I wasn't going to make a move on Sasha, but then I thought, fuck it. Life's short. So here we are. Two coffee warriors tending to our women."

Our women.

Christ on a bike.

"Good luck," I told her. "I hope the morning coffee strategy pays off."

She went to walk away, then turned back. "Oh, and I know we both have to head home today, so nudge your legal team. Let's sort the details quickly though. I'm playing a bunch of festivals starting in a few weeks, the album launches on July 23rd, then everything gets a lot more tricky." She paused. "I can't wait to see the first watch."

Another excellent reason why I couldn't spend the next few weeks having earth-shattering sex with my business partner. Roka could make or break Voss Watches' future, and I needed every functioning brain cell focused on that opportunity. Roka's album launch signalled the end of my first three months. A time to think about how far I'd come.

"Absolutely," I said. "I'll make it quick and painless, I promise."

Now I just had to work out how to apply that philosophy to whatever the hell was happening between me and Eliza.

Chapter Twenty-Two

When I made it back, Eliza was sat up in bed, the sheet placed in a way that was definitely not helping my new-found commitment to keeping things more professional. Her tits were perky and seemed to whisper "good morning" as I walked in. I did my best not to trip up and fall face-first into them.

"Coffee delivery," I announced, aiming for casual and probably landing somewhere around mildly unhinged.

"You're a goddess." She got on all fours – *really not helping* – and reached for her drink as I set it down on her bedside table. "I was just lying here wondering if it's possible to die from dehydration. And also wondering if you'd run off home having realised what a terrible error you made last night."

Her words were light, but I knew there was an edge to them. I glanced up, brave enough to meet her gaze.

"Is that what you think?" If she said yes, I wasn't sure what face I was going to pull. I didn't regret it. But I knew we had to talk about it.

She shook her head almost before I'd finished my question. "No. Not at all."

Okay.

Well, *okay.*

I took a steadying breath. We had a lot of things to work out. But we had all day. So long as Eliza put some clothes on, everything might be fine.

Emphasis on *might*.

She settled back under the covers, took a sip of her coffee and made a noise that reminded me exactly why I was in this mess. Then she patted the empty space beside her.

"You've got far too many clothes on. Why don't you get undressed and come back to bed to have coffee and pastries."

Pastries? Last I heard, we didn't have any pastries.

But ever eager, Eliza jumped out of bed. I was learning she was very comfortable being naked, and that I was very comfortable with her being so.

She grabbed a basket of pastries I hadn't seen before.

"Where did they come from?"

"Somebody just dropped them off." Eliza lifted up a pot of yoghurt, and tipped the breakfast basket so I could see its contents. "There are fresh croissants, pain au chocolat and those cute custard tarts I can never resist. Still warm. Plus, there are two scones with jam, and this." She held up a mini can of squirty cream. "Apparently it's for the scones." She gave me a flirtatious smirk.

My body whooped with delight and begged me to get naked. My brain, however, wasn't having any of it.

"Eliza, we really need to talk about last night…"

But she was already crawling over the bed like a predatory animal, all long limbs and silky skin. When she got to me, she got on her knees, and before I could finish my very sensible sentence about maintaining professional boundaries, she kissed me. Properly kissed me, with the kind of thoroughness that made my brain flip the sign on its front door to 'Closed'.

"This can't happen again," I mumbled against her mouth, even as I was kissing her back.

"Absolutely not," she agreed, her hands already finding the hem of my sweatshirt. "Terrible idea."

"We have to focus on getting the job done…" I added, although I was helping her pull the bloody thing over my head.

"But today's Sunday, day of rest," she whispered, and then she was kissing my neck and I forgot why I'd objected in the first place.

In moments, I was naked on the bed, with Eliza on top of me, eyebrows raised in triumph.

"You're pretty easily persuaded, just so you know."

I blew out a breath. "You're very persuasive. Especially when you're naked." Her tits begged to be touched, but I was still battling with myself. I think she saw something in my face, because she held up both hands, rolled off me, and pulled me to a sitting position.

"Why don't we have our coffee first, and eat. I don't know about you, but I'm starving. You made me work hard last night."

"I remember it well." I leaned over and got my coffee, deflated that she'd pulled back. I was very aware I was a mass of contradictions this morning.

"I met Roka outside. She was getting coffee for her and Sasha."

Eliza raised a solitary eyebrow. "It wasn't just us that got lucky last night, then." She passed me a plate, then a croissant.

As soon as I bit into it, I realised just how hungry I was.

Between the getting-on-stage, the courtyard, and then the very exclusive after-party, there had been a lot of drinking and not much eating.

Not of food, at least.

Eliza finished her croissant, then immediately reached for the pain au chocolats, and handed one to me.

I bit into it, and let out a moan.

"You're irresistible. Do that again," she told me. Then she leaned over and kissed me again. Thoroughly, purposefully, so that my stomach flipped, and I groaned louder than I had for the pastry.

Damn her.

When I opened my eyes, her mouth was still inches from mine.

"I know you want to talk," she said, her gaze dropping to my lips without any pretext of subtlety. "But can't we just enjoy this for what it is? Two people, taking a weekend away, embracing nature?"

I snorted. "This is embracing nature?" I gestured towards our boujee surroundings.

She shrugged. "We had sex in a fucking forest. That is enough nature for me."

"You are full of surprises, you know that? You have been one person all my life. Annoying. Infuriating. Gorgeous. But then, I get you in this tent, and you become this smouldering sex goddess."

Now I really wanted to slam my head in a door. Why the hell had I said that?

Eliza perked right up at that description. "Sex goddess? Please put that rating on my TripAdvisor."

"I'm sure you score highly, don't be modest." I paused, glancing up at her. "And please forget I said that. My mouth runs away with me sometimes." To ensure nothing else stupid came out of it, I stuffed the rest of my pastry in my mouth.

Eliza sipped her coffee, put it on her bedside table, then shuffled closer to me, shifting the breakfast basket to one side. My clit woke up. I gulped.

The darkness in her eyes, the intention in her face. I recognised it from last night. I wanted it so badly again.

My mind blanked as Eliza ripped open the last half of her pastry, ran her finger along the warm chocolate and smeared some on my stomach, then my nipple.

I gasped. I hadn't been expecting that.

Then, with no pause, she got on all fours again – godammit, the woman was insatiable – and licked the chocolate off my stomach ever-so-slowly.

It was at that point I decided that perhaps she was right. We should enjoy this for what it was.

Plus, there was no way I'd stop her licking the chocolate off my nipple.

When she did, I groaned again, as she swirled her tongue around it, then sucked hard. When she pulled back, she made sure to lick her lips fully, her tongue hanging out of her mouth suggestively.

She grinned at me, reached behind her, and grabbed the squirty cream.

"In my own bed, I might not do this. But we don't have to clean it up." She shook the can and popped the lid. Then she tipped back her head, opened her mouth, and squirted some cream into it.

My whole body shook with want. Maybe it was the way her blonde waves caught the light, tousled from our night, or how her toned body flexed as she knelt on the bed, all casual dominance. It was like she'd flipped a switch, turning our old issues into this delicious game: her leading, me melting.

She shook the can again. "You into it?"

I salivated, then nodded.

"Open your mouth, then."

The things that simple sentence did to me. It was just four normal words, nothing fancy. Yet, somehow, coming out of her mouth this morning, they transformed into something so hot, they burned the bed.

Eliza leaned over and squirted cream into my open mouth. It tasted deliciously sweet. I closed my mouth, letting it ooze down my throat, while Eliza placed her mouth next to my ear.

"Now prop yourself up on your elbows, and spread your legs."

I nearly choked on the cream, as my mouth went dry.

But she was serious. I could tell from the look in her eye. Mischievous. Hungry. Like she'd won this round.

I took a deep breath as Eliza slid between my legs, and pushed them apart. Then she shook the can, and squirted a line of cream up one thigh – shit, it was cold – then the other.

Holy mother of the universe.

A pulse throbbed between my legs.

Eliza flicked her gaze to mine, grinned, then licked the cream off one thigh, then the other. Her tongue was warm and teasing, sending sparks up my spine.

The anticipation of what might happen next was almost too much to take. But I didn't have to wait long. Within moments, her hot breath was over my very core, and I couldn't pull my gaze away as she shook the can once more.

"Should I take a bite of scone first? Spread some jam on you, too?" The smirk on her face was priceless, a callback to our snarky past, now laced with lust.

"You can do whatever you like. As long as you put your tongue on me very soon."

Eliza raised both eyebrows. Then she licked her lips, placed the nozzle over my cunt, then sprayed.

The sensation was like chilled lightning against my natural heat. Cool, fizzy bursts that made me gasp, the sweetness mingling with my own arousal.

"You like that?" she asked.

I nodded. "Strangely, yes."

"This brings a whole new meaning to creaming yourself, doesn't it?"

Then she lowered her head, and swiped her tongue through the cream, before she buried her face in me and didn't come up for air.

Eliza was like nothing I'd ever experienced before in every way possible. She'd always pushed my buttons, but at least now she was doing it the right way, driving me wild with relentless laps and flicks that coiled tension like a spring.

I arched into her, as my fingers gripped her hair hard. The tent's canvas flapped in a sudden breeze that matched my ragged breaths. She didn't stop for mercy, even though the cream was long since gone, replaced with model's own.

Her fingers dug into my bum cheeks as she pressed her face to me, her tongue and fingers working overtime. When she curled herself into me and her tongue vibrated on my clit, I finally broke, thighs clamping around her as I came undone in sharp, shuddering waves, my cries cutting through the morning quiet. I no longer knew who I was with Eliza, but I was just fine with that. This weekend was showing me none of that mattered. I could be whoever I wanted for 48 hours.

My orgasm still coursed through me when I pulled her up. She surfaced with a smug grin, lips glossy, and yanked me into a messy, cream-smeared kiss.

I shook my head as I stared into her clear blue eyes.

"How are we going to work together next week when I know you can do this?"

My phone beeping broke the moment.

I rolled over. A message from my sister, Katy.

I frowned, then remembered. Margot was doing Sunday lunch.

Shit. Shit. Shit.

"What's wrong? That is not a happy face." She rolled her face beside mine.

I shook my head. "Margot's doing lunch today, and I forgot. Can we pack up quickly and get out of here? Sorry to bust the party."

She shook her head, then climbed on top of me, grinding herself on my thigh.

I closed my eyes and sucked in a breath.

She moved her mouth to my ear. "I was kinda hoping I

could get creamy," she said, voice deep. "Then sit on your face and you could lick it off."

Heat burned through me.

Now that was all I hoped for, too.

I pulled her face to me and kissed her hard.

"If you drive really fast, I can squirt really fast."

She licked my neck from top to bottom, then snagged my lip between her teeth.

"I bet I can squirt faster."

Chapter Twenty-Three

When I answered the doorbell to Katy six hours later, I was still reliving every last moment of the night before, and this morning. Because Eliza had given me a whole lot to think about. Having Sunday lunch with my family wasn't the best way to decompress, but at least I'd be fed, and there would be wine.

"You look like you had a good time at the festival," Katy told me. "I don't care how much sleep you didn't have, because it honestly cannot be as little as me. But please sober up and get your head in the game. I need you to be on top form today, because Margot has sprung a surprise."

I slammed my front door shut and walked over to Katy's grey People Carrier, where Bryce was at the wheel. He shot me a pained smile. I waved at my nieces, both strapped into car seats and kitted out in pink, looking like butter wouldn't melt.

"Before we get in the car, what's the surprise?" I braced myself.

"There's been a change of venue. Margot told me last night that things are getting serious with Max, and she wants us all to meet him in a more informal setting. Lunch has been switched to his house in Highgate today, and he's cooking."

My mind blared, but it took me a moment to connect the dots. If Max Carpenter was cooking at his house, that meant we were having lunch where Eliza lived.

Also, that Eliza would be there.

With my whole immediate family.

The same woman I'd spent the past 24 hours having outrageously hot sex with.

This weekend had already proved it could rival anything that had gone before in weirdness. But now, it was taking it that step too far.

"No," I told her.

"No?"

How to word this? "I mean, Margot's the best chef. I don't want Max's cooking. Can't we tell her we want to have it at her house?"

Katy looked at me like I was mad. "Feel free to call her, but she sounded all frothy and happy, like this was a big deal when she called this morning. I figure, we have to support her. She's supported us enough over the past couple of years."

There was that.

I closed my eyes.

This was going to be an utter disaster.

I slid open the door and said hi to Bryce.

"Morning, favourite sister-in-law." Always his favourite joke.

"Aunty Boppy!" shouted Lily.

"Guck girl!" said Vivien, sucking on her fist and pointing at herself with her other hand.

"That's right, you're going to be good girls for lunch, aren't you?" Katy told them.

I wasn't sure the same could apply to me. The shock of what was about to happen was a little too much. My brain could not compute.

* * *

If you'd told me this morning when Eliza was riding my face that we'd be sat with both our families around a dinner table having Sunday lunch in a few hours, I would have laughed. Yet, here we were, with Margot in high cackle mode, so wired and wanting everything to go well, her jaw hadn't unclenched since I walked through the door.

And what a door it was. Margot didn't go for men without money, and Max certainly fitted the bill. When Eliza told me she was living with her dad temporarily, she'd forgotten to mention the pool and games room, sweeping driveway and the small matter of seven bedrooms. We could all move in here and still never see each other. However, right now, there were eight of us huddled around the dining table, and it seemed like a criminal waste of so much house.

I reached over and helped myself to another Yorkshire pudding, figuring that carbing up was a good thing to do in the face of so much 'what-the-actual-fuck-ness'.

"How was your pop star, and did she agree to the deal?" Margot asked, her floral dress dipping just enough to catch Max's attention.

"She did." Eliza's voice was like hot honey being poured on me.

I wanted to lick it.

I needed to calm the fuck down.

But honestly, I was still recovering.

"She agreed to the whole deal, but we've got to move fast before her summer festival schedule kicks in," I added. "She agreed to wear the brand, she loved the idea of a special edition, and she even proposed a future single tie-in."

I couldn't look at Eliza, so I focused on my lunch. Roast beef with all the trimmings. It was very good. Max could cook.

Could his daughter cook, too? Would she ever cook for me?

Stop it.

"That's incredible!" Margot picked up her wine, staring at us both. Could she detect anything? I had to put my game face on and act like nothing happened, otherwise she undoubtedly would.

"It really was." I risked a look at Eliza, then had a flash of her riding my face again. Blood rushed to my cheeks. This is why you should never see your family in the first throes of a thing.

Not that we were a thing.

"Roka was great, she even got us on stage, and we met a few famous faces. The whole thing was like a weird, fever dream."

Eliza nodded, her cheeks flushed, too. "We went backstage, front of stage, stayed in an incredible glamping tent."

"I couldn't believe you agreed to camping," Max laughed. He was way more ripped than I remembered, his biceps on show beneath his short-sleeved shirt, his stubble perfectly set to 5pm. "My daughter is not known for her love of the outdoors."

"Even you would have been okay," I told Margot, who was also famously allergic to nature. "This was five-star camping with champagne, a hot tub, pastries brought to your tent in the morning, a coffee cart whenever you needed it."

Why had I mentioned the pastries? I glanced down at my nipple that Eliza had recently sucked dry. Glitter cascaded through me.

"Did you meet anyone famous?" Katy's face lit up. "Did you meet Lady Gaga? She's playing today."

Eliza reeled off a few names, and Bryce and Katy made impressed noises.

"They were all really lovely. I met a woman this morning in the tent next to us. I'm sure she's an A-List actor, but you know me and faces."

"I do," Katy replied. "Poppy is not fazed by famous people, mainly because she has no idea who the hell they are 99% of the time." She shook her head, then sipped her wine. "I was saying to Poppy when I picked her up, it must have been a late one because her eyes are still bloodshot. Tell me what time you were up 'til. Let me relive my youth."

I really didn't want to do that. My temperature rose smartly, and suddenly it was all a little bit much. I ate a mouthful of potato, then pushed back my chair.

"I'll fill you in when I'm back. Just nipping to the loo," I said.

Eliza immediately jumped up, too. "I'll show you where it is. I need to plug my phone in. Poppy hogged the charger last night, and it's nearly out of juice."

I slipped into the downstairs loo and gripped the edge of the basin, staring at my reflection in the pill-shaped mirror. My cheeks were flushed, my eyes still had that telltale glassy look that came from too little sleep. In fact, I looked exactly like someone who'd spent the weekend having the best sex of her life.

The door opened behind me and Eliza slipped in, turning the lock with a soft click.

"Sorry," she said immediately, leaning against the door. "I had no idea this was going to happen today. I assume you didn't, either?"

"Believe me, I would have mentioned it. Or at least made up a mystery illness which meant I couldn't come."

I shook my head, then suddenly we were both laughing. Quiet, slightly hysterical laughter at the absurdity of sitting around a family dinner table pretending we hadn't been doing unspeakably filthy things to each other mere hours ago.

The laughter died as we looked at each other properly for the first time since we'd arrived. The small space was charged, intimate in a way that made my pulse quicken.

Eliza licked her lips, then stepped closer, and before I could think of all the reasons this was a terrible idea, she kissed me. She made a habit of doing that, and I made a habit of falling for it.

I kissed her back for a few long, unhurried moments, before I came to my senses and pressed my fingertips to her chest.

As she leaned back, she inhaled deeply. "Sorry. It was just kinda torture sitting with you and not touching you."

"I meant what I said earlier, and I thought we agreed," I whispered, conscious of six other people sitting just down the hall. "This was a one-time weekend thing. We can't keep doing it. It's not part of the plan."

"I know."

She looked so hurt, my heart contracted. I didn't want to be the cause of hurt to Eliza.

"It's just… I can't stop thinking about this morning. About your fingers inside me, about the way you—"

"Eliza." I couldn't take it if she was going to start talking like that, as if it wasn't already playing like a really insistent movie in my mind. "I get it. But we can't."

She backed me up against the sink. "We agreed it was a weekend thing, right?" She kissed my lips, ever-so-gently, her breath hot. "It's still Sunday."

Something inside me snapped. If this was the last chance I was going to get to kiss her, maybe I should take it. Plus, she was right.

It was still Sunday.

"Fuck it." I cupped her face between my palms, and kissed her with a ferocity that surprised even me.

She didn't need a second invitation. In moments, her hand slipped inside my shorts, finding the edge of my knickers. If I had resolve left, it crumbled completely. We kissed again, deeper this time, urgent and desperate. Her fingers found me already wet, already wanting her despite every rational thought in my head.

I had to bite down on her shoulder to keep from making noise as she worked me with the kind of precision that suggested she'd been paying very careful attention to what I liked. Then my own hand found its way between her legs, and we moved together in perfect, silent rhythm, our breathing harsh in the small space.

When I came, it was in muffled, shredded silence against her mouth. My body heaved as I caught my breath, and focused my attention on her. She followed moments later, trembling against me as I held her upright. We clung to each other, and I hoped that we'd been as silent as I thought, but I had no idea.

We stood there for a moment, foreheads pressed together, trying to catch our breath and process what we'd just done.

"This is insane," I whispered, to her and to myself.

A few seconds later, I did up my shorts, washed my hands, checked my reflection and kissed her lips. "You're going to be the death of me."

I slipped out first, leaving Eliza to follow.

Back at the table, I picked up my wine glass with hands that were definitely *not* shaking and rejoined the conversation about Katy's latest work drama as if I hadn't just had a quickie in the downstairs loo.

A few minutes later, Eliza appeared, holding up her phone charger triumphantly.

"Found it!" she announced cheerfully. She plugged it in, then slid back into her seat.

I held my breath for a full minute, but nobody gave us a weird look or seemed any the wiser.

But I was wise enough to know this spelt trouble.

Chapter Twenty-Four

By the time we'd polished off Max's sticky toffee pudding (which was obscene in its perfection and exactly what my hangover needed), I'd had enough wine to blur the edges of the past 24 hours. In particular this surreal lunch. One where my aunt was introducing us to a man, which had never happened. And one where my toilet trip had proved one of the most entertaining of my life.

Max turned out to be surprisingly good company too, telling stories about his early days in buying and selling companies that had us all in stitches. Perhaps he wasn't the cold-hearted businessman I'd thought he was. He topped up drinks, made us all feel very welcome, and complimented Margot at every opportunity.

As for my aunt, she was as relaxed as I'd seen her around a man she was dating, her voice getting to a normal octave level within half an hour of us sitting down to lunch, which was good going. I wanted only the best for Margot, and perhaps Max was it. Maybe he'd also met his match in her.

The man could cook, too. I made a mental note to ask him for the pudding recipe, assuming I could ever look him in the eye again without thinking about what I'd done to his daughter in between courses.

The drive back was blissfully uneventful – even the twins slept the whole way until Katy dropped me home – and by the following week, I was back in full work mode, sending the negotiated contract terms over to Roka's management team. I'd structured it as generously as I could without Margot having me sectioned: decent money upfront, royalties on sales, and creative control over how her image was used. Plus, the percentage to charity we'd agreed on.

I fired off a quick message to Roka.

> Deal sent to your team. Hope it's what you're looking for. Thanks again for an incredible weekend.

Her reply came back within minutes: a thumbs-up emoji followed by:

> You're a legend. I'll get back to you soon.

It was in the hands of the pop gods, now.

I touched the photo of my mum and Gran on my desk, hoping they were happy with the contract. The photo was outside the Goldloch plant when they'd expanded ten years ago. They both wore broad grins, unaware of what was coming their way.

I glanced up through my clear walls to the office opposite, the place where my mum took her final breath, currently empty. When she worked full-time, it'd been Margot's space. She'd encouraged me to take it over, but I couldn't do that.

Not yet, at least.

My next call was to Fiona in Scotland, because when Roka signed, we were going to have to up our production and be ready. She answered on the second ring with her usual brisk efficiency.

"Poppy, hen! How are you? How did it go with your mega pop star, and when are you coming back up to the Highlands to give us all a big hug? I told our Ronnie, and he was very impressed. Knew who she was and all! But then, you know gay men and divas. They love them and are them."

I grinned. "Tell Ronnie, if she says yes, which I think she will, he might even get to meet her. She was very keen on the idea of visiting Scotland."

Fiona hooted down the phone. "A pop star in Goldloch. Imagine! Someone who might be bigger than Marti Pellow."

"You're not claiming Rod Stewart?"

"He's a performative Scot, hen!"

I grinned at that. Nobody in Scotland claimed Rod Stewart.

"Anyway, it's looking hopeful. She made all the right noises when we saw her, and we sent over the contract today."

"Fantastic news! I've already started looking at production schedules. Obviously, we've already launched the latest watch, we just need to put her signature on the back for her special edition. Did you get the final imagery?"

I nodded. "Yes, I've asked for her signature and the number 23. Then we just need to think about packaging with her face on. I know we said we'd take it up a notch with our next launch. Maybe we could do it for Roka's special edition, too."

"We can certainly try, hen. Ronnie is buzzing about it. Plus,

I've spoken to Simon down the job centre, and he's got some people on standby."

That's what I loved about Fiona. She already knew what it was going to take to make this work, and she'd take charge. Fiona was worth her weight in gold. I made a mental note to visit again soon, and give Fiona a bonus. She deserved it.

"But anyway, I'll show Eliza when she's here next week."

I blinked. Eliza was going to Scotland? That was news to me. Why hadn't she told me? Or invited me? I pushed my thoughts to one side.

"Any luck with the council? What did Harvey say? Was he up for resurrecting that slightly derelict building while we set up the pre-order?" I knew I was jumping ahead, but the contract was as good as signed.

Why had Eliza not mentioned going to Scotland?

Fiona chuckled. "Having the head of the council as a husband certainly has its perks, that's for sure. Most council business takes months, sometimes more. But when I control what he eats and how much he gets to kiss me, things speed up a little. He thinks they'll approve it, but he's also been sniffing around some other options. There's an old textile factory about 15 minutes from here that's in far better nick and might be a better option. Could be perfect for what we need."

"Keep me posted. And I will try to make it up to see you very soon, I promise."

I was just hanging up when Margot swept in, looking more animated than I'd seen her in a while. She settled into the chair across from my desk, pulsing with energy.

"I have to say, Poppy, I'm genuinely impressed with how you've handled these couple of months. You've seriously got a lot done in ten weeks. I've had the pressure taken off me, and you and Eliza have handled it all beautifully."

"Did you think I wouldn't?" She'd clearly thought I'd be a trainwreck.

"We haven't exactly been keeping track on each other's lives since your mum died, have we?" It was a statement, not a question. "But this Roka thing? It's smart. Really smart."

From slapping me down to bigging me up in 60 seconds. Sometimes I hated working with family.

"I always said I could do this if you gave me a chance."

Margot stared at me, then gave a slow nod. "I can see that. Just make sure you see it through. The job's not done yet."

She dropped my gaze. For some reason, dread washed over me.

"I wanted to ask also…" She paused, twisting her hands in her lap.

This was not my cool, assured Aunt Margot. Was she about to renege on our deal? I frowned, waiting for her to finish her sentence.

"I wanted to ask what you thought about Max, and Sunday lunch? I really do want you to like him. He's the first man in a long time I've cared about this much." She glanced up at me, her cheeks suddenly flushed. "I need to know how you feel about him. It matters to me. You and Katy, Bryce and the kids. You're my family now, and while I don't need your blessing, it'd be nice to have it."

I blinked. Margot going all coy and shy was not on my bingo card this week. But if she was going to be vulnerable, perhaps I should be receptive to it. Plus, he had made a very good dessert.

"I really liked him. He was warm and charming, and he can cook. I don't see anything in the con pile for now. It's all pluses."

That was a small white lie. His big con was that he wanted to buy Voss Watches from underneath me, and Margot held the key. If she fell for him – she might already have done so – that presented a problem. But I'd cross that bridge when I came to it.

My phone buzzed with a call from Eliza, and a familiar flutter of panic mixed with something far more dangerous fizzed through me. I was sure I was transparent, but when I glanced up, Margot was too wrapped up in her own love life to notice mine.

"I should take this." I gestured at the screen. "It's Eliza, and she had a big meeting this morning."

Margot nodded and waved a hand, but didn't get up.

I swiped the green call button.

"Are you sitting down?" Eliza's voice was bright with excitement.

"I am."

"Good, because I have news. This morning went really well, and I've managed to score us a meeting and a tour with SwissTok."

"Wow." They were a major name, doing big things in our arena.

"Wow is right," Eliza replied. "They're willing to give us a factory tour, talk about their production processes, maybe share some insights about scaling up luxury manufacturing. I think this is a trip we should both be involved in."

My brain immediately went to two places: first, that this was actually a brilliant opportunity to learn from one of the best in the business. Second, that spending time alone with Eliza in Switzerland was definitely going to end with us in bed together.

Also, was she going to tell me about Scotland? I couldn't ask her with Margot there.

"That sounds really valuable," I said carefully.

"It could be game-changing for understanding how to position ourselves in the market with our next launch. Also, we could get ideas for the Roka packaging. I was thinking we could fly over soon?" She paused. "I'm heading to Scotland next week to work out the production plans with Fiona and Ronnie. Just decided this morning. I thought it best to be there, show them we care."

"Do you need me to come too?"

Was she avoiding me again?

"No, you're on the Roka deal, and you're doing great. We can be more effective separately, get more done. When I get back, we'll head to Switzerland the week after. That way, when my three months is up, you've got loads of ammo to show Margot."

When she said it like that, it made sense. "Do you want my assistant to book Switzerland?"

"I'll do it," she replied. "And don't worry, I know it's work. I'll book two rooms."

She hung up, and I stared at my phone for a moment, wondering what I'd just agreed to. She could book two rooms, but even though this was work, I doubted we'd use them.

"Was that Eliza?" Margot asked.

I nodded. "She's got us a meeting with SwissTok to talk branding and upscaling."

"Excellent. You two are quite the pairing." She narrowed her gaze. "Only, are you okay going to Switzerland? You haven't been since—"

"I'm fine," I interrupted. I wasn't going to think about the last time I was there and what my mum asked me.

Margot clasped her hands in her lap, stared at me, then nodded. "Okay, then. This is what I mean about you stepping up and taking things seriously. I'm very impressed."

If only she knew how seriously I was about to complicate everything.

Chapter Twenty-Five

I woke up the next morning feeling as if someone had parked a small car on my chest. The sensation was so intense I couldn't draw a proper breath, and for a moment I lay there in my rumpled sheets, staring at my perfectly smooth ceiling, trying to work out what the hell was happening to me. Was I having a heart attack? If so, it was *really* inopportune timing.

But somehow, I didn't think I was. My skin prickled, and I had the distinct, bone-deep certainty I wasn't alone in my bedroom.

"Mum?" I whispered to the empty room, feeling immediately ridiculous but unable to stop myself.

The presence – because that's what it was, a presence – seemed to get stronger at the sound of my voice. I'd felt this before, in the months after she died, but never this intense, never this urgent. It was like she was trying to push something important into my consciousness, something I was too dense or too distracted to pick up on.

If Amina was here, I'd have run into her room screaming. But she was at Noelle's place. Instead, I fumbled for my phone and dialled Sage's number before I could talk myself out of it. She was the only person I knew who wouldn't immediately suggest therapy when I told her I could feel my dead mother hovering around my bedroom like an anxious ghost. In fact, she'd positively encourage such thoughts.

"Poppy." Her voice immediately soothed me. Maybe Sage was half-medium, half-therapist. Perhaps that's what all mediums were.

"Sage, I'm really sorry to bother you—"

"It's no bother." When she said that, I believed her.

"It's just… I think my mum's here. In my flat. I can feel her, and it's freaking me out."

"Okay, take a deep breath."

I did as I was told and was immediately calmer.

"Are you feeling pressure? Like she's trying to get your attention?"

"Yes, exactly that. Like she's pressing on me. Like she wants to tell me something."

"Do you want me to come over?"

She didn't live far from me. It wasn't so much of an imposition. Plus, I did owe her a coffee.

"If it's not too much trouble?"

"Message me your address."

An hour later, Sage stood in my living room, inspecting my space with open curiosity. Most people walked into your house and sat, glancing at things. Not Sage. She picked up my photos, stroked my entrepreneurial books, inspected my money plant. Her bangles chimed as she put down a photo of Amina and me at university.

"That was the year before we met on our MBA course," I told her, filling the silence. I already knew Sage was super-comfortable with nothing being said.

"I recognise the top you're wearing. I always thought it

looked good on you. You should wear more autumnal colours."

I nodded like I was definitely going to remember that.

But Sage wasn't here to give me fashion advice.

"Thanks for coming over at such short notice. Can you sense anything?"

"Oh, they're definitely here." She glanced to one corner of our lounge, then the other.

I followed her gaze, but I couldn't see anything. It was unnerving and maddening.

"You were right to call me. Have you felt this before?"

I nodded, and all the hairs on my arms stood up. "A few times, but I thought it was just me and how I was feeling that day. Like I got out the wrong side of the bed. But after meeting you, it's opened my eyes to other possibilities."

I perched on the edge of my red velvet sofa, feeling like a guest in my own home. "Why is she here? What does she want?"

Sage closed her eyes, tilting her head like she was listening to something I couldn't hear. The silence stretched out until I was ready to scream, and then she opened her eyes and looked directly at me.

"She's always here, always looking over you. She wants you to know that."

Goosebumps unfurled across my body.

I hugged my arms to my chest, and held my breath.

"But she's specifically here to issue a warning about something or someone. She's telling you to be careful."

Icy fear slithered down me and I tightened my fingers on my arm. "Can she be more specific?"

"She's showing me a number 23. She says to take care of yourself."

Number 23. Was she talking about the new launch? Was Roka going to do a number on me? I couldn't believe she had either the time or the inclination. Plus, anything we agreed to was in a contract.

My mind immediately went to Eliza, who'd come up with the '23' idea initially. The dread that followed was so intense, nausea swelled inside me. I didn't want to believe it, but who else could it be? My own sister wouldn't betray me. It couldn't be Fiona, who was about as straightforward as a person could be and had been nothing but loyal to our family business.

Maybe Margot? But that made no sense. She had her doubts about me taking everything over, but she'd said she'd give me a fair crack of the whip. Plus, she was family.

Which brought me back to Eliza. I reminded myself that I hardly knew her at all. Yes, she said all the right things, but she'd only been back in my life for a few months. People weren't always what they seemed, especially people who fell into your life at convenient moments offering exactly what you needed.

But if that were true, why would she be going to Scotland to smooth things along? Unless she had an ulterior motive for doing that?

My head swam, and not in a good way.

"Can she give me a name?" I hated how small my voice sounded.

Sage shook her head slowly. "She's fading now. I think she might have been here too long. Does '23' mean anything to you?"

"Too many things right now. It means everything."

After Sage left, I poured myself a coffee and walked into my home office, trying to make sense of what Sage had said. The Voss business plan was pinned to my white board, showcasing the hours I'd spent on it before actually making it happen. I couldn't have done it without Eliza's help. She was also a key cog in where we wanted to end up.

The rational part of my brain knew that mediums were hardly reliable sources of information. But the part of me that had felt my mother's presence, that had woken up unable to breathe couldn't dismiss it so easily.

I thought about Switzerland, about spending two days alone with Eliza, about how easily I'd agreed, despite knowing it would complicate everything.

Maybe that was exactly what she was counting on.

* * *

The following week, I got the email from Roka's people. The contracts were signed and sealed: it was all systems go. The magnitude of the achievement made me grin as I pushed back my office chair and stared out over the capital. We'd done it. I wanted to punch the air, but it seemed a little weird.

The first person I wanted to share the news with was Eliza. I picked up my phone and called her. She was still in Scotland. It went to voicemail. I exhaled, then tapped out a message.

> We've got Roka's signed contracts.
> All the prep work was worth it! Xxx

I stared at my phone, waiting for a reply. She wasn't online. I checked my watch. It was just gone 2pm. Where was she? I tried Fiona too, but she didn't pick up either.

Nobody else would understand. Maybe Margot? I peered across the hall, but she wasn't in her office. She rarely was these days, choosing to work from home more often than not. I dialled her number.

"Poppy. What can I do for you?" Finally, somebody answered.

"I just wanted to let you know that Roka's signed, and I had to tell someone!" She was third choice, but she'd do.

"That's incredible. It's never done until it's signed, you know that. You've done it, kid."

"Thanks." I blushed, despite myself. I didn't need Margot's approval, just like she didn't need mine when it came to Max. However, it was nice to have.

"I'm hoping this proves I can do the job at my three-month appraisal."

Margot paused for a long moment before she replied. "It can't harm anything, can it?"

Two hours later, my phone pinged. I picked it up, like I hadn't been checking it constantly while mainlining coffee all afternoon. Finally, a message from Eliza.

That was it. For the biggest win of my career, the deal that could save everything: a thumbs up emoji. No call back, no excited response, not even a proper message.

I stared at that pathetic little yellow thumb until my eyes hurt. Something was wrong. This wasn't just Eliza being busy or distracted. She was avoiding me, and I needed to know the reason why.

Chapter Twenty-Six

The skip outside Eliza's house this Saturday afternoon was full to the brim with broken tiles, chunks of plaster, and an awful lot of garden debris. A sign in her front garden told the world the name of the construction company doing the demolition, should they want their house beaten up, too. Eliza had told me it was an extensive renovation, but I hadn't appreciated the scale until I arrived at the front door.

I knocked on the door, which was ajar, but I was pretty sure nobody was going to hear me over the hammering and drilling coming from close quarters. I called out as I stepped inside, my voice echoing off smooth plastered walls with dangling wires and the occasional punched hole.

I walked past three builders having a coffee and phone break, and spotted Eliza out the back, directly in my eyeline. I walked through the half-installed kitchen and out the bifold doors, to where Eliza stood in what would be an impressive courtyard garden when it was tidied up, but was currently full of excess tiles, a cement mixer, three bikes, and a ton of roofing material.

"I'm not going to do that, and it's not fair of you to ask me." Eliza's voice was firm, with an edge to it I hadn't heard before. She had her back to me, so it was only when I stepped closer that I realised she was talking on her phone.

I took a tentative step back, not wanting to be caught earwigging.

"I am holding up my side of the bargain. You're the one going back on what we agreed." She lowered her voice. "I've told you before, I'm not doing that. Especially not now."

Who was she talking to and who was she talking about? Did it have anything to do with me? All my senses went prickly.

"You know what, I don't need this. I've agreed we'll speak tomorrow. Just leave me to have my Saturday in peace." She paused while whoever was on the end of the line said something. "And that's the reason I am where I am." Another pause. "Yep, see you then."

When the conversation ended, she stuffed her phone into the pocket of her baggy jeans, and shook her head.

I wanted to let her know that I was here, but this was a really inopportune moment to announce myself. However, short of teleporting out the door, then coming back in as if I'd heard nothing, that wasn't about to happen. I cleared my throat.

When I did, Eliza spun around, then clutched her chest.

"Oh my god, it's you." She blushed furiously, then glanced over my shoulder. "Did you just arrive?"

I nodded to give her the reassurance she wanted. "Just walked through the door. I shouted, but then I saw you out here."

She patted her back pocket, and wouldn't meet my stare. "Right. I didn't hear you." She pulled back her shoulders and took a deep breath. "Welcome to my humble abode."

As well as her baggy jeans, Eliza wore a blue sweatshirt that brought out the colour of her eyes, and was far more casual than her normal style.

She'd clearly been on site many times, and knew what to wear. I was the numpty who'd shown up in black jeans, and was surely going to leave with them covered in a thick layer of dust. There was already dust in Eliza's hair, along with a smudge of something dark across her cheek. Maybe she'd fare better out of the rat race than I'd given her credit for.

I pushed aside my unease as much as I could. If I'd turned up five minutes later, I wouldn't have heard what I did. Eliza could speak to whoever she wanted. This was her house, and her life. When it came down to it, we were work colleagues, who had sex once a month at weekends.

Which was a hugely depressing description of our relationship.

We walked back into the half-finished kitchen, and I fished in my bag and handed over the Farrow & Ball paint charts that I'd told her I'd drop off this morning, now she was back from Scotland. I'd redecorated my own flat using them last year.

"Thanks for bringing these around, I appreciate it." She placed them on a pile of flat bags of concrete currently serving as a makeshift table.

"No problem. They might have changed the colours a bit since last year, but the key ones will still be the same." I glanced around. "I know you said you were renovating, but this is something else."

She stood, and gestured around the space. "It needed it, there was a lot of damage. Plus, this whole downstairs was a series of smaller rooms. I took it back to brick, opened it up, extended as you can see, and put in more glass and an island."

Even though I knew the project was due to finish in a couple of months, it was still hard to visualise completely. Max was once a property developer, which meant this didn't faze Eliza as she'd grown up around it. It's probably why she was so unflappable in business, too. Eliza knew she could take on projects, break them down into smaller pieces, and get them done.

Was that how she was viewing me? Charming me, getting me into bed, softening me up so her dad could buy the company and profit big time?

My heart told me not to be ridiculous. She wasn't a money-grabbing thief.

Yet my head and my mother's warning told me to tread with care. I itched to ask about the phone call, but knew I wouldn't.

"When I started this, I was hoping this was going to be the place I could call home, you know?" Her voice was quiet, delicate. "Somewhere I can be who I really am, away from my dad and all his expectations. But lately, I've been thinking maybe I need to move further away, make a proper break. I could rent this out or sell it. Start again."

My eyebrows shot up, but my stomach filled with a thousand pebbles. "You're thinking of moving? But I thought you were excited about this house."

And what about us?

Maybe that's why she'd been avoidant.

She dropped my gaze and stuffed her hands in her back pockets. She stretched her neck, and I longed to run my fingertips up it.

"I was, and part of me still is," she said. "It's going to be amazing when it's done. I'm just not sure it's my long-term plan. Dreams change, and who I want to work with might change, too." Her gaze met mine again. "The last few months have opened my eyes and made me realise what's important. Do you know what I mean?"

I nodded.

I knew *exactly* what she meant.

We stood there staring for a few moments, as heat rolled through me. Her fingertips touched mine, and sparks ignited on my skin.

"I'm glad we reconnected, Poppy. I really hope you're going to be in my life for good, even after all this. I need you to know that. I mean, *properly* in my life."

The way she said it, the intensity behind it, made something twist in my stomach.

I liked Eliza. The feelings I had for her were becoming impossible to ignore. But I couldn't shake the sense I was missing something important. And how was I going to be in her life if she was going to leave?

"Would you like to grab an early dinner?" she asked. "There's this place nearby I've been wanting to try."

What could I say? *I'd love to, but the ghost of my mother warned me not to.* I didn't want Eliza to think I was crazy.

I wanted her to think I was sexy and cool.

I wanted her to fixate on me.

I wanted her to want me, whether it was wise or not.

But still, I couldn't ignore what I knew.

"I'm not sure that's wise."

This was the first time we'd seen each other this week,

with Eliza extending her stay in Scotland to nine days. Was this what had prompted the talk of leaving?

I'd told her we had to keep things professional, and she'd stuck to the rules, only talking to me about work. I'd spent the time in a permanent state of disappointment and longing.

Her face fell slightly, but she recovered. "How about just a drink then? There's a pub literally two minutes away."

I should have said no. Every rational part of my brain was screaming at me to make my excuses and go home to my pristine flat where the ghost of my dead mother would pat me on the back for my sound life choices.

However, I was not known for making those.

The pub turned out to be a gay bar, intimate and dimly lit, with rainbow flags draped artfully around the space. The clientele were in their 20s and 30s, with more piercings and tattoos than an average bar. Eliza ordered us both a beer, then found a corner booth.

She could have sat opposite me, but instead she slid into the booth beside me, until our thighs touched.

I stopped breathing. She smelled so good, even though I could still see the plaster dust in her hair. Before I knew what I was doing, I leaned over and wiped the dirt smudge from her cheek. When my fingers touched her skin, she shuddered.

When our gazes locked, my earlier resolve around Eliza melted like chocolate in the hot sun.

"I missed you this week." When she spoke, her eyes never moved from my lips.

Her gaze was an aphrodisiac. Hell, *she* was an aphrodisiac.

Those blue eyes, the colour of the brightest ocean, saw

straight through every defence I'd tried to build over the past week. Sitting this close to her, I could smell that subtle perfume she wore. It reminded me of expensive hotels and summers by the loch.

"How was Scotland?"

She shook her head wistfully. "Incredible. I stayed at the pub again. Marcus turned out to be a barman I could confide my problems to with ease, and Harvey cooked me a mean steak and chips. I was spoilt, but it was nice to get away. My dad's been rubbing me up the wrong way of late." She sighed. "I've been sleeping at the house since I got back two days ago. Working from the café up the road."

I frowned. "Sleeping at the house can't be comfortable." I'd been there. "And why didn't you come into the office to work?"

She squirmed a little. "I didn't want to burden you with my personal problems."

I called that for what it was.

"Bullshit. You've been avoiding me ever since Sunday lunch at your dad's. It's not cool to fuck me in a loo, then bugger off to Scotland without a word."

Eliza winced, her mask slipping for a moment. "I'm sorry. It's not just about us. It's also about my dad. About living and working together, trying to navigate our relationship. We might just have run out of road." She paused, and I watched her fidget with her Voss watch: a nervous habit I'd never seen from someone usually so controlled. "But yes, it's also a bit about us. What we're doing."

I frowned, studying the way her shoulders had hunched, how she couldn't quite meet my eye. "We're not doing much if every time anything happens, you run away. You know it's a pattern that's played out in my life. I don't need you to emulate it just when I was starting to put a little trust in you."

She sucked in her cheeks, that sharp bone structure becoming even more pronounced, and nodded. Her usually immaculate blonde hair fell across her face as she looked down, and she pushed it back with an unsteady hand. Her breath was laboured, and for some reason, it made my breath stutter, too.

"I haven't dealt with it very well, and I apologise. It's just everything at once. Job. Love life. Home. Nothing is concrete, and it's unsettling me."

The vulnerability in her voice caught me off guard. Part of me wanted to stay angry – it was safer that way – but seeing her like this made something protective stir in my chest. She looked so sad, I almost felt sorry for her. But she had to hear this.

"I get that, but we've been working on the Roka deal for the past three months. When the contracts got signed, I was thrilled. I expected more than a thumbs-up emoji."

Eliza winced, then splayed her hands.

"I agree. But I figured if I reacted too much to Roka, it would be acknowledging what happened at the festival, which is all tied up with Roka."

She tapped her head with two fingers and gave an apologetic shrug. "It made sense in my head at the time. I was more focused on helping out, getting the watch production in place, and securing the SwissTok details. Plus, you told me we couldn't happen again. I wanted to make it easier for both of us. To tread carefully. To manage the situation."

"Did it work?" I knew the answer, but somehow, I wanted to hear her say it.

"It made it worse." She reached for my hand, and I let her take it.

At her touch, the air in my lungs froze. For a moment, everything stopped. Her eyes snapped to mine, searching for something.

"You should go up to Scotland too, by the way." Her voice was quiet now. "It's a breath of fresh air, literally and metaphorically. Plus, there's Harvey's steak."

"I offered, but you told me no." I wanted to stay mad at her, but I couldn't.

She nodded. "I needed a little space this time. But next time, maybe we could go together."

"Maybe."

She shimmied an inch closer so our shoulders touched.

The contact sent flames shooting through me, and suddenly I was right back in that glamping tent, remembering the way her skin had felt under my hands: soft, warm and addictive. How she'd made me feel like I was coming apart at the seams, like every nerve ending in my body had been rewired specifically for her touch. The way she'd looked at me afterwards, pupils dilated, lips swollen from kissing, like I was something precious she'd discovered.

Even now, just the brush of her shoulder against mine was enough to make my breath catch. Her sapphire gaze was doing that thing again, that slow, deliberate sweep across my face that made me feel like she was memorising every detail of me. When her eyes lingered on my mouth, heat pooled low in my stomach, the same insistent want that had consumed me all week.

"Poppy." She said my name like she was savouring it. It sounded like a promise of all the things we could do to each other if I just stopped thinking and let myself fall.

But my mother's warning was still there, a persistent whisper at the back of my mind, even as every cell in my body was screaming at me to close the distance between us and damn the consequences.

Eliza took the decision out of my hands, and I didn't push her away.

In seconds, we were kissing like teenagers. Her hands were in my hair, mine were gripping the front of her shirt, and for a moment, the nagging sense I was walking into something I didn't understand got swallowed up in the pool of our mutual want.

When we finally broke apart, we stared into each other's eyes, both breathing hard. My heart beat out of my chest, and I had no idea who I was or what I wanted. All my rationale went out the window when Eliza kissed me. That had never happened with anybody else before, and it terrified me.

Eliza fixed me with her gaze, opened her mouth like she was about to say something, hesitated, then lowered her eyes.

I missed the burn of her lips already.

What had she been about to say? Something big, or a guilty secret?

A chill breeze swept over me. I sat up, glancing around. My heart thundered in my chest. I was so confused.

I pressed my index finger to her lips. "Whatever you're going to say, don't."

She took a deep breath, and kissed my fingertip.

Desire dripped through me.

"I was going to say, it's Saturday," Eliza clarified. "Which is the weekend."

"Uh-huh."

"Could we be a two-time, weekend thing?"

Before I knew what I was doing, I was kissing her again. She was like a drug, and I couldn't get enough.

Chapter Twenty-Seven

I woke up in my bed, tangled in Eliza's limbs, her hair tickling my shoulder and the smell of her skin making me want to bury my face in her neck and never come up for air. Last night, we'd submerged ourselves in each other; so much so that this morning, I was still underwater, drowning in a warm Eliza sea. My whole body ached, but it was the sweetest ache imaginable.

"Morning." Eliza turned her head to me. We'd ended up in bed together on June's first and last weekends. Could that almost be construed as a relationship? I shook myself and gave her a sad smile.

"Morning."

She rubbed her eye with her knuckle. "I'm not gonna lie, I've had more enthusiastic greetings."

To make up for it, I leaned in and kissed her. When I pulled back, the smile on her face was wide.

"Much better. You should have led with that." She kissed me again, then rolled onto her back. She exhaled before she spoke, keeping her eyes to the ceiling.

"I want you to know, whatever this is between us, I'm not sorry. I know it's complicated, but I don't care. It's too good to ignore."

The fierce certainty in her voice made something flutter

in my stomach. "Good," I replied, pressing a kiss to her collarbone. "Because I'm not sorry either."

I glanced around the room, half-expecting to feel that crushing presence on my chest again. Was my mother watching this? The thought should have been mortifying, but I couldn't bring myself to care.

"Just so you know, I've got things planned today." Eliza stretched in a way that made her breasts sit up and beg for attention. "We're nearly at the end of our initial three months, and I've got meetings about what might come next."

Three months. Our working relationship had an expiration date, and it was approaching faster than I wanted to think about. After that, I wasn't sure what might happen.

Could we try to make a go of it if we weren't working together full-time? I wanted to ask, but I was afraid of the answers. So I did what all good Voss women had for decades before me. I swallowed my feelings and painted on a smile.

Oblivious to my inner turmoil, Eliza slid out of bed, all graceful limbs and golden skin. I temporarily lost the ability to form coherent thoughts.

Watching her get dressed was its own form of torture. The way she moved, the little smile she threw over her shoulder when she caught me staring. I was pretty sure she knew what she did to me.

"Stay for brunch," I told her, having a flash of inspiration. I wanted to make the most of this moment, whatever it was. "I'll make scones. With my gran's proper recipe." Now I had the quantities written down, it was easy.

Eliza paused, reaching for her jeans. "Like when we were kids?"

"The very same." I sat up, desperate to stretch this bubble of intimacy as long as I could.

Her smile was tight, and I could see the war between duty and desire playing out across her face. "I really should—"

"An hour. Two, tops. It is Sunday, after all."

Something in my voice – the barely concealed pleading, maybe – convinced her. "Nobody has ever made me scones before."

Twenty minutes later, we were in my kitchen, me in shorts and T-shirt, and Eliza in one of my oversized sweatshirts that somehow looked better on her than it had ever looked on me. The sight of her padding around my space in my clothes made my heart do crazy gymnastics. She made us both a mug of tea while I got the rolling pin and mixing bowl, then she slid onto a stool opposite me.

"When my gran made these, I used to sit on her stool and watch, just like you're doing. When I was old enough, she let me help." I started to pull ingredients from cupboards.

"What's the next project? I know you've had meetings with your dad over the past couple of weeks, but you haven't divulged much." I chopped the butter into small cubes, then tipped flour into my large mixing bowl. I had no idea what Eliza was up to once we were done. Her work life was a mystery outside of Voss Watches.

"However, if you're riding in on a white horse to help another damsel in distress, maybe I don't want to know."

She grinned, then moved behind me, sliding her arms around my waist, placing her mouth next to my right ear lobe. I melted back into her warmth. "No rescuing. I'm a one-damsel-at-a-time kinda woman."

She placed gentle kisses on my neck, the vibration sending shivers through me. My fingers stopped kneading the butter and flour, as my brain short-circuited.

"It's nothing exciting. Just boring business stuff. Another company my dad's looking at helping." Her hands settled on my hips possessively. "But I don't want to waste what little time we have today talking about my dad."

Did I catch something in her expression when I glanced back? A flicker of guilt that made my stomach clench with worry? The uncertainty screwed with my mind, but I pushed it away. Not now. Not when she was here and warm and mine, even if only temporarily.

"Where's the baking powder?" I muttered, opening the cupboard above the microwave, then the big larder shelf. It wasn't on the baking shelf where it should be, but I recalled Amina had baked a Victoria Sponge last weekend. She had a habit of not putting things back where they belonged.

I was still searching when I heard my gran's voice, clear as day: "Middle shelf, behind the honey, love."

I froze, my heart hammering. I glanced around the kitchen, but could see nothing.

"You alright? You look like you've seen a ghost." Concern dotted Eliza's voice.

I reached up behind the honey and found the baking powder, my hands trembling.

"My gran used to help Katy find things in her house after she died. Katy told me, and I thought she was being kooky. Then you told me about your mum's experience, too. I think Gran just told me where to find the baking powder."

Eliza's smile broadened. "I hope I'm this useful when

I'm dead." She paused. "I loved your gran. Remember we were going to set up a stall in front of Loch Cottage selling her scones?"

Our childhood dreams were so innocent.

"I remember she wasn't like other grans," Eliza added. "She went to work, ran her own company, which was kinda badass."

"Badass is right," I replied, regaining my voice. "But she was also kind, and always had time for me. There was never a problem she couldn't solve with tea and a scone. She was far from a traditional grandmother, but her scones were the one thing she held tight."

I resumed rubbing butter into flour, the familiar motion soothing my racing heart. When I breathed in again, I could smell my gran's favourite lavender perfume. There was nothing lavender in this kitchen. I didn't freak out. Rather, it made me smile.

"Scones were her thing, but she didn't share the recipe with outsiders. Said it was a family secret." I smiled, thinking of her telling me this as a kid. "It turned out, the secret was soaking the fruit, then sprinkling flaked almonds on top. I made them throughout my childhood, but I recently found the full recipe. This is the first time I've made them properly again."

"I'm glad you think I'm trustworthy enough to share it with."

I snagged Eliza's gaze. "Me, too." This wasn't just breakfast; this was me letting her into something precious, something I'd never shared with anyone else. This was me being vulnerable. Something I could never have imagined when we first met.

"Do you want to help?"

"I would love to."

I guided her through the process, our bodies moving around each other with surprising ease. When I needed to reach past her, she'd shift just enough, her hand brushing my back. When she needed something, I'd hand it to her before she asked, like we'd been doing this dance for years instead of minutes.

"It's great doing this with someone else."

"Anyone would do?" she replied, bumping my hip.

I rolled my eyes. "You know what I mean." The feelings I had for Eliza sloshed inside me, but they were always at war. I changed the subject to stop them bubbling up.

"How are things with your dad and Margot?" I tried to keep my voice casual, while grabbing the cutter for the scones.

"Still going strong, as far as I know. Margot's on a spa weekend with her girlfriends, hence Dad snagging me for work."

Her meeting up with her dad was normal. They worked together. But the phone conversation from yesterday flicked through my head. Had that been Max? Was it about Margot? Or worse, me?

I ground my teeth and focused on the here and now.

As I cut the scones, Eliza glazed, then we put them in the hot oven.

"Make sure it's hot, that's the secret," my gran always said, tapping the side of her nose.

Once the door was shut, I put a pot of coffee on, and we chatted about Roka and how well the deal was going. Pre-sales were pouring in, and she'd agreed to wear our watch in her next music video and on tour. The ad was already on her socials, and it was driving a ton of sales.

But after a while, our chat stopped. Then, Eliza pressed me against the worktop, slid a hand up my arse, and kissed me for so long, it felt like I was imprinted on the counter.

When we broke apart, her thumb traced a line down my cheek, and I stared into her eyes. It was such an intimate gesture that something inside me cracked open.

This felt real in a way that terrified me. It wasn't just about our chemistry, it went deeper than that. She made me want to tell her about my fears, about the way I felt like I was drowning most days, but I was faking it until I made it.

The timer saved me from examining that feeling too closely. I pulled out golden, perfect scones while Eliza poured the drinks, and we ate them warm with butter and jam, sitting at my kitchen island in morning light that made everything soft and easy. Eliza closed her eyes with the first bite.

"Your gran knew what she was doing, and so does her granddaughter," she said, licking butter from her thumb in a way that made me forget my own name.

"Thank you."

She sipped her coffee. "You must really miss her. Your mum, too."

"More than you can possibly imagine. But the way to keep them alive? Bake scones. And keep Voss Watches in the family."

Eliza nodded, picked up her phone, and winced. "I really do have to go now, though."

"I know." I didn't want her to. I wanted to keep her here

in my kitchen forever, eating scones and looking at me like I was something worth staying for.

When she finally went to leave, we bumped straight into Amina coming home. I'd clean forgotten they hadn't met before.

"Amina, this is Eliza," I said, trying to sound casual and probably sounding anything but.

"Good to meet you." Amina shook Eliza's hand, keeping an admirable poker face. "I've heard a lot about you."

"All good, I hope."

"A-stars all the way."

"Sorry it's short and sweet, but I have to run." Eliza's gaze lingered on me. "Thank you for brunch. The scones were perfect. See you at the airport, if not before?"

After she left, I flopped onto the sofa like a deflated balloon, still able to smell her perfume on my top.

Amina settled into her armchair opposite. "How's 'keeping it professional' going?"

I honked out a laugh that sounded slightly hysterical. "Absolutely acing it, as you can see."

"What happened to 'this won't happen again'?"

"During the week, we're completely professional." I knew how ridiculous it sounded.

"And at weekends, you're completely unprofessional? Goddit."

"It seems that way."

She flopped down beside me, her expression softening. "You seem to actually like this woman. Hence I want to point out that you could work together and have a relationship. Office romances happen all the time." She tilted her head. "What am I missing? Because you look terrified."

The concern in her voice made something in my chest loosen, and I filled her in on Sage's visit and my mother's warning about not trusting someone close to me. I didn't tell her about the phone call yet. I hadn't fully processed that.

"She might not have meant Eliza," Amina replied. "Did she say a gender? She could have meant Max. Or maybe you just had a bad dream and Sage isn't all she's cracked up to be." She paused. "And I heard an airport being mentioned? You're going somewhere with her again?"

"To Switzerland. But it's work, and it's during the week."

Amina rolled her eyes. "Keep telling yourself that." She paused, her brow furrowed. "But are you okay, going to Switzerland? You've got a lot of history there. Plus, you haven't been since your mum asked you to join the company and you told her no. Isn't that going to stir emotions?"

I was determined to squash that particular fact *very* far down. I already had enough emotions brewing without adding more to the pot. "It's going to be fine. Two days, get the job done, come home." I was such a good liar when I wanted to be.

She shook her head, but her eyes were kind.

"How is it really? Because you look thoroughly ravaged, but also… relaxed. More so than I've seen you in ages." She glanced over to the kitchen counter. "And you baked scones. You haven't done that since your mum died, either. These are big steps. Maybe Eliza is good for you."

How could I know? I could only trust what I felt in the moment.

When I was with her, it felt like flying.

"Our connection is off the charts. We get each other in ways I didn't know were possible. Like she sees parts of me

I didn't even know existed. I honestly never expected this to happen, and it's scrambled my brain."

Amina's mouth dropped open. "Oh, honey. This is so much more than just a shag. That's what I said when I met Noelle."

"It's not that simple." But even as I said it, I knew she was right. The thought of losing Eliza made me feel physically ill.

"If her intentions are good, it might be that simple." Amina paused. "Plus, if you're going to Switzerland overnight, your weekend rule is about to be comprehensively destroyed."

I groaned and pulled a cushion over my face. Despite everything my mother had tried to warn me about, despite the fear and uncertainty, I had no intention of stopping it. I was already in too deep, and the thought of stepping back felt impossible.

Chapter Twenty-Eight

The SwissTok factory was built into the mountainside like a modernist cave, growing out of the rock as if it had always belonged there. Floor-to-ceiling windows offered views across the stunning valley. Rolling green hills dotted with chalets, Lake Geneva gleaming like hammered silver in the distance, and the majestic Alps rising beyond.

Standing there, breathing in the crisp mountain air – pine and wildflowers and pure freshness – I was suddenly 15 again. Slouched in the back seat of that rental car while Mum and Gran marvelled at being back in their beloved European mountains. All I'd wanted was Spain with my friends, beaches and absolutely no alpine scenery. I hadn't returned since Mum died. It had been too much.

But now, I was here to learn what I needed to carry on her legacy. How she'd have loved this: research trips always made Mum giddy with possibility. Which only made me more determined to make every moment count.

"We're so excited to have you here, Poppy." Gabriel shook my hand. "I loved your mum, and it's a pleasure to meet you, all grown up. Welcome to what we like to call, 'the home of modern luxury'."

Gabriel took us inside, then gestured to the production floor below. He was impeccably dressed in a way that screamed Swiss precision: tailored suit, perfectly groomed beard, smooth skin. I would lay bets that Gabriel had a moisturising routine. "We don't just make watches here. We create lifestyle statements for the digital age."

"Which is exactly the vibe we're going for, too," Eliza told him.

The last trip I'd come on with my gran – I must have been 18 – I'd sulked throughout, whining about the lack of Wi-Fi and how my gran dragged me on hikes up "pointless hills".

"Each piece combines traditional Swiss craftsmanship with cutting-edge technology," Gabriel continued, leading us down to the production floor. "3D-printed titanium cases machined to tolerances of one micron, movements that sync with satellites for perfect timekeeping, sapphire crystal displays that can show biometric data."

The workshop floor was a symphony of old and new. Master crafters worked alongside robotic precision tools, hand-finishing components that had been shaped by computer-controlled lathes. Holographic projections showed tolerance measurements while artisans used techniques passed down through generations.

"This is incredible," I murmured to Eliza, watching a crafter use laser engraving to create microscopic details on a watch face while a computer mapped every stroke. "It's like they've found the perfect balance between old and new."

"And look at the packaging," Eliza whispered, gesturing to the finishing station. "Each box is bespoke 3D-printed bioplastic, but designed to look like traditional Alpine wood. Sustainable luxury. We could do something similar with the Highlands."

The presentation area was more like an art gallery than a showroom. Each watch was displayed like a sculpture, with interactive screens showing the owner's journey: from initial design consultation through to final delivery by a white-gloved courier.

"Our customers aren't buying watches," Gabriel explained, his eyes lighting up as he got into his stride. "They're buying into a narrative, into a moment."

He pulled up a holographic marketing presentation that made my head spin with possibility. "Social media integration, influencer partnerships, limited-edition drops that sell out in minutes. We never put things on promotion because we don't need to. These are bespoke watches which are now must-have lifestyle accessories for those who value time and something special in their lives. You can't put a price on that."

"How do you manage the demand?" Eliza asked.

"We have carefully curated waiting lists. VIP preview events. We build up, show customers their watch being made, give them a timeline, make it an event. We make people feel special for being chosen to spend a lot of money on a watch." Gabriel smiled with the satisfaction of someone who'd cracked the code. "Exclusivity isn't just about the product: it's about the entire experience."

* * *

That afternoon, we sat on the terrace of our hotel, spreading papers across the table as the sun began its descent behind the mountains. Lake Geneva stretched before us, its surface broken only by elegant white sails and the occasional ferry churning across to France. The view was so beautiful and familiar, it made my chest tight with old grief and a fresh future.

I pulled out my laptop and tried to focus. "We could integrate some of this tech – not the satellite syncing, that's overkill – but maybe smart features that connect to phones?"

"And the lifestyle marketing, which you'd already identified. He just made it come to life." Eliza's voice had an excited edge that made my stomach flutter. "We're not selling watches, we're selling lifestyle. Also, the story of the independent British woman who swooped in to save her family company, who values intricacy and quality in a throwaway world."

"She sounds like a nerd." But I couldn't help the smile that spread across my face.

"She's the coolest nerd I know," Eliza told me. "Also, she doesn't know it, but she's beautiful and brave. I don't think I've told you that enough. Taking risks is vital for any business, but it takes guts."

I nodded. I was thrilled that Eliza thought I was brave.

And beautiful.

She had said beautiful, right?

But it did take bravery. I knew what was at stake. My future. My nieces' future. Then a familiar panic began to creep in, the same anxiety that had plagued me since childhood. "But what if I bugger it all up? What if we spend all this money, and we fail?"

Eliza gave me a small shrug and a smile. "At least you tried."

Dread slithered through me.

"What if we're too successful? What if we take orders we

can't fulfil? What if we scale too fast and everything collapses and all those people who believed in us are disappointed? I can't take Margot's 'I told you so' look."

"Pops." Eliza reached across the table and covered my hand with hers, her touch warm and grounding.

I didn't correct her when she called me Pops this time. She'd earned the right.

"You are a brilliant businessperson. You get people. Your mum and gran," she looked around, "who may or may not be here, they'd be so proud of you."

Her observation made me sit up. "I hadn't even thought they might be here. I figured we'd be safe in Switzerland. But I guess spirits don't have to book plane tickets to travel to another country, do they?"

"Not if all the movies are to be believed." Eliza looked me direct in the eye. "But if they are here, they're protecting you. Nothing more."

I furrowed my brow. "Do I need protecting?" I shook off her hand and sat back. All my old fears about trusting people, especially Eliza, roared back to the front of my mind.

"I don't think so?" Now it was her turn to frown. "I just meant, they're looking after you because that's what family does. It's what they'd do if they were here. It's what Margot wants, even if she thinks that means selling the company."

"Has she told you that?" Eliza sounded very sure when she said it.

From being bold and brave, I was now a spiralling mess. This conversation had turned quickly.

She shook her head. "It's no secret that's what she wanted at first. But I think you're causing her to reconsider."

I wished she sounded more convincing. "Has she said something to you?"

But Eliza shook her head some more. "No, nothing."

I puffed out my cheeks and squeezed my hands together. Suddenly, the weight of everything landed on me. What we were doing. What was about to happen with Roka.

Plus, we were *here*.

Switzerland was such a beautiful country. But for me, it would always carry so many emotions and memories. Love. Hate. Grief. Maybe Amina had been right to be worried.

I blinked back tears, my vision blurring as I looked out over the lake. I couldn't meet Eliza's gaze.

"Sorry, I'm being ridiculous. It's just, sometimes, it all comes rushing back that they're not here anymore. That I'm doing this alone."

Eliza jumped up and sat next to me. She went to take my hand, but I shook my head.

"Please don't be nice to me or I'll fall apart. I really don't want to do that when I'm here with you for work."

She stared at me, her eyes shiny.

Dammit, she was beautiful. I'd always thought so. But now her styled brows and her perfect mouth held weight in my heart. She wasn't just a pretty face anymore. My feelings went way deeper, and there was nothing I could do about it.

"You're not doing this alone, Poppy."

That was all it took for the tears I'd been holding back to start properly falling. I reached for a tissue. Thankfully, Eliza didn't try to comfort me too much, and I was grateful. Too much sympathy would end me.

"I was here with my mum the year before she died." My

voice was quiet, thick. I daren't look anywhere but straight ahead. "Gran was already gone, and Mum wanted to come back to the places we'd visited as a family."

Mum's favourite thing to do in the evening was wander through the village, get a drink and a bite to eat. Soak up the local atmosphere. She always far preferred that to a posh restaurant. She liked to support small, local businesses. Which was how Voss Watches had started out.

I wiped my cheek with the back of my hand, but more tears followed. I stared out at the lake, the one Mum loved the most: even more than Goldloch. I saw now that Switzerland had a lot in common with Scotland: the scenery, the beauty, the welcome. It was why they'd loved it here.

"Mum kept talking about how Gran would have loved to see how the villages had changed, pointing out things she remembered from our trips when I was younger. We sat by this same lake and she told me about all her dreams for the business. How she would love me to be involved. I wasn't interested."

My breath hitched. "Somewhere in the back of my mind, I thought I would take over when it was time. I thought we had years to figure it all out. And now she's gone too, and I'd give *anything* to have them here now, to see what we're doing."

The tears flowed a little more, but I didn't feel judged. Yes, we were here for business, but this business was always going to be personal. Margot and Amina had both known it. I'd tried to deny it, but it hadn't got me very far.

"They would have loved this. Mum would have been taking photos of every detail, and Gran would have quizzed Gabriel for far too long."

Eliza was quiet for a moment, then she moved closer and

wrapped her arms around me. I melted into her warmth, breathing in her familiar scent while my shoulders shook.

"I remember how excited your mum got about new technology," she said softly against my hair. "She would have been fascinated by the 3D packaging. And your gran would have charmed Gabriel into giving us all his suppliers and trade secrets."

I choked out a laugh. "You're not wrong there." I sniffed. "When we're on the cusp of something amazing, I want to call them and tell them everything."

"They'd be so proud." Eliza stroked my back. "You're doing exactly what your mum dreamed of. You're honouring everything they both taught you while pushing the business forward."

I pulled back slightly, wiping my eyes with my sleeve. "That last trip here, Mum kept saying she wished Gran could see how beautiful it still was. She missed her so much. And now I miss them both." I exhaled. "Why didn't I get that time was precious? Why didn't I agree to do this sooner?"

Eliza cupped my face gently, her thumbs brushing away fresh tears. "But you're here. You're doing it now. That's not nothing, Poppy."

Something in her voice, the tenderness and certainty, made my whole body tingle with... I wasn't quite sure what. She'd known them both, and somehow that made her comfort feel even more precious.

"Thank you," I whispered.

"For what?"

"For remembering them with me. For being here. For

helping me. For not thinking I'm completely unhinged for crying about this during a business trip."

Katy's words came back to me: "She doesn't seem like a villain." I'd never thought that more than now. Maybe Mum meant someone else entirely.

"This was never going to be just a business trip." Eliza gave me a sad smile. "Plus, we can't be too successful. We're only taking pre-orders at first, not shipping the watch until it's ready. We're offering exclusive updates, inviting them into a golden-circle moment. Remember the email Fiona sent last week, and you gave the green light?" Her tone was gentle but confident. "Scarcity marketing, like Gabriel said. Make it special. People are buying a ticket, and then we ship when it's ready."

I smiled, still shaky from crying. I did remember, of course. "I appreciate all the help you've given me."

Eliza shook her head. "It's a team effort. You're the key contact, dealing with the star, legal and marketing. I'm helping the Scotland team with logistics, while working on my mental health, too." She sighed. "Plus, Andrew is working up the pre-order system. Turns out, Andrew has his uses after all."

"Sounds like you've got it all figured out."

"Just trying to do my bit. But you have the final say."

"Who would have thought you'd ride to my rescue these past couple of months, when you tried to undermine me for years?"

Eliza shook her head. "Everything that happened was accidental. I never intended to undermine you. We've been playing cat and mouse for at least a decade. I even got married in the interim. You could say we've been playing the long game."

The sexual tension that had been simmering between us all day suddenly crackled to life, intensified by the emotional intimacy we'd just shared. I was acutely aware we were alone on this terrace, and that the golden-hour light made everything look soft and romantic. Eliza's hair was catching the breeze in a way that made me want to reach out and touch it.

Instead, I forced myself to look back at my laptop, though the screen was blurry through my lingering tears. "Roka's shooting next week when she's back in the UK for another festival. Then she launches her album two weeks later at 23:00 on July 23rd, and the watch pre-order will get super-charged off the back of that. It's already up for super-fans. We've got 50 influencers lined up for the big launch, social media ads ready, select newspaper and airport ads primed."

"You're creating a moment together." Eliza's voice was warm with something that sounded like pride. "This is going to be massive. I predict you might crash the internet."

My phone buzzed with a call from Fiona, and I grabbed it gratefully, needing the distraction from the way Eliza was looking at me.

"Hi Fiona, how are things?"

"All good here, love. Just wanted to check in. I know you're worrying about capacity, but we've got plans in place. The new 3D printing setup arrives next week, and I've got three more craftspeople lined up if we need them. We can handle whatever comes our way."

Fiona's surety made calm run through me. I wasn't doing this alone. I had a team behind me who were backing me all the way.

Even so, I had to check. "You're sure we can do this?"

"Poppy." Fiona's voice was firm but kind. "Take care of yourself. That's what your mum would want, and in lieu of her, I'm the closest thing you've got to a mother figure telling you to stop panicking and enjoy what you're doing."

The words hit me unexpectedly hard, especially after my tears about Mum and Gran. Fiona was right: she was the closest thing I had to a maternal presence.

"I know," I managed. "Thank you."

After I hung up, Eliza eyed me with concern. "Everything alright?"

"Yeah, just… Fiona looking out for me, like always." I stared out over the lake, where the last light was painting the water gold. "Sometimes I focus so much on the people I've lost, I forget the people I still have."

"You're not alone," Eliza told me, and when I looked up, the intensity in her gaze made my breath catch, and a sonic boom explode in my body. I gripped my leg for something to hang on to.

The silence stretched between us, loaded with all the things we weren't saying. The weekday rule felt increasingly ridiculous when she was sitting there looking at me like that, when she'd just held me while I cried.

"We should probably get ready for our dinner reservation," I said finally, though I made no move to pack up.

"Probably," Eliza agreed, but she didn't move either.

Chapter Twenty-Nine

We never made it to dinner.

Instead, Eliza suggested we walk into the village, and something about the way she said it – gentle, like she understood I needed to move, to breathe – made me nod. The path wound down through vineyards, past stone walls covered in climbing roses that released their perfume into the evening air.

The village was small and perfect, like something from a fairy tale. Cobblestone streets, wooden chalets with flower boxes overflowing with geraniums, and a little church with a bell tower silhouetted against the darkening sky. Most of the shops were closed, but warm light spilled from restaurant windows and we could hear the gentle murmur of conversation and clinking glasses.

We wandered past a fountain where water trickled over worn stone, and Eliza slipped her hand into mine. I didn't pull away. The sparks I'd come to expect when our fingers met didn't stun me this time. Rather, they warmed me. Here, it felt like the perfect thing to do.

"Your mum loved evening walks through the village, didn't she?"

I glanced at Eliza's heart-shaped chin, her strong jaw, her

just-right ear lobes. She was taking charge. She was looking after me. The butterflies in my stomach soared.

"How did you know that?" The observation caught me off guard.

"I remember her telling me, and also, I remember you moaning about it when you were younger. How you just wanted to be on your iPad after dinner, but she always dragged you out for a walk, a drink, a chat."

I closed my eyes and shook my head. "That sounds like something I would have said. Mum loved the old buildings and streets, being connected to history."

Eliza squeezed my hand gently. "It's time to make your own traditions in Switzerland. But they can be the same as your mum's, too. That might make them extra-special."

I expected to be overwhelmed with memories, and I was, but not in a sad way. Instead, I could feel Mum here with me, smiling at the washing on the lines up high, waiting for the church bell to ring. It was nice to do it with Eliza. It was extra-nice that she understood.

We found ourselves in the village's main square, where strings of lights had been hung between the buildings and a few couples were dancing to music from an accordion player sitting on the church steps. It was utterly romantic, the kind of scene Mum would have stopped to photograph from every angle. On the far corner, a flower seller sold roses of all colours. Should I run over and buy a bunch for Eliza?

I immediately rolled my eyes. That was way too corny. I had no idea what this was and what Eliza thought it was. One thing I did know: we were nowhere near corny.

"Dance with me." Eliza held out a hand.

Perhaps I was wrong and we'd arrived at corny?

"Here? Now?"

"Your mum never let self-consciousness stop her, did she? She would have been the first one up dancing."

Before I could protest, Eliza pulled me into the square, and her arms slid around my waist as the accordion player launched into something slow and beautiful. Other couples smiled at us as we swayed together under the fairy lights, and I found myself relaxing into Eliza's embrace.

"Your mum loved you," she whispered into my ear as we twirled. "I know you had your differences, but she would love what you're doing, too. Just like I do."

My whole body vibrated with her words. I'd never doubted my mum's love. But Eliza was right: I needed validation from someone who got what I was doing. Margot wasn't going to do it, and my dead relatives didn't perform to order.

Getting it from someone who was alive and on my side was the next best thing.

Eliza paused, pulling back so I could see the vulnerability in her face.

"You're amazing, Poppy. Who you are, what you're doing. I always thought that when we were younger. I always loved being your friend. Our years apart are behind us, and now I want to be more than that. I want to be the one you rely on. I know I wasn't part of your plan, but I hope I can become your whole plan. I want you to know, I'm falling for you."

My brain seized up at her words. I never expected to dance in a village square with Eliza. I never expected her to say something like that.

"This can't be happening," I said, as if my ears had deceived me.

She held me closer, her eyes serious in the soft light. "It is happening. And you can panic about it, or you can get used to it, because I'm not going anywhere. I know this is complicated, but we can work it out. I *want* to work it out." She gazed into my eyes. "And I think you do, too."

Somewhere in the back of my mind, I could hear Mum's voice from years ago: *Be careful who you trust, darling. People will say anything when they want something.* But looking at Eliza in the fairy lights, dancing with me in this perfect village square like we were the only two people in the world, I pushed the words away.

This was genuine.

She was genuine.

"Of course I do," I admitted. "That's why I'm terrified."

"Good." She cupped my face. "Let's feel the fear and do it anyway."

* * *

The walk back was different. Charged. Every brush of her fingers against mine, every sideways glance, every moment when our shoulders touched as we navigated the narrow path felt deliberate. The careful distance we'd maintained had collapsed entirely.

In the hotel lift, we stood on opposite sides, but the air between us hummed with tension. Eliza's eyes never left mine, and I could see my own want reflected back at me. When the doors opened, she held out her hand.

"Your room or mine?"

"Mine," I said without hesitation, leading her down the corridor.

I managed to get the door open, and we tumbled inside, immediately reaching for each other. Her hands tangled in my hair, mine gripped her waist, and when she kissed me, it was hungry, desperate. Decidedly not weekday material.

I knew now that my crush on Eliza went way back. That I'd inexplicably taken my frustrations out on her for not being age-appropriate when I was 12 or 14, and carried that into my adult life.

Eliza had always been around, but we'd been in different phases of our lives. She'd been busy building a career and getting married. I'd been busy avoiding my family, Voss Watches, and her.

Not anymore.

Eliza had landed back in my life at the same time as Voss had, which was always going to be a potent cocktail to deal with. But Eliza had helped me over the past few months. She'd also made me see that I could do this. That my mum was proud of me. That running towards my problems was always better than burying them and running away. She'd helped me with work and my personal life, and now, I couldn't see a future without her in it. Which scared the living hell out of me, but also, made me realise that I'd never had this with anyone else before.

There was a fine line between love and hate, and for me, it had always been Eliza. That thought had crystallised when she asked me to dance, and my body almost levitated. Dancing with a woman in a public square wasn't something I'd normally entertain. But with Eliza? She made everything seem possible. She was the definition of what could be. Of what might be.

The other thing? She'd always taken the lead. Now, I was determined to top her. I loved what Eliza had given me so far, but today, it was more than time to turn the tables.

When I pushed her down on the bed, she seemed to understand and acquiesce. Our mouths met in a tumble of limbs, fitting together perfectly. I wanted to remove every item of her clothing, but I also wanted to take my time. Every other instance we'd come together naked, it had been fast and furious, as if it would never happen again. At one point, I'd been sure that might be true.

Now, I gazed at her silver St Christopher necklace that hung down past the mole on her right breast, drinking her in. A few moments later, my gaze climbed back to her full, pink lips, and I shook my head.

She'd been right under my nose all my life. I'd avoided her because of stupid pride, and then our lives had gone in separate directions. In a roundabout way, my mum's death had brought us back together. If I was looking for a sign from the afterlife, surely this was it?

But now, I wasn't going to think about my mum, my gran, or Voss Watches. I was going to focus all my attention on the way Eliza's eyes burned with want when she looked at me. The way the edges of her mouth turned upwards when I slowly unbuttoned her blue shirt. The way her toned muscles flexed as she shook free her bra. The way she moaned when I took her nipple into my mouth and sucked.

Long minutes later, after I'd peeled away Eliza's clothes and then my own, I settled my naked body against hers. The first touch of skin to skin pulled matching gasps from our throats: that moment when pretence fell away and you're left with nothing but each other.

My mouth found hers, and we kissed like we were drowning, like each press of lips could anchor us to something real in a world that felt so uncertain. Every time she arched into me, something cracked open in my chest: not breaking, but blooming. This wasn't just desire; it was something that made me forget every reason I'd had for keeping my distance.

When she came up for air, my hands roaming her arse, she took my hand and placed it over her core. "Please," she begged. "I need to feel you."

But I wasn't going to be that easy. I wanted this to be memorable, just like Eliza was to me. Always had been. I skated my fingertips around, up and over, never quite getting to the point, and Eliza moaned in my ear.

"That's it," I whispered right back. "I want you wet and ready for me."

That pulled another moan as I pushed her legs apart, playing with her until she squirmed and her eyes sprang open, breathless.

"If you're trying to kill me, please don't. I want this orgasm before I die."

"I promise to keep you alive just long enough." I circled her a few more times, before slipping just the tips of my fingers inside.

She screwed up her face and lifted her hips off the bed.

I grinned, teased her a little more until she hissed, then slowly eased myself back in, slid between her legs, and began to fuck her.

And honestly? I could wax lyrical about the noises she made. The agony and ecstasy on her face. The way her hips thrust against me as heat rose up her body in faint pink streaks. She sat up halfway through, her eyes wild as I fucked her some more, wrapping an arm around my neck and pulling me to her.

Her follow-up kiss was intense. And when I slid my thumb over her clit, we both groaned at how ready she was.

Fucking her like this, kneeling together, her begging for release was the greatest privilege of my life. It only took another couple of seconds for everything to topple, and Eliza Carpenter to come in a rush all over my fingers. To come so hard, she squirted over my hand.

When she did, her eyes sprang open. I didn't let her dwell on it. Instead, I brought her to climax again, and when she pushed me away, spent, and fell backwards, I kissed my way up her body, finally placing a hot, wet kiss on her mouth.

She was still getting her breath back a few minutes later when she opened her eyes. "Check you out being all masc."

I gave her a tiny smile. "I can turn it on when I want to."

"I'm well aware."

Her eyes never left me when she spoke.

"That was incredible, by the way. I might be dead, but I'm happy."

I turned up my smile. I was still caught in her Eliza forcefield and resistance was futile. Her declaration earlier had freed up something inside me, something that made me want to show and tell Eliza what I wanted. I'd done the first. Now, with my true feelings swirling around my body with abandon, I had to do the second.

"I want you to know, I'm falling for you, too." I kissed her lips one more time. I couldn't keep away. "Completely, utterly, totally." I stared into her bright eyes, and she gave me the sexiest, surest smile imaginable.

"I'm super-glad, because it would have been really awkward otherwise." She paused. "One caveat, though. You think we can stay here forever?"

"I'll check with Margot and Fiona. I'm sure they'd be down with it."

Chapter Thirty

The notification sound on my laptop had been going off constantly for the past hour. I'd given up trying to keep track of individual orders and was just watching the numbers climb on the dashboard.

True to her word, Roka had trailed the new watch all over her socials this week, and pre-orders had come in as soon as she did. But it was nothing compared to what happened when she fully launched at 23:00 last night. The campaign had surpassed my expectations, and it'd only been a few hours.

My only sadness was that Eliza wasn't in the office to share the excitement with me. Her dad had her on the next project already, but she'd told me she was going to try her best to get in to see me today. I hoped she did. Since we got back from Switzerland, she'd bounced between my flat, her house and her dad's place, but she'd seemed distracted. No matter her declarations in Switzerland, once we were back in our real lives, she withdrew a little again. I was getting tired of the games. I didn't need them.

My phone rang, and Roka's name flashed on the screen.

"Poppy! Have you seen the response? It's crazy!"

I shook my head, not quite believing that a world-famous

pop star was taking time out of her promotion schedule of her new album to call me about our watches.

"I know, I can't believe it. The website keeps crashing from all the traffic."

"I'm not surprised. The campaign is gorgeous. Really. I've done a few partnerships before, and most of the time I forget about the product the second we wrap filming. But I keep looking at this watch and thinking I'd genuinely buy one if you hadn't already given it to me."

My chest swelled with pride. The whole team had worked really hard with the designers and production teams getting the product right. The marketing was about letting people know, but it meant nothing if the actual product itself didn't cut the mustard.

"That means everything coming from you. Your album is going great, too."

"It's all about collaborating with the right partners. You and Eliza are that. Seriously. I wish you all the success in the world."

After she hung up, I tried Eliza again, but it went straight to voicemail. I fired off a quick text instead.

> Roka just called! She loves it! Sales are off the chart. Where are you?? Xxx

An hour passed. Margot arrived and did a happy dance in my office when I told her about the response, which I appreciated. However, I was very much aware there still hadn't been a reply from Eliza. Why was she not answering, on today of all days? Where was she? What was she doing? Negative thoughts clawed at the back of my mind, sinking their nails in deeper and deeper until I had to send another message.

> The website's crashed twice from traffic. Fiona's freaking out in the best way. Call me! Xxx

By 5pm, I'd sent another unanswered message and was starting to feel pathetic. Had I misread everything in Switzerland? Had she regretted our confessions the moment we got back to London? But she'd been the one to say she was falling for me first. I knew she had other things to do this week, but I'd thought after working on this deal for months, she'd want to share in the celebrations. It was reminiscent of when Roka signed. It was weird.

Moments later, my office door burst open, and Eliza appeared with a bottle of champagne in one hand and a bouquet of flowers in the other, out of breath like she'd been running. Her cheeks were flushed pink, and her chest rose and fell as she tried to catch her breath.

"I'm so sorry I've been MIA, today of all days." She rushed over to me, her usual composed stride replaced by something more urgent. "I had Dad on my back, I had to meet my colour stylist and make final paint decisions, and I didn't get a second to check my phone properly."

She set the champagne and flowers on my desk. Her expression softened, the worry lines around her eyes easing as she took my hand in hers. For a moment, everything was exactly as it should be.

"I'm so proud of you: you made this happen. The Roka deal started with you, and it ends with you."

"It was a joint effort, but I'm so glad you're here." I wanted to kiss her, but this wasn't the environment. Our offices had glass walls, and I didn't want Margot walking in and finding out like this. "Sorry for the many messages this morning. I was excited. Our marketing team kept calling with news and it's been a bit overwhelming."

"We can be overwhelmed together in the best possible way." She grinned, then picked up the champagne. "Shall we pop this now?"

I shook my head. I never enjoyed drinking in the office. I wanted to save our champagne for when it was just the two of us.

"Not yet. I'll put it in the fridge for later." I paused. "Are you coming to mine after work?"

Something flickered across her features, and my euphoria vanished as quickly as it had arrived. Did she have some place better to be? Yes, she'd told me she was falling for me. But then she'd returned to a familiar pattern. Maybe she said that to all the girls. We hadn't even declared we were a couple yet.

So far, our relationship had been more actions than words. Perhaps that needed to change soon.

"Knock, knock!"

I looked up to see Margot leaning against the doorframe. Perfect timing.

"The dream team, together again." She gave us a slow clap as she walked in. "Even though I already saw Eliza this morning when I stayed over with Max."

Almost as soon as she said 'Max', he appeared at the doorway, too.

"Dad!" Eliza's pitch elevated.

"I just popped by to take Margot to an early dinner."

He walked in, then leaned over my desk, hand outstretched. Max's stubble was trimmed to perfection, and his suit fitted like a glove.

"The launch looks fantastic. I've seen the images all over socials, and Roka has really kept up her side of the bargain. For someone who has a reputation for being difficult, you turned her into an easy customer."

I shook his hand, but couldn't shake the prickly feeling in my bones.

"My advice, though?" He didn't ask if I wanted it or not. "Don't let up. Ride this wave. The launch looks fantastic, but the launch isn't where you make your money. Building on a launch is where you make your money. Focus on getting the orders fulfilled on time. Then you need to keep pushing. Keep focused. Stay aware of new opportunities."

I tried not to bristle, but I knew I was failing. He spoke to me like I didn't have an MBA, like I'd never been in business.

I understood people, because I'd been taught by the best. Plus, I knew full well that launch was just that: a start. You had to keep pushing, otherwise your launch might break down. I could tell Max about the social media influencers we had rolling out over the next couple of weeks, about the product placements the team were working on across TV and film.

Hell, we'd even sent Voss Watches to a host of top sports and entertainment figures. Including the England soccer captain Ashleigh Woods, who was engaged to Princess Victoria.

If either of them was seen wearing Voss, it would catapult the brand even further still. But I didn't want to blow his mind that I might know what I was doing.

"Plus, whatever happens with the company – whether you carry on, or whether you sell – this collab shows what a strong proposition it is. What legs it's got." He smiled at Margot, then at me. "You win either way, right? Which is what business is all about."

Beside me, Eliza stiffened.

Meanwhile, Margot's smile faltered by a fraction. Other people might not have noticed, but I knew my aunt.

Suddenly, I felt like I was the only one in the room not in on the joke. Only, the joke wasn't all that funny. Was there something I needed to know?

I glanced at Margot, who stared at my desk like it was the most interesting thing in the world.

Meanwhile, Eliza had picked up the champagne and was studying the label like she was about to regale me with the bottle's grape composition at great length.

The only person meeting my gaze was Max.

"We're not selling, Max. If I do well and prove myself, Margot promised me that."

She nodded. "So long as the numbers stack up and Fiona's okay. A promise is a promise." She kept nodding a little too long.

I wasn't reassured.

Max checked his watch – not a Voss – and clicked his fingers. "We should get going," he told Margot, before spinning on the ball of his foot and pointing at Eliza. "We still on to meet later as you were so busy doing other things today?"

I could sense Eliza's squirm beneath her nod. "I told you earlier, it's totally fine. I'll see you at the club."

Margot and Max bid us farewell. However, the office after their departure was a very different place to when they arrived. Now, it felt stained. Rife with things left unsaid.

I turned to Eliza. "You didn't see your dad today? Were you lying earlier?"

She shook her head, the crease at the top of her nose deepening.

"Of course not. He just wants to meet in person. We had phone chats."

I was fairly sure she was lying.

"Will you still be able to come and drink the champagne with me after meeting with your dad?"

She nodded, but didn't quite meet my eye. "Absolutely. This is a big day. The first of many."

Chapter Thirty-One

The printer jammed for the third time that morning, producing half a page before grinding to a halt with an ominous whirring sound. I smacked it harder than necessary, which only made it beep angrily at me. I was in no mood for a printer to give me trouble. I had enough of that from people in my life, never mind inanimate objects.

Maybe not people in general.

Just one person.

Eliza.

She hadn't made it to my flat last night, sending apologies and promises, just like she had for the past couple of weeks, along with a cryptic message.

But I didn't trust words. I trusted action.

Eliza's actions were showing me in shocking clarity that she was pulling away, and there was nothing I could do about it. She was my worst fears imagined. But at least we hadn't started calling each other girlfriend.

Hadn't said the famous three words.

It didn't count that I'd allowed myself to think them.

For now, I'd flushed them down the romance plughole.

I was readying myself to make peace with that. Be a mature adult. This had been an exciting interlude. Three months of push and pull, with hot sex thrown in. But now, it seemed like Eliza was calling time. I wrestled with the paper tray while balancing my phone between my shoulder and ear.

"We're looking at eight new hires minimum." Fiona's voice was bright with excitement. "Ronnie's training them up. And we're pressing ahead with the new premises as Harvey has fast-tracked our council application."

I finally freed the crumpled page and fed in a new sheet. "That's incredible news. How's the building coming along?"

"You should see it, Poppy. It's like watching history come back to life. We're keeping a bit of the old machinery as a nod to the history of the place, and our new equipment arrives next week. You need to come up and see it properly. Bring your brilliant sidekick back, too. She was quite the hit when she was here. You both need to see what you've achieved and what lies ahead."

Brilliant was not a word I'd use to describe Eliza right now. "I'll speak to Eliza when I see her."

I had no idea when that might be. Was this what Michelle had to deal with? Eliza going into work mode, always being on, never having an off switch? Had she fucked Michelle and left her alone before the bed was even cold? Perhaps Michelle had reason to be as mad and move countries to shake Eliza from her system.

The printer finally cooperated, spitting out the first 48

hours' numbers. Eliza had told me I should print it out and frame it. I'd noticed she liked to print out emails like she was from the 90s. I just wished she was here to share it with me. Without her, without my mum or gran, the success felt a little hollow. Margot couldn't be counted on, and Amina and Katy had both chosen the same time to be away. It was just me, dealing with this alone. At least I had Fiona to share the excitement.

Maybe Fiona might adopt me if I asked nicely.

"Can I ask you something?"

"Anything you like, you know that."

"When Mum took over the business, did she ever feel like she was doing it alone?" I felt guilty even voicing it, because Fiona had been by my side every step of the way. "You know what I mean? Like the buck truly does stop here?"

She took a moment before she replied.

"I think that comes with being the boss, hen. Even though your mum had me and your gran, I'm certain she felt alone at times. It's lonely at the top. Plus, she never had a spouse to talk to after your dad legged it."

Fiona tutted. "But she spoke to me and we talked things out. She always worried about the future, providing for you girls. It spurred her on to do what she did. You know, I'm always here if you need a sounding board, or a shoulder to cry on. I just assumed Eliza was doing that for you."

I was learning the hard way, that assuming was a mug's game.

Chapter Thirty-Two

After talking to Fiona, it only made me determined to get to the bottom of what was going on. Because she was right. Eliza should be by my side. Even if we were just friends and colleagues, she at least owed me that.

Hence, after lunch, I got on the Victoria line and headed over to her place in Walthamstow, my stomach churning with a mixture of anticipation and dread.

The sound of drilling greeted me as I approached the Victorian terrace. Through the bay window, I could see ladders and a woman in overalls painting the walls a lovely shade of olive green. I smiled as I recalled Eliza telling me she hoped it didn't make her want to drink gin martinis every day. I knocked on the front door, my heart trying to make a break for it.

A man answered the door, his bald head slick with sweat.

"Hi, sorry to bother you. Is Eliza here?"

He shook his head, wiping sweat from his forehead with the back of his hand. "She was here earlier, but she left about half an hour ago. You're Poppy, right?"

I was impressed he remembered me from last time.

I should have left then, should have respected her privacy and gone home. But something compelled me to step inside when he asked if I wanted to see the progress since I was last here, curiosity overriding my better judgment.

It'd come on a fair bit. The floors were down, covered with a protective top layer. The quartz kitchen counter-tops gleamed in the sunlight streaming in, with expensive-looking units installed top and bottom, now with gold handles. Meanwhile, the exposed beam was waiting to get its first coat. Had Eliza gone for bright yellow, or the more muted pale blue? She'd pondered both in Switzerland.

That thought sent a wave of affection, mixed with annoyance through me. I knew this woman. I knew what she worried about, what she wanted. Why was she shutting me out?

I turned to leave, but changed my mind and climbed the staircase, my footsteps echoing in the emptiness. The landing was painted a warm sand colour, with doors leading off to three bedrooms and a bathroom.

Eliza's bedroom was at the front of the house. I pushed the door open and immediately a knot formed in my chest. Eliza had left her dad's palatial pad to sleep here, in what was very much a work in progress? A king-sized bed in the middle of the room, a suitcase, and a single wooden chair with a pile of clothes slung over it. The floorboards were still bare, awaiting carpet. It looked like a place someone was running to or hiding in, not living.

I walked over to the window. What was I missing? I balled my fist at my side as I turned back to the bed. That was when I saw my name on a page, folded on top of Eliza's suitcase.

My heart skipped a beat.

I shouldn't snoop, but I couldn't help myself. I picked up

the paper, and smoothed it out. It was an email from Max to Eliza. Sent three days ago.

> Eliza,
>
> I need you to focus on the task at hand. The longer this drags on, the more complicated it becomes. Do exactly what we agreed: get the company in the best possible state, then persuade Poppy it's time to move on. She listens to you. Sweet-talk her if you have to, but get it done.
>
> Get this one over the line, and as I told you last week, the company succession line is clear. The world will be your oyster, as they say. But don't let personal feelings cloud your judgment. This is business. Poppy will understand once the dust settles and she has all the money in her account.
>
> Dad

The paper shook in my hands as I read it again, then a third time, hoping I'd somehow misunderstood. But the words were crystal clear, each one like a knife to my chest.

Sweet-talk her. Personal feelings. This is business.

I thought about Switzerland, about the way she'd kissed me like she meant it, the way she'd got me up to dance, looked into my eyes, and told me she was falling for me. Had all of it been calculated? Part of some elaborate plan to manipulate me into selling?

The betrayal hit me like a physical blow, stealing my

breath and making my legs unsteady. Eliza and Margot both. I stumbled down the stairs and out the door, my mind reeling.

Every kiss, every touch, every word.

It had all been a lie.

Chapter Thirty-Three

I sat on a bench in the green opposite Eliza's house for 20 minutes, the email clutched in my hand. The words kept swimming in front of my eyes, each one a fresh stab of humiliation.

But beneath the hurt, something else was building. Anger. White-hot, clarifying anger. I wanted to scream, or hit something. I glanced up, then walked to the nearest tree, drew back my foot, and kicked it.

Wrong move.

I staggered backwards, pain shooting through my foot. Was this why people hit things in times of stress, to take their minds off things? It'd certainly achieved that.

I hobbled back to my bench.

I wasn't going to let this destroy me.

I pulled out my phone and called Sage, my hands still trembling.

"Hi Poppy, how are you?" Her voice was soothing as always.

"I need to see you. It's a bit of an emergency. Can we meet somewhere?"

"I'm at your sister's place right now. Do you want to come over?"

Katy was back from holiday? That was the best result possible. Relief swept through me. "I'm coming now."

I jumped on the overground to get to Katy's, the email folded in my jacket pocket, the physical proof of Eliza's betrayal burning against my ribs.

My sister opened the door almost as soon as I knocked, her familiar face creased with worry. "What's wrong?" She pulled me into an immediate embrace, and I sagged into it. I needed her arms around me more than she knew.

Sage appeared behind her, dressed in a hot-pink trouser suit, not at all her usual style. Her concerned face told me everything I needed to know about how I looked.

I stumbled into the living room, feeling like I might collapse. Everything felt surreal, like I was moving through water.

"Mum," I said, my voice cracking.

Katy's eyebrows shot up.

"Is Mum here?" I asked Sage. "I need to talk to her."

Sage and Katy exchanged a look, the kind that said they were worried about my mental state.

"You know it doesn't work like that." Sage guided me to the sofa and sat beside me.

"I'll get you tea. Tea always makes things better." Katy reappeared a few minutes later with a mug of hot tea. "I added emergency sugar, because it looks like you need it." She paused, sat on the armchair to my left, and reached over to take my hand. "What's going on?"

I pulled out the email with shaking hands. "She was right. Mum warned me about betrayal when I saw you last time, and she was right. It's happened, and everything's fucked, and I don't know what to do."

I handed Katy the email, and her sharp intake of breath echoed my own devastation from earlier.

"Oh, Pops. Oh, honey."

Pops. I'd let Eliza call me that.

I'd opened up, let her back in. I thought she was going to leave, which would have been a kinder cut. The deception was extraordinary.

"I thought she cared about me. I thought Switzerland meant something." The words poured out in a rush. "But it was all just manipulation. She was playing me the whole time, getting me to trust her so she could convince me to sell. It was all to further her career."

My voice was getting higher, my throat constricted. I could hear it happening but couldn't stop it. I was determined not to cry.

"And the worst part? I was falling for her. *Really* falling. Like, thinking that she could be the one who I'd been waiting for. The game-changer. I thought she understood me, but at the end of the day, she's just like Mum, putting business over personal. She used me. Now she's ghosting me."

"Have you spoken to Eliza about this?" Katy put the email on the coffee table. "I know the email is pretty damning, but Eliza doesn't strike me as that person."

"Maybe that's why she's so good at what she does. You don't see it coming." I turned to Sage. "I know you're not an answering service, but I don't trust my own judgment anymore. I need to know what my mum thinks. What I should do."

Yes, I was hysterical. But if I couldn't be hysterical in these circumstances, when could I be?

Sage sighed, her expression conflicted. "I've told you before—"

"Please." I was begging now, and I didn't care. "Just try. Please."

Katy squeezed my shoulder. "Maybe just this once?"

Sage closed her eyes, her breathing deepening. The room fell silent except for the distant hum of traffic outside. I held my breath, desperate for some sign, some guidance from beyond.

Then, the candle flames flickered, and I caught it: that familiar scent of jasmine and vanilla, the perfume Mum always wore.

Sage went very still, her eyes snapping open but looking unfocused, distant.

"She's here," she whispered. "She clearly heard you."

My heart leapt. "You can see her properly this time? What does she say? What should I do?"

Sage shook her head and put her finger to her lips.

I glanced at Katy, who was sat bolt upright, a terrified look on her face. She'd told me she was drawn to these sessions, but she found them mildly disturbing, just thinking that Mum and Gran were in the same room.

Sage held up a finger. "She says that you have to look after yourself first."

"I get that," I replied. "But things have happened now. What do I do about them?"

There was a long pause. Sage's eyes seemed to be tracking something I couldn't see, and the jasmine scent grew stronger.

"She says go with your gut. Trust your instincts, they won't lead you astray. And..." Sage paused, tilting her head as if listening. "She says you can never disappoint her, whatever you choose to do."

Before I knew it was happening, tears streamed down my face, but they felt different from the devastated sobs I'd been fighting all afternoon. These felt cleaner, somehow, like they were washing away the confusion and self-doubt. Deep down, I did know what to do. I'd just been afraid to do it.

"Is she still here?"

Sage nodded slowly. "She's with your Gran. She's hugging her."

When I looked up, Katy was crying, too.

"Can you tell them both I love them and I miss them?" I told Sage.

The candles stopped flickering. The jasmine scent began to fade. Sage blinked several times, coming back to herself.

"You don't have to tell them that. They know it already." She paused. "Wow, that was a strong signal. They wanted to come through. They did, loud and clear. Did it help?"

I wiped my eyes, feeling steadier than I had since finding that email. "It really did. If nothing else, there's not much that'll take your mind off your problems than a visit from the afterlife."

Katy shoved me and Sage to our right, then slipped in beside me on the sofa and hugged me tight. "I'm scared shitless but also a blubbering mess. I always thought ghosts were out to get you until they turn out to be your family."

"Most spirits aren't out to harm you. They just want to exist peacefully, and help their loved ones," Sage told her.

I thought about Eliza's face when she told me she was falling for me. About the way she'd pulled away of late. About her saying she wanted to run away from it all.

Even though she'd betrayed me, pieces of the puzzle still lay scattered, refusing to fit together. Because beneath all the evidence, beneath the cold reality of what she'd done, something in me rebelled against the simple narrative.

I knew what I'd felt when we were in bed together: the way her breathing changed when I touched her, the way she'd cried out my name. You couldn't fake that kind of vulnerability, could you?

"I think," I said slowly, "I need to confront Eliza before I decide what to do next."

Katy jumped up and came back with her car keys. "Take my car. I can collect it from you tomorrow when the girls are at nursery. Or do you want me to drive?"

I shook my head, but took her keys. "Thank you, but no. This is something I have to do myself."

Because whatever game she'd been playing, whatever instructions she'd been following, the woman I'd been with in Switzerland had been real. I was sure of it. And if there was even a chance that her feelings had been genuine, that maybe she'd been caught between her job and her heart?

I owed it to both of us to find out the truth.

Chapter Thirty-Four

The drive to Max's house was like travelling towards my own execution. I nearly turned the car around twice, until I persuaded myself it was better to know the truth than live in ignorance. I wasn't sure if I believed it, but my foot stayed on the accelerator.

The email sat folded in my passenger seat like evidence of a crime. Which, in a way, it was. I put the radio on, but even Radio Six's lunchtime show didn't soothe me.

I'd rehearsed what I was going to say a dozen times, but now I was pulling into Max's still-very-large driveway, my carefully planned words scattered like leaves in the wind. The anger that had sustained me throughout the drive was giving way to something more complex: hurt, betrayal, but underneath it all, a desperate hope that somehow I'd misunderstood everything.

Eliza's car was parked outside. At least the drive wasn't in vain.

But then, disappointment sank through me. Was this where she'd come to discuss exactly how she was going to fuck me over?

I got out of the car, then walked the ten steps to the door at the slowest pace possible, my legs made of lead.

I rang the doorbell, but then heard gravel crunching behind me. When I turned, Eliza was there, a frown creasing her forehead. Her cheekbones could still slice bread, but there was a real sadness behind her ocean-deep gaze.

Despite my plight and the reasons for me being there, my body responded to her the way it always did. With an internal high five, and an immediate need to touch her. I physically yanked myself backwards to stop that happening.

"Poppy." Her voice was barely a whisper. "What are you doing here?" She glanced left to right, as if expecting three of me.

"We need to talk." I pulled out the email, and held it between us like a weapon. "About this."

Her eyes dropped to the paper, and the colour drained from her cheeks.

Right at that moment, I so wished I didn't have to do this.

"Where did you get that?"

This was the bit where I had no excuse. I hadn't actually snooped, but I hadn't exactly *not* snooped either. I gulped, then tried to find the words. Anger fizzed up my system. I was here now, and I'd seen the email. Did it matter how I found out?

"You've been distant since we got back from Switzerland. You know that." I paused. "I wanted to get to the bottom of it. I decided to go round to your house, but you weren't there. The builder invited me in, so I had a look around, just to see how it was going. I was curious, I guess. I wasn't snooping. But then I went to your room and found this."

She didn't say anything, just stared at me, her mouth slightly open.

"Was it all a lie? Did you get me into bed just to make sure I played the game your way and got your dad the best price for the company?" My voice cracked as I spoke. Now I said it out loud, it was absolutely worse than I thought.

Right at that moment, the door opened, with Max behind it. The absolute last person I wanted to see right now. Then, seconds later, Margot walked up behind him.

When she saw me, her face fell. I expected a better poker game from her. Max, though: his game was perfect.

"Poppy! What a nice surprise. Come in, come in."

I turned and stared at Eliza. I'd come to talk to her, to see what defence she had. But Max and Margot were all tied up in this, too. Should I get it all over in one go? Rip the plaster off right away? Unless I ran now, I didn't really have a choice.

Eliza gestured for me to go inside, and against my better judgement, I did. But once the door was closed, I struggled to breathe.

"What brings you this way? It's not exactly local."

"This email." I waved the piece of paper at Max.

He frowned just like his daughter had when she saw me, then held out his hand. "I don't know what this is about, but can I see?"

But Eliza stepped between us. "I know this looks bad, but it's not what it seems…"

"Isn't it?" I waved the email again. "Because it looks like it is exactly what it seems to me. 'Sweet-talk her.' 'Don't let personal feelings cloud your judgment.' 'This is business'." Each quote felt like swallowing glass. "You told me I wasn't business. That Switzerland wasn't business. But this? This makes it way harder to believe."

"Switzerland was real. Everything between us has been real." She looked me in the eye. "I couldn't fake that if I tried."

I heard a gasp from my left, then realised Margot didn't know about us. Nobody did.

Well, they did now.

"Then why is this email even in existence? You've been tense and avoidant, and I kept thinking, 'it's not what it seems'. However, it turns out, it's even worse."

Margot stepped closer. "Poppy, what does the email say? And what's this about you two? Are you together?"

"No," I stated.

Eliza stepped back, like she'd been slapped in the face.

"Maybe for a little while we were, but not now."

Margot looked to Eliza, then to me.

Max folded his arms across his chest. "This is all making a bit more sense to me now. I didn't think my normally rational, business-savvy daughter would suddenly turn on a deal we'd agreed on months ago. But you slept together. Feelings got involved. It all becomes clear."

He shook his head and sighed.

As for me? Max had just answered all my questions in one go. I wanted to go sit on the grand piano stool to my left, lean over and vomit on Max's pristine Italian tiles.

Instead, I said: "A deal you'd agreed on months ago?"

Eliza shook her head in double-quick time, then dropped her gaze to the floor. Maybe she was thinking about vomiting on her dad's tiles, too.

"It was the original plan, yes. To let you have a go so that you couldn't say we didn't let you try." Her voice was so quiet I had to strain to hear it.

She cleared her throat and finally looked at me.

"But you have to understand, nobody thought you were going to pull off something this big. Plus, I thought you hated me. I thought our relationship would blow up long before now. I thought I could persuade you because, as far as I knew, you hated the company and never wanted to work for them."

Each word was like another cut, deeper than the last. I took a step back. "But you planned to manipulate me right from the start." A chill ran through me. This was deception beyond words, almost beyond feelings.

"I thought you were faking it at the start," Eliza said. "Then I found out you'd changed. And then, when I got to know you and what the company meant to you, I changed, too. You have to believe me."

She stepped closer, and I could see tears gathering in her eyes. "You changed me. These past few months have changed me for the better. You made me confront my life, made me move forward instead of just drifting. If you want to think the worst of me, you can, but I would never do anything to hurt someone I love. And I do love you, Poppy. Even though you're standing here looking as if you want to rip my head off."

"Everything you've said and done has been based on a lie." I shook my head, numbness creeping through me. I turned to Margot. "And you. My own aunt selling me down the river. What happened to giving me a chance, to seeing what I could do?"

Margot stepped forwards and grasped both my arms with her hands.

"You don't know what's best for you sometimes. Giving you a poisoned chalice that's killed your mum and Gran? I wasn't going to do that." Her words were choked.

"You might be mad now, but you'll thank me in the long run. Plus, Max isn't even the buyer now. Thanks to your efforts, the price tag has gone up and we've managed to get a new party in the watch space. Voss will be folded into SwissTok and our range kept on as a legacy range. It's a great bit of business and means that you can now do what you really want to."

"This is what I really want to do!" She still didn't get it. "You've seen how hard I've worked over the past few months. It wasn't to spite you. It was to inspire myself and everyone in the company. I went to SwissTok to learn, not to showcase my skills."

"He's interested in keeping you on. He was impressed by you. If that's something you want, Gabriel is open to it. Everyone wins. No responsibility, but you still get to work on whatever's next."

"Nobody wins. I don't win. Mum and Gran don't win." And what about all the staff at Goldloch? What about Roka's contract? The more I considered all the implications, the angrier I got. Maybe Mum had been warning me about Margot, not Eliza.

"The only people who win here are you, Eliza for getting the deal done, and no doubt Max is taking a consultancy fee."

He held up both hands, his smile showing me he had no remorse. "Business is business, Poppy. You know that."

But I shook my head again. "Not the way I do business."

Eliza ran her hands through her hair, and for the first time since I'd known her, she looked genuinely rattled. "I've been trying to make this right since we got back. Trying to talk these two around, thinking about my future and where it's going to be. I wanted to work it all out before I came to explain to you. But then SwissTok got involved, and it all got far too complex. So yes, I have been avoiding you."

"No shit."

"It's why I moved out of Dad's house. I told him I wasn't going to do this anymore, that I wouldn't manipulate you into selling. We've been fighting about it for weeks." She glanced towards Max, and for a moment, his mask fell. "We were just arguing half an hour ago. I'm fed up of arguing, so I went for a walk. When I came back, you were on the doorstep."

I stared at her, trying to process what she was saying. "None of this changes the fact that you signed up to deceive me. You, Max and Margot all had a plan to let Poppy play at being in charge, before telling me no anyway."

Her calling me Playgirl Poppy in our train carriage came back to me now, like someone was shouting it through a megaphone. Anger sloshed through my veins. She'd never changed her view. She still saw me as a stupid kid who knew nothing.

"If what you're saying is true and you didn't use me, why didn't you tell me this was the plan once everything changed? You could have done that. That would have been the right thing to do."

My anger came and went, swiftly replaced by total, chilled numbness.

"Did you think about telling me just before you fucked me in Switzerland? Or did you think that every orgasm I had would get you that step closer to the perfect deal? Was I just a stepping stone? A convenient fast-track to taking over your dad's company?"

"No!" Eliza's voice echoed through the hallway. "Everything I told you was true. I've been considering my future. I printed out the email to show Dad his own words written down, hoping they might jog some piece of his conscience. Show him what he was asking me to do." Her head slumped forward. "But then I left it at the house. I wanted to put this right before you ever found out. That was my logic. I can see now that it was flawed."

"You were colluding with the enemy all along."

"If we're honest, you knew the situation from the start," Max added, his voice not quite so cocky now. "That there was a strong possibility Voss would be sold."

"I didn't know it was a foregone conclusion." The hurt bled through again, making my voice crack. "I trusted Eliza. I trusted Margot until she got together with you. Even in my wildest nightmares, I wouldn't guess you were all just waiting for the right moment to cash out."

"It's not a foregone conclusion," Margot told me, not looking at Max.

"It is if Max has brainwashed you. I'm not yet 30, so I don't have a say. Katy wants what's best for her daughters, and a lump of cash would suit her just fine." The full scope of my powerlessness hit me now. "I hope you all had a good laugh at me trying to make everything right."

Eliza's face crumpled, her usual polished composure dissolving in an instant.

"Everything I've ever said to you has been real. About the business, about my life, about how I feel about you." She glanced at her dad, then Margot.

"I love you, and that makes doing this deal problematic.

I think Margot should listen and take into account what you've done since you took over. The Voss brand is on everyone's lips and that's down to you.

"As for me?" She turned to her dad. "Take this as my verbal resignation. I think we've come to the end of the road with our business pursuits. It'll be better to have you just as a dad, not as my boss. This is one deal I can't finish."

I gaped at her words.

The problem was, I loved her right back. Even standing here, feeling like my heart had been fed through a shredder, I could feel that treacherous pull to her. But love wasn't enough when the foundation was built on lies.

"You know what the problem is?" I said, my voice breaking completely now. "I fell for you, too. Hard."

Hope flickered across her face, but I crushed it before it could take root.

"But how can I ever trust you again? How can I know what's real and what's just part of some elaborate game?" I took a step back, putting physical distance between us before I lost my resolve. "There's only one thing I can do."

"Poppy, please—"

I shook my head. "It's too late, Eliza. I have to go."

I turned and walked away before she could say anything else, before the sight of her tears could break down what was left of my defences.

I didn't trust myself to look back.

Chapter Thirty-Five

The drive back to Hackney was stop-start as I hit the evening rush hour. The whole drive was filled with a kaleidoscope of brake lights and choked breaths. I left the radio silent, craving space to untangle what had just happened, but my thoughts moved like oil on water. Each time I tried to grasp one feeling, it slipped away, contaminated by another.

I climbed the three flights up to our flat, but my legs felt borrowed from someone else's body. The key trembled against the lock like a tuning fork, taking four tries before the door finally opened. The moment I stepped inside, the familiar smell of Amina's vanilla candles nearly broke me.

My flatmate looked up from the sofa where she was folding laundry, took one look at my face, and immediately dropped the T-shirt she held. Behind her, the neon sign screamed *Queer & Fabulous!* at me. I felt anything but.

"What's wrong? Why do you look like that time I shrunk your favourite jumper by accident?"

I opened my mouth to speak and nothing came out except a strangled sob. I sank onto the sofa beside her, pulling out the crumpled email with shaking hands.

"It was all a lie. All of it."

Amina read the email twice, her expression growing more thunderous with each line. "What the actual fuck?"

My thoughts exactly. "I confronted her. Just now. At her dad's house." The words came monotone. "She said it wasn't what it looked like, but then she admitted it was the plan all along. To manipulate me into selling."

Amina let out a low whistle, shaking her head. "I'm so sorry, Pop Tart. I know you were into her, even though you were trying your best not to be."

"She said she was trying to make her dad see sense. That I changed her." I sniffed in a very unattractive manner. "She said she loves me in front of her dad and Margot."

"That makes it all better then, doesn't it?" Amina's voice was sharp with sarcasm. "She only planned to emotionally manipulate you for a few months, but then she had a change of heart. What a saint."

"Amina—" Even I wasn't quite sure why I was jumping to Eliza's defence.

I was damn sure she didn't deserve it.

"No, Pops. There are no ifs and buts here. When somebody shows you who they are, believe them." Amina turned to face me fully, her dark eyes blazing. "This woman has been playing you since day one. She studied you, then figured out exactly what buttons to push, what vulnerabilities to exploit."

The brutal honesty hit like a slap, but I needed to hear it. "I feel so stupid."

"You're not stupid. You had your doubts but she won you over. She was good, I'll give her that. But she doesn't have your best interests at heart." Amina pulled me into a fierce hug.

"You've been hurt by people who were supposed to protect you before. She was supposed to be your mentor, your business bodyguard. She wasn't supposed to sleep with you, make you promises, and then break your heart."

The parallel between Eliza's betrayal and all the times people had let me down before – first Gran, then Dad, then Mum – was too close to the bone.

"I really thought she was different," I whispered into Amina's shoulder. "In Switzerland, when she told me she was falling for me, I believed her."

"Maybe some of it was real," Amina said more gently. "People are complicated. She might have caught feelings, but that doesn't make what she did okay."

My phone had been buzzing intermittently for the past hour, but I'd been ignoring it. I didn't want to hear whatever Eliza had to say. Now it rang again, the shrill sound cutting through our conversation.

"It's probably her." I didn't check the screen. "I don't want to talk to her."

"Good. Let it go to voicemail."

But a short while later, there was a sharp knock on the door.

Amina and I looked at each other.

"If it's Eliza, I'm going to commit murder, just so you know." Amina scowled as she got up to answer it.

But it was Katy's voice that echoed from the hallway. "Poppy?" She bustled in and gave me a tight hug. "You're not answering your phone, and I was worried."

"Shit." I'd forgotten about Katy. After leaving hers earlier, she'd made me promise to text her updates.

Amina moved her laundry from the sofa and Katy sat where it had been.

"Shall I put the kettle on?" Amina asked. It was a rhetorical question. Tea made everything better.

"What happened?"

I told her everything. About confronting Eliza, then the admission that it had all been planned from the beginning. Katy listened in stunned silence, her expression growing more horrified with each detail.

"That manipulative cow," she said finally. "And I liked her! I thought she was genuine."

"She's good at what she does." Then a memory of what she did to me flashed through my mind. I wasn't lying. She was good. "She fooled us all."

"But this affects more than just your love life," Katy said, her practical mind already jumping ahead. "If they're planning to sell the company…"

"Then we're all fucked." The reality of it was starting to sink in properly now. "Max has Margot's ear, you need the money, and I'm still nine months from having any control. If they decide to sell, there's nothing I can do to stop them."

Katy was quiet for a long moment, and I could see her working through the implications. The share dividends helped with the girls' expenses, but a lump sum from a sale would secure their futures completely.

"What are you going to do?" she asked finally.

"I don't know." I hadn't assessed my options yet. It was too soon. "Fight it, I suppose. Maybe talk to Margot. See how far along this new deal is. Talking her out of a deal with Max was one thing. I could play on the fact that all our staff would lose their jobs. That the Highland base would close. But with SwissTok interested? I think Gabriel would keep the Highlands on. It wouldn't be so catastrophic. But it would mean we'd lose what Mum and Gran took so long to build."

Katy rested her head against the sofa. "Why do you want to keep the company this much? If the numbers stack up, this deal is the best we could possibly hope for." She paused, choosing her words carefully. "Is it just grief, or do you actually want this?"

I took a deep breath, then shook my head. "It's not just grief. I want to do this because it's the right thing to do. Also, because I don't want to be haunted forever by an unhappy ghost."

Katy smiled then, taking my hand. "What Eliza did was terrible, and I know you're hurting. Sleep on it, but if you still want to run the company, then I'll speak to Margot, too. But this is also your chance to walk away."

I couldn't do that. I was all in with Voss Watches, just like I was with Eliza. Unfortunately for me, I had no control over either of their outcomes.

"I can't just give up," I said. "This company is all I have left of Mum. If Margot can't see that, then she doesn't know me at all."

"Then fight." Amina put three steaming mugs of tea on the coffee table. "Margot loves you. Make her wake up and see what's in front of her."

I nodded, feeling something hard and determined crystallise in my chest.

It was time to speak to Margot without Max in the room.

Chapter Thirty-Six

Roka's latest track thumped in my ears as I hurtled around Victoria Park, trying to process everything that had gone on. I'd put so much into the past three months, truly channelling the spirit of my mum while her ghost followed me around with a clipboard scoring my every move.

It'd been exhausting and exhilarating in equal measure: the late nights strategising, the easy chemistry with Eliza, the intoxicating rush of calling my own shots. For the first time, I understood what Mum meant about being your own boss. The responsibility I'd always dodged? It came with a freedom I'd never tasted. No one else's schedule, no one else's agenda. Just mine. It was what I wanted now. It was what Eliza wanted, too.

A couple jogged past, matching Fitbits glinting in the morning sun, and something lodged in my throat as I rounded the corner by the lake. Eliza and I could have been like them, unstoppable together. If both our families had just stepped back, stopped orchestrating from the wings, perhaps we could have made it work: the business, us, everything.

Now Margot was handing it all to SwissTok like a consolation prize. Every sleepless night, every breakthrough moment, every careful decision: wasted. She'd made up her mind before I'd even walked through the door. The realisation sat bitter in my mouth.

I was driving to see her tomorrow. I'd intended to go this morning, but Katy and Amina had persuaded me to take a day to cool down and get my gameplan together. Not go in too hot-headed. It was good advice. Katy had already messaged to say Margot had retreated to her Cotswolds house alone. That was where I'd have to go.

My phone buzzed through my earbuds, cutting through the playlist. Fiona's name flashed on my watch face. I slowed to a reluctant stop, already dreading this conversation. She knew what a takeover could mean for the Goldloch setup, no matter what the initial good intentions were.

"Hi Fiona." How much did she know? How much would I have to explain about the takeover, about what it meant for Goldloch, for everything we'd built?

"Hello to you, my favourite interim CEO and saviour of Voss Watches."

I grimaced, catching my breath.

"Before you say anything," she continued, "Margot called me this morning. Told me about SwissTok."

That blindsided me. Of course she had.

"I'm not naive, hen. I knew this was always possible, regardless of how brilliantly you performed." She paused. "Incidentally, I downloaded Roka's singles – that girl's got real talent. You chose well. Harvey and I had quite the kitchen disco last night."

Despite everything, that coaxed a smile from me. Fiona had this gift for finding light in the darkest corners, while I seemed magnetically drawn to the shadows.

"I'm sorry I couldn't keep it in the family. But I'm seeing Margot tomorrow—"

"What will be, will be. When you're not holding the reins, you trust those who are to do right by everyone. You're still interim CEO, and I have complete faith in you."

If only I shared that confidence.

"How do you stay so relentlessly optimistic?"

Her laugh crackled through the connection. "Decades of practice, love. Your mother faced takeover pressures too, you know. She considered selling more than once but couldn't bear to let go. That means something profound. But she wouldn't want you doing this for her memory. You have to want it for yourself."

"I know that." The words came out sharper than intended.

"I'll tell you another strange thing. I had the most vivid dream about your mum last night. Clear as day, wearing that gorgeous dress she wore to Katy's wedding. Remember? Her eyes absolutely sparkled."

A lump formed in my throat. I could picture it perfectly. Mum walking Katy down the aisle, radiant in powder-blue silk. Only five years ago, though it felt like another lifetime.

"The strangest part? She made me tea."

I actually laughed. "Maybe she's finally got domesticated in the afterlife."

"If miracles are going to happen, I suppose it would make sense it's there. Then she sat with a plate of your gran's scones."

Every nerve in my body suddenly came alive. I could taste them: buttery, perfect, exactly as Eliza and I had made them that magical morning. The memory turned acrid in my mouth. I really hoped I hadn't ruined my gran's scones forever.

"She told me to persevere, that everything would work out. Said she was grateful I'd always been there for the family. Then she pulled out that Montblanc pen she treasured."

I bent forward, hands on my thighs, suddenly unsteady.

"She told me I'd made the right choice about the facility: reusing the old premises instead of building new. Which is excellent timing, since we've just signed the lease." Fiona chuckled softly. "When I woke up, I swear I could smell her perfume lingering."

A punch of grief hit then: raw, immediate, overwhelming. I sniffed, trying to capture Mum's perfume, but I could only smell freshly cut grass. In the distance I could still hear the rumble of the lawnmower. Somebody had been busy this morning.

"I just hope SwissTok honour everything," I told Fiona, verbalising my thoughts.

"Or maybe your mum knows something you don't? She was very relaxed about everything in the dream."

"Fingers crossed she's in the know. I'm not 30 until next March. I don't have a say in the fate of Voss until then. It's all in Margot and Katy's hands."

"I'd say you should talk to Katy. She called me last night, too."

It seemed like everyone had got to Fiona before I managed it.

"Whatever happens, come see us. See the new facility, get excited about the Roka prototype. I sent you a sample—"

A wasp appeared near my ear, its buzz unnaturally loud in the humid air. I shrieked, eyes squeezed shut, flailing wildly in the universal dance of wasp terror.

"—while you wait for it to arrive."

"Sorry, Fiona," I gasped, spinning around frantically. "Wasp attack. What did you say?"

"I was saying if the sample hasn't arrived, Eliza has one."

Another reminder of how thoroughly she'd infiltrated every corner of my world.

"We need you up here. Eliza absolutely loved it. The lochs and glens gave her the clarity she needed about her future. They might do the same for you."

She'd contaminated my gran's scones and now the Scottish Highlands too. My initial wariness about Eliza had been spot-on. The dead weren't the threat: it was the living who could destroy you.

"Once I know where things stand, I'll definitely visit," I said. "I could use the escape, too."

"You're always welcome to stay with us, although I know you prefer your independence. Eliza stays at the pub. I can have Marcus reserve you a room, too."

"Perfect."

"One last thing, hen. Whatever Margot's decision, there's reasoning behind it. She's not heartless: she's doing what she believes is right under impossible circumstances. Try to remember that."

Chapter Thirty-Seven

For the past few days, it felt like all I'd been doing was driving to showdowns. At least this time, I wasn't behind the wheel, as Katy had insisted on coming with me. Plus, now I'd confronted Eliza, this was truly the final reckoning.

While Katy drove at speed – she didn't know how to do anything else – I stared out at hedgerows that blurred past in shades of green. We'd barely spoken since leaving London, both of us wrestling with our own versions of what we'd find when we reached Margot. The radio had kept us company, providing background noise to our crowded thoughts.

Her cottage sat tucked behind an overgrown hedge at the end of a narrow lane, its thatched roof and honey-coloured stone walls looking like something from a postcard.

I'd been here a couple of times before, and I was always struck that Cotswolds Margot wasn't the aunt we knew: the one with the Mayfair penthouse and the driver. Cotswolds Margot was usually far more relaxed and laissez-faire. Which version were we going to see today?

When we pulled up, Katy killed the engine and sat for a moment, staring at the cottage through the windscreen. Then she thumped the steering wheel with the heel of her hand and blew out a long breath.

"Right. Before we go in there and potentially have our hearts ripped out again, I need you to know something." She turned to face me properly. "Whatever you decide about the company – keep it, sell it, turn it into a bloody artisan cheese operation – I'm with you. After how she's behaved, my half is your half. Margot doesn't get to steamroller us anymore."

Hearing those words, it was as if someone had lifted a crushing weight from my chest. For months, I'd felt like I was fighting this battle alone, carrying the responsibility for both our futures. But here she was, my big sister, finally standing beside me.

I was not going to cry before we even got in the door.

"Katy—"

"I mean it, Pops. I've been a rubbish sister, letting you carry all this alone. But you can count on me from now on. And who knows, once the girls are in nursery, I might even want a job."

She gave me her cheesiest grin, and it lightened the mood, even though tears still pricked my eyes. However, these weren't the frustrated, angry tears I'd been crying of late. These were tears of gratitude that somebody was finally in my corner.

"Oh, and I wanted to give you this." She held out a blue box.

I knew what was inside: Mum's favourite Montblanc pen. I started to protest, but Katy shook her head.

"You earned this. Mum's pen should be involved in running the company. It should be yours. She would have wanted you to have it, too."

"Thank you," I said. "But honestly? The thing I want most from today isn't about the company. I want our family back.

I want to understand how Margot could keep secrets from us, lie to us, and still expect us to trust her. I want my aunt back, not this corporate stranger."

Katy nodded, then reached over to squeeze my hand. "Then let's go get some answers. And maybe our aunt back too, if she's still in there somewhere."

Margot answered the door in jeans and a jumper. Without her usual designer armour – even though I'd no doubt the jeans and jumper were a label – she looked more fragile. The vulnerability in her eyes was stark and immediate.

"I've been expecting you," she said simply, stepping aside to let us in.

The interior was nothing like her gleaming London pad. Here, there were exposed beams and worn flagstones, along with mismatched furniture that actually looked lived-in. Books were stacked on a dresser and a side table, her reading glasses abandoned on the coffee table. Margot actually relaxed here.

We got water and settled in the lounge, the windows partially open to let in some July air. A cafetiere of coffee was half-drunk, the dirty coffee cup sat next to it. Margot motioned for us to sit on the sofa, while she sat on the armchair opposite. She took a deep breath, then looked at us with defiance.

"I know you're both furious with me, and you have every right to be. To the outside, what I did looks terrible. But there's something you need to understand about why I pushed so hard for the sale. And not just any sale: the right sale."

Katy and I exchanged glances from the sofa, its cushions soft with age and use.

"Your mother came to me," Margot continued, and my blood went cold.

Not more visitations.

My mum was not relaxed in death.

"Not in a dream, not in some mystical vision," Margot clarified. "She came to me three weeks before she died. It was almost as if she had a premonition her aneurysm was going to happen." She shook her head, remembering, her face grey. "Anyway, she was very insistent. She made me promise to sell the company if anything ever happened to her."

That snippet of information sucked all the air from my body. Beside me, Katy went rigid. I reached out and took her hand.

She squeezed it tight.

"She said she couldn't bear the thought of you two carrying that burden, especially you, Poppy. She'd asked you, and you'd told her you wanted nothing to do with it. She knew how the responsibility ate away at relationships and happiness. She wanted you both to be free to choose your own path without the weight of family legacy crushing you."

"But she loved Voss," I said. "It was everything to her."

"She loved you more." Margot's voice cracked, and she balled both her fists in her lap. "She made me swear I wouldn't tell you. She wanted it to seem like business, like my decision. That's why I was so adamant about selling, but I had to wait for the right buyer so we could secure the Goldloch jobs. I was keeping a promise to her. I never intended to undermine or hurt you."

The cottage seemed to spin around me. Every assumption I'd made about Mum's wishes, about honouring her memory, about my duty to the family legacy – it was all bullshit. She'd actually wanted the complete opposite.

I thought back to all the times with Sage, what she'd said. Mum had sent me warnings, and told me she was proud. She'd never said she wanted me to run the company. I'd read that into it because of her life.

I decided there and then, perhaps it was best to live my life with the guidance of the living, not the dead. To look forward, not back.

I vaguely recalled Eliza telling me that during our time together.

She was wise, that one.

"But I can't do it anymore." Margot sat forward, stroking her chin. "I'm not the villain in this story. These past months, watching you throw yourself into the company, seeing how much you've grown and what you've accomplished – your mother would love it. And maybe, just maybe, she was wrong about what would be best for you."

Before I knew what was happening, silent tears dripped down my face. This was the first honest conversation we'd had since Mum's death about what she wanted and why.

"I thought I was disappointing her. That I was failing everything she built."

Margot closed her eyes and shook her head slowly. "Oh, my darlings."

She stood up and walked over to us, holding out her arms.

We both stood and fell into her, months of grief and confusion finally finding their outlet. Margot hadn't hugged us since we were kids. This embrace felt like coming home after being lost for years.

"You could never disappoint her," Margot whispered. "Never."

Katy was crying too now, and she wrapped her arms around both of us, the three of us clinging together in this cozy cottage sitting room, all the pretence and lies stripped away.

When we finally pulled apart, tear-stained and breathless, I found my voice again. "None of it made any sense, but it does now." I shook my head. "I'm sorry for anything I said that was out of line."

Margot smiled, then shook her head. "Consider it forgotten."

We all sat, this time in a row on the sofa.

"Is Max here?" I winced as I asked.

Margot shook her head. "I told him to stay in London, I needed a little time." She exhaled. "But I hope you're okay with him. He wasn't the one pushing the sale. It's true I asked him to push Eliza, but he was doing it for me. He was uneasy about it." She shook her head. "As was Eliza. What a mess."

Where was Eliza right now? My heart lurched thinking about her. I missed her.

"But you and Max are still together?"

Margot nodded. "Very much so. I hope you like Max, because he's here to stay. He makes me happy, and I hope I do the same for him."

Katy reached over and squeezed Margot's hand with her own. "We like him very much, don't we, Pops?"

I nodded. "We do."

"He looks out for me, takes care of me," she said softly. "And that hasn't happened since your mum died. She was my best friend. I miss her so much." Margot glanced up at me. "Don't let what's happened stop you from being with Eliza, either. She stuck up for you, and pushed back on what Max was asking her to do. He was surprised. She normally did whatever he asked of her. She's got feelings for you. If you like her too, don't let it slip away."

I bit my cheek and nodded. I couldn't speak about Eliza too right now. That was for another day. Perhaps tomorrow. Tonight was all about us.

We sobbed and hugged, and talked for another couple of hours about how we're going to be honest going forward, about the weight of secrets we'd all been carrying. Margot made tea and brought out home-made fruitcake that her neighbour dropped off, which was off-the-charts delicious. By 6pm, we were emotionally exhausted, but happy.

I was going to get my family wish, and that was the best thing of all.

"The SwissTok deal: shall I tell Gabriel it's off?"

I nodded. "I know Mum didn't want to burden us, but you're not. I want this."

"And who knows, once the girls are at school, I might want a job at Voss, too," Katy added.

Margot snorted. "Felicity will be rolling her eyes wherever she is. Both her daughters in the business when she thought you didn't care at all. How wrong she was." She shook her head. "We all need to talk a lot more about what we want."

"Agreed." Katy said. "When the time comes for the company to be passed down to the next generation – if that's what they want – I don't want this happening again."

"But if we're being honest, there is something I want from you, Margot." I shifted on the sofa until I snagged her gaze. "Not business-related, not about the company. I just want my aunt back." My voice caught. "I want the woman who used to let me help her put on lipstick when I was little. Who taught me how to order wine. Who was Mum's best friend before she was ever anything else."

Margot's eyes went shiny, and she groaned. "You're going to set me off again." She reached for a tissue from the box beside her mug, and blew her nose. "But I'd like that, too. Maybe we can actually talk rather than be polite at our Sunday lunches from now on."

I smiled. "Especially if Max is cooking, then we can focus on the wine."

That drew a laugh from all three of us.

"There's something else." Should I say it? It seemed trivial, but we had just agreed to be honest with each other. "There was something Eliza shared that irked me. She said when you were at Max's, you made her a mean fried egg. I know it sounds ridiculous, but I got jealous. I wanted you to cook me a fried egg. She's not your niece. I am."

Blood rushed to my cheeks.

Perhaps that was oversharing.

"You want me to make you a fried egg?" Margot's smile broke through her tears.

"Is that the most pathetic request you've ever received from a grown adult?"

"Not even close. Last month, Max wanted a butterscotch Angel Delight after a particularly hard day. Whatever makes you happy." She gave me a rueful smile. "I like Eliza. She deserved a fried egg for what I was putting her through. I've apologised to her, and I want to apologise to you both, too. But it was done with the very best of intentions."

She stood, smoothing down her jeans. "Though I should

warn you, my fridge currently contains two bottles of champagne and some questionable cheese. We'll definitely need to raid the village shop for eggs."

"Perfect. Nothing says family reconciliation like a quest for eggs at the local Co-Op."

Margot laughed, the sound lighter than I'd heard from her in quite a while. "Stay the night, both of you. We'll go to the pub for dinner. They do an excellent steak-and-ale pie, and the fish and chips have great mushy peas."

"Will there be more crying?" Katy dabbed at her mascara.

"Almost certainly. But also wine, so it balances out."

Margot opened her arms again, and this time when we fell into her embrace, it was less a tearful reunion and more like three women who'd finally figured out how to be in the same room without family pressure weighing them down. We weren't staying because we had to. We were staying because we wanted to.

"Right then." Margot pulled back with renewed energy. "Family dinner it is. Fair warning, though: I might actually be terrible at this whole emotional availability thing. I've been practising on Max, but he's very easy to please."

"We'll muddle through," I said. "We're British. It's what we do."

* * *

Hours later, when I was lying in bed full of pie and wine and scrolling my phone, a message popped up. It was from Eliza.

My heart did one of its best somersaults, and I pushed myself up further in the bed.

I swallowed hard, then clicked.

> I'm sorry how we left it, but I hope you know that everything I said and did was real. I didn't fake any of it, Pops. I've sent a first-class sleeper ticket to your email. I'm in Scotland. Please come join me. Fiona and the gang would love it. But not as much as me. E xxx

The 'Pops' felt right.
And perhaps Eliza was right for me, after all.
The only way I'd find out for sure was to go to Scotland.

Chapter Thirty-Eight

The last time I was on a sleeper train to Scotland, I was wary of Eliza and what might happen if I let her back into my life. The memory of our awkward carriage-sharing made me smile. I could never have foreseen falling for her, or the spectacular mess that would follow.

But now, as the Highlands rolled past like the world's most expensive screensaver, I found myself semi-optimistic. Maybe it was the wise lack of gin this trip, or the plush first-class cabin. Or perhaps it was because I finally had some idea what I was doing with my life.

Eliza clearly had an affinity for this place: she kept fleeing here like some sort of corporate refugee. Perhaps there was something in the Highland air that induced clarity, or at least the illusion of it.

Despite everything, I was looking forward to seeing Eliza. With Margot restored to her rightful position as my aunt – and the company crisis resolved – Eliza was the final piece of the puzzle. Whatever happened, at least I'd know where I stood.

The train pulled into Goldloch, and I dragged my wheelie suitcase through the usual platform chaos, feeling slightly seasick from the train's rocking motion now I was back on solid ground. As I cleared the barriers, I spotted a familiar figure waiting on the other side, and couldn't suppress the grin that took over my face.

Eliza was clad in tartan trousers that should have looked ridiculous, but somehow made her look like she belonged, her blonde hair catching the morning light. Just the sight of her made something in my chest do an embarrassing flip, like my heart had just woken up from a very long sleep. She held a sign that read *Poppy Voss, CEO, Voss Watches* in bold black letters, as if she were the world's most strangely attired chauffeur.

I shook my head as I approached. When I was close enough, she turned the sign over. The reverse side declared: *I'm Sorry. Can You Forgive Me?*

I stopped just short of her. To her left, two teenagers wandered past in a passionate clinch, oblivious to the world. We weren't there yet.

Eliza lowered the sign and offered a tentative smile. "I wasn't sure if this was endearingly romantic or mortifyingly cheesy." She tilted her head, studying my expression. "Judging by your face, I'd say it's landing somewhere in the middle?"

"It's very *Love Actually*, which was nobody's finest hour."

"In my defence, I'm significantly less stalker-y than Andrew Lincoln.'

I raised a single eyebrow. "You did send me train tickets to travel the length of the country."

She grinned. "But I gave you a choice and didn't kidnap you. And I wore tartan trousers to make you feel at home. Can we agree it's a good start?"

Eliza reached out her hand and took my suitcase.

I let her.

"I wasn't even sure you'd get off the train," Eliza admitted, shepherding me towards a red Mini Cooper. "But I thought, on the off-chance you did, I should be here. I'm glad I took the gamble."

"And you've got a car, now?"

"I hired it for a bit."

As we drove through the village, Eliza waved at various locals like she was running for town mayor. She pointed out the butcher chopping in her shop window – "A female butcher. Everyone's very excited!" – along with where to find the best coffee, and which road worked better for avoiding tourist traffic. It got me wondering, how long was "a bit"?

At the pub, Marcus greeted me with a hug, then launched into easy banter with Eliza about some local drama involving the postie and a territorial cockerpoo. This wasn't casual acquaintance. Rather, this was the familiarity of someone who'd become part of the furniture.

Once I dumped my bags in my room, Eliza turned to me.

"Are you hungry, or can I show you something first?" There was a strange energy radiating from her.

"So long as we can get a coffee on the way, you can take me where you need to."

We did just that, then drove down to the loch, stopping right on the shoreline beside Loch Cottage. In the overgrown garden, the estate agent's sign still proclaimed it was for sale, though something about Eliza's expression suggested that might not be entirely accurate anymore.

I stared at the cottage, its stone walls the same weathered grey, the windows still crooked in their frames like sleepy eyes. The wild garden spilled towards the water in a riot of Scottish roses and brambles, exactly as I remembered it.

"What are you showing me?"

I had an inkling.

She nodded towards the cottage. "This."

This was the place we'd invented stories about as children, the one we'd sworn we'd buy someday when we had money. The cottage that featured in every daydream I'd ever had about the best view to pair with a morning coffee. About a life that moved at the speed of seasons rather than quarterly reports.

"Eliza." My voice was a whisper. "Please tell me you haven't—"

She reached into her pocket and pulled out some keys.

"You've bought it?"

She shook her head. "Not yet, but I've put in an offer, and it's been accepted. I just need to give the nod, and it's mine. But I didn't want to do that until you arrived."

This was still making zero sense. "You're buying a house here? But you're doing one up in London." I had to say the words out loud to make sure I wasn't hallucinating. When she told me it wasn't necessarily the house of her dreams, I never thought she meant it.

Eliza's mouth quirked up at one corner. "It's just a house, not a home. I can rent it out. Or maybe keep it as my London base. I have some plans, if you want to listen."

She got out of the car and we walked up to the front door. It was still the same powder blue, although it could do with a lick of paint.

"What I want and need has changed. This house?" She put the key in the lock. "It's always been the dream, hasn't it? I bought the house in London because I needed somewhere to live, and my dad told me to buy a doer-upper. I did what he told me. I'm tired of doing that. It's time I did something for me."

She walked into the house, and I followed. Finally through the front door after all these years.

I took in the faded floral wallpaper that was probably fashionable sometime in the 80s, the carpets that had seen better decades, and the kitchen units that looked like they'd been installed when microwaves were still a novelty.

But I also saw the gorgeous stone fireplace with its carved mantel, the thick walls that would keep out Highland winters, the high ceilings with their original beams still intact. Light poured through windows that faced directly onto the loch, and despite the dated decor and musty smell of a house that had been empty too long, there was something familiar about it.

Standing in what would be the lounge, looking out at water that stretched to mountains, something settled in my chest that I hadn't even realised was unsettled. It was like coming home to a place I'd never actually lived, but had been dreaming about my entire life.

I brought my gaze back to Eliza.

"What do you think?" she asked.

Emotion stirred inside me, something between wonder and panic. "I think you bought our cottage."

She shook her head. "Not yet. But I very well might."

I folded my arms across my chest, suddenly needing a barrier. "I just got off a train, and this is a lot. Explain it to me again."

She took a steadying breath. "You know I quit my job with my dad."

I shook my head. "I didn't. I know you did in the heat of the moment, but I wasn't sure if it was real."

"It's real. In fact, it's the best decision I've made in years. Being up here made me realise what I actually need." She took a deep breath. "You know that Andrew wants early retirement; he wants to go travel the world."

Fiona had messaged me the news when she heard. Andrew had been with Voss for 30 years. I nodded.

"Fiona needs someone to step in to his role. She offered me the job." Eliza rushed on before I could respond. "I know she usually hires without consulting the CEO, but this felt different. I couldn't take it without getting your okay."

"This is quite the departure from a few months ago." I was still trying to catch up.

"You genuinely wanting to run Voss made me see that I definitely *didn't* want to run Dad's empire. He can sell it or find someone else to handle the corporate machinery. I want to work for something I actually care about, something hands-on and meaningful." Her voice grew warmer. "Something like this incredible family-run watch company with a brilliant CEO who's not even thirty yet."

She paused, a hint of her dazzling smile appearing. "Quite an attractive CEO, too."

My cheeks warmed despite everything.

"I know this is overwhelming," she added quickly.

Speechless didn't begin to cover it. This wasn't just a career change: this was Eliza completely rewriting her script. I was happy for her, but disappointment filled me like cold water. She was moving on, building something new, and I had no idea where that left us.

Then a thought flickered to life just like Amina's neon sign: could I live here too?

"After I left London," Eliza continued, "I came back here to help Fiona and Ronnie. The lease on the old factory is sorted, and I've been involved in recruiting the new staff, and getting all the admin sorted. Turns out I'm quite good at the practical side of things when I'm not drowning in boardroom politics.

"I'm sorry I wasn't in touch, but I wanted to give you space to cool off. I hope you know by now I was trying to get Dad and Margot to change their plans. I wasn't trying to undermine you. I believed in you."

Her face told me that was true. "I know. Margot told me."

She exhaled. "Thank fuck. I'm sorry for being elusive, too. I didn't handle it the best."

"You didn't."

Eliza licked her lips. "I'm also really sorry for declaring my undying love in the middle of an argument in front of my dad and Margot. That was unforgivable." Her face crumpled with embarrassment. "Can you forgive me? For all of it?"

I looked at her standing there in our childhood dream cottage, hair slightly mussed from the Highland wind, wearing tartan like she belonged here, asking for forgiveness for loving me badly instead of not loving me at all. The disappointment I'd felt moments ago was transforming into something else entirely.

Something that felt dangerously like hope.

"I think there might be some leeway." I wanted to forgive Eliza. I knew she'd been my cheerleader, not my saboteur.

Eliza's face lit up, and she reached for my hand. "This place needs some work, but I love the bones of it. I love where it is. I especially love it when you're in it." She grinned. "Come on, let me show you the best bit."

She led me down the narrow path to the water's edge, a couple of minutes' walk to our log and our small wooden jetty. The water was mirror-still, reflecting the mountains like something from a tourism poster. Eliza swept the log of debris, and gestured for me to sit.

I did as she wanted.

"Remember we used to come here as kids? We used to dream about living in that cottage?"

She nodded towards what could be her future home.

"Dreams can come true. And I want them to come true with you." She sat next to me and took my hand in hers. It fitted perfectly.

"Even though I told you I love you in the worst possible circumstance, I meant it. I want to tell you again, in one of our favourite places in the world."

She swept a hand, and I took in our surroundings. The absolute peace and tranquillity, the gorgeous scenery, the even more gorgeous woman beside me.

Eliza snagged my gaze, and the silver flecks in her eyes sparkled as she spoke.

"Poppy, I love you, and I would really love it if you'd consider moving here permanently. Look around, it's not a bad option. If you need to be in London, it's easy enough. But in between times, we could try building something here. Slow down a bit, try a different pace of life." She paused. "And if you say yes, Loch Cottage is big enough for two."

I stared out at the loch, and the Highland air filled my

lungs, crisp and clean in a way that made London's exhaust fumes seem like a distant memory. When I raised my gaze back to her, something had shifted inside me. It was what I'd always wanted as a kid. Now, Eliza was offering me the chance to make it real.

"I've never entertained the idea fully before, but it sort of makes sense when you say it." Why had I never thought it possible to wake up to this view every day? Eliza and the loch, and mornings that began with mist rising off water?

"Think about it. I don't need an answer right away. But you could keep your London flat with Amina if you wanted, and be there whenever you need to be."

"She's been talking about moving in permanently with Noelle."

Eliza's eyebrows lifted. "Maybe it's a sign. I could keep my house as our London pad, and we could both use it when we need it." She paused. "I know one thing. I miss you when you're not with me. Wouldn't it be better to be together more, wherever that might be?"

The pure honesty of her statement hit me hard. Perhaps the simple solution really was the best option.

"You'd be in the same place as Fiona, Ronnie and me. In some ways, it makes sense."

"That's true. Plus, I could wear tartan trousers more often and nobody would bat an eye."

"Already things are tipping in my favour."

I shook my head, staring at Eliza. The woman who'd spent her life in tailored suits and killer shoes was stood in DMs, tartan trousers and a massive black woolly jumper, looking more relaxed than I'd seen her.

"If I say yes, you've got no hidden agenda? You're not a secret spy for your dad?"

She gave me a sad smile. "My dad has gone back to being my dad, which I'm really pleased about. My mum is really excited to come back here, too. She'd be even more excited if you were here as well." She shook her head. "I'm on your side, Pops. I always have been, even when I was too stupid to show it properly."

I reached for her then, and she met me halfway. Our lips met, and we finally kissed. My heart roared its approval, as my whole body tingled with possibility.

When we broke apart, I rested my forehead against hers. "This cottage, then: it definitely has room for two?"

Her eyes lit up. "Plenty. Amazing views, too." She patted the log. "And I hear the stone skimming competition is really strong." She smiled. "Is that a yes?"

"It's definitely an 'I'll think about it'."

She kissed my lips again. "Good enough."

I stared at her, then shook my head. "I can't believe you bought our cottage."

She took both my hands in hers. "Isn't it about time?"

Epilogue

Eight Months Later

I rolled over, and rebounded off Eliza for the third time that week. I was still getting used to permanently sleeping in the same bed as her. Still surprised that another warm body was lying next to me. But it was something I was thrilled about. Two weeks in, and the novelty of waking up next to her hadn't worn off.

"Did you just smack your nose again?"

I smiled as Eliza rolled over, her face adorably creased with sleep.

"Uh-huh."

"You really need to get used to the fact we live together."

"I do. But you're the first person I've ever lived with. It's only been two weeks. My body needs time to adjust to its new circumstances. Plus, I'm on Highland time now."

Eliza rolled her eyes, then pressed her warm lips to mine. She smelled delicious: freshly baked.

"Are you ready for the circus that's coming to town today?"

I scrunched my eyes shut and wrapped myself around her like a koala. I hadn't looked outside yet, but I already knew the snow would still be piled high in our garden and beyond.

"No," I whispered.

Today was a big day for Voss Watches. Roka was arriving with Sasha for a spot of PR. It was also Fiona's last day, and we were throwing a big party to celebrate her. As soon as she installed Eliza, and I told her I was moving here, she informed us she was going to retire.

"It's time, hen. But I'll still be around, don't you worry. The company is in safe hands with you, Eliza, and Ronnie."

"You think anybody would notice if we don't turn up?" I asked. "Maybe we could become invisible, like the people who used to live here when we were kids?"

Eliza grinned, then kissed me again. "I forgot about them." She looked wistful. "Do you think they actually were ghosts? And if so, are they still here?"

I frowned. "I've had enough ghosts to last me a lifetime. If they are, at least they're not chatty like my family." I paused. "Talking of which, did I tell you Sage is coming today?"

Eliza shook her head. "You did not."

"Bryce couldn't get the time off work, and Katy didn't want to drive up on her own. Sage offered to share the driving and the childcare."

"Is she bringing any spirits with her?"

I rolled my eyes. "Have you ever known my mother to miss a big occasion? I've no doubt they'll be here. I just hope they respect the event and shut up. I've had enough time worrying about them. Now it's time to trust our instincts and do what we think is right."

I tucked a strand of hair behind Eliza's ear and stared at

her beautiful face. She was all mine. Sometimes, I couldn't quite believe I got so lucky. What I'd been searching for had been right in front of me all along.

Eliza ran a hand down the side of my body, and I burrowed into her. She kissed my shoulder, then the top of my head. "I'm getting up now, because we should get going. But I'm making bacon sandwiches first. Got to keep the CEO fed so she can perform today."

I groaned and rolled onto my back.

It was still lonely at the top, but at least I had Eliza beside me now.

* * *

"Oh my god, I am such a fan. Thank you so much for coming, for wearing Voss watches, for your music, just for everything you do."

When Ronnie said he was Roka's biggest fan, I hadn't realised he was serious. But last night in the pub, he'd told me he had all Roka's albums in every format, including a signed gatefold that he'd paid hundreds of pounds for. Now, I was going to have to prise her hand out of his death grip.

"Okay Ronnie, let the woman have a coffee before you propose marriage."

Ronnie glanced at me, releasing Roka reluctantly. "It's just, I don't think I'll ever get over today."

I really needed to extract Roka before she called security.

However, she'd clearly met her fair share of Ronnies.

"Before you go, let's snap a selfie," Roka told him. "Do you have your phone?"

She was a pro, and Ronnie almost levitated with joy.

Then Eliza and I took Roka on a tour of the factory, where she shook every hand, posed for countless photos, and said all the right things. Once she'd spoken to the media about her upcoming single, 'It's About Time', we brought her back to our reception lounge, where Sasha was waiting. Roka kissed her as soon as she saw her.

"You two are official now, I assume?" Roka asked, snaking her arm around Sasha's waist.

I nodded, recalling that first kiss in that Brooklyn bar. Roka had been there from the start.

"Eliza bought a cottage, got a new job up here, and I moved in. We're now Highland lesbians, and very much together." I threaded my fingers through Eliza's to prove the point. Nothing had ever felt so right.

Showing she was thinking the same thing, Eliza kissed my cheek.

Roka beamed our way. "It's about time."

It'd only taken us two decades.

"Talking of which: what time is the party tonight? I met Fiona when I arrived. How cool is that woman?"

"The party will get going after work. And yes, Fiona is the absolute best. Way cooler than her son, Ronnie, who is not normally such a fanboy," I said.

Roka grinned. "He was fine. And if I didn't already have a mom, I'd want Fiona to adopt me."

I laughed. "My sister and I are already in the queue."

Hours later, the party room at the factory complex was a mass of people all drinking, chatting and eating the delicious food prepared for us by the local deli. Eliza had got a good deal because she was on first-name terms with the entire village.

Living with her was like living with a local celebrity. In Goldloch, Roka's star was totally eclipsed.

I grabbed a flute of champagne from a passing tray, and walked up behind Eliza, who was chatting to Margot and Max. They were staying at the pub, but were due for dinner at Loch Cottage tomorrow night. Our first dinner guests as a couple.

"Great turnout. You must treat your staff very well. Everyone seems happy." Max gave the room an appreciative glance.

"You should take a leaf out of our books, Dad," Eliza told him, with a wink.

He rolled his eyes, but smiled. "That's up to Alicia now. I told you I promoted her and she's in interim charge? She's doing a good job, too. Soon, my life won't be appeasing staff. It'll be whisking my future wife on exciting adventures and working on my golf handicap."

Eliza shot me a look, and my gaze went to Margot's ring finger. Sure enough, there was a large rock on it.

"When did this happen?" I pulled Margot into a bruising hug, and she looked the most bashful I'd ever seen her.

"Last week. We didn't want to make a fuss to upstage your big party and Roka being here. But Max has brought some vintage champagne up with us, so perhaps we could pop it tomorrow night?"

This softer, more vulnerable version of Margot was going to take some getting used to, but I was here for it.

I reached over and shook Max's hand. "Congratulations. Do we need the traditional 'treat my aunt well or else' conversation?"

Max laughed, his smile accompanied by a certain sparkle. He was a catch, and no mistake. Just like his daughter. "She's already given me her minimum expectations of a husband. I've promised to study them well."

Eliza hugged them both. "So long as you don't want me to be a bridesmaid, I'm delighted for you."

Katy and Sage walked over with champagne in their hands, and we told them the news. I'd never seen Katy look so stunned.

"The woman who told me marriage was a patriarchal trap is getting married?" Katy shook her head. "I have to hand it to you, Max. You must have some sweet-talk to turn Margot's head."

Sage clinked my glass with her own. "Are you settled in okay? What a gorgeous place to live. Katy pointed out your cottage on the lake when we drove in, too. Quite a change from Hackney."

"Polar opposite. But sometimes, change is good, right?"

Sage gave me her wise nod. "Change is inevitable."

"I have to ask," I said, lowering my voice to a whisper. "Is there anyone else here tonight?"

She gave me a knowing smile. "They're always here, Poppy. But I think you're more settled now, which means they are, too." She squeezed my arm. "You've got this. You can do this from here. They're always here if you need them."

At the allotted time, Eliza and I got up on stage. She tapped the microphone, and eventually, the crowd hushed.

"Thanks everyone for coming. I know having free food and drink makes it a real draw, but I hope most of you are here to wish Fiona good luck in her retirement. I, for one, want to say this place won't be the same without her. Where are you, Fiona? Come on up."

Fiona bounded onto the stage, waving like she'd just won the lottery.

Eliza hugged her before continuing. "Goldloch has truly changed my life. I first came here as a kid with the Voss family for summer holidays, and I loved it then. Mistakenly, I thought you had to be Scottish to live here. But since moving in, I can honestly say you've all made the transition seamless. I sold it to Poppy by saying we could see how it goes, but I think I'm here for life."

A huge cheer went up from the crowd. Eliza gave me a cheeky wink.

"Thank you to Fiona for being my mentor." Eliza turned to me. "And to our CEO, Poppy, for showing me true courage and grace under pressure. And for knowing that even though this was not part of the plan, sometimes taking the road less travelled is where the adventure is."

She passed the microphone to me, and I hugged her. "You're too good," I whispered in her ear, before taking a deep breath. Eliza was more the public speaker. My heart thumped in my chest as I looked out at the sea of people. Most of them worked for me. It was a lot of responsibility. But it was also something I was going to give my all. I spotted Sage in the front, hand to heart. She gave me an encouraging smile.

She was right. I *could* do this.

"Exactly one year ago I persuaded my Aunt Margot to give me a chance to run the company. I had no idea what I was getting into, and honestly, if I had, I might have run for the hills. Now it turns out, by moving here, I *have* run for the hills, but this time in a positive way."

Laughter rippled through the crowd. Fiona gave me an encouraging smile.

I took a deep breath and carried on.

"I never wanted to run the company when I was a kid, but I always loved it here. When Mum died, the world went a bit grey, but moving here, the colour is starting to flood back.

"Now Voss Watches is a globally recognised brand thanks in no small part to our collaboration with an international pop star – take a bow, Roka! – and also thanks to Eliza Carpenter. I could not have done any of this without her. She's been my touchstone, my mentor, my sounding board, my shoulder to cry on. But as much as she's been one hell of a business partner, she's also proved to be one hell of a life partner, too." I turned to her. "Eliza, I love you. Thanks for suggesting we move home."

The crowd went crazy for that one.

"Finally, to Fiona, the beating heart of Voss for so many years. Thank you for it all, and I hope you know I have you on speed dial in my phone."

Fiona grinned, then made a heart shape with her fingers.

"You will always be welcome back here," I told her. "You are Voss." I turned back to the crowd. "Thank you to each and every one of you for making this company what it is. I look forward to getting to know you all over the next few months."

Only when I put down the microphone did I realise my hand was shaking. I took a deep breath and glanced towards Eliza. She walked up, a rueful smile on her beautiful face.

"Took you months to tell me you loved me, now you're announcing it to huge crowds?"

I grinned. "Is that okay?"

"More than okay," she replied.

* * *

After the party, we walked home. The paths were clear of snow, and the moonlight sliced the loch like a silver knife. The evening couldn't have gone off any better. We'd presented Fiona with an all-expenses trip to Switzerland as her retirement gift, along with a fat bonus to spend while she was there. The band had played, everyone danced, and now we were tired and it was just gone midnight. However, having swerved all but a couple of drinks all night, I wanted a whisky in the moonlight in front of an open fire.

Eliza got it going, while I fixed our drinks.

Half an hour later, warmth circled the room.

"When we were kids, my dream was to live here and have hot chocolate in front of a fire while it snowed outside." I smiled at the memory.

"Nearly right. We swapped hot chocolate for whisky." Eliza smiled, then took a sip of her drink. "Can you believe Margot and Dad's news? I didn't see that coming."

I shook my head. "Nobody did. Are you okay that our families are going to be connected?"

"We kinda already are." She cleared her throat. "Actually, I'm a bit miffed."

I frowned. "Why?"

"Because if anybody was going to propose to a Voss woman, I wanted to get there first. Dad kinda stole my thunder."

I tried to untangle her words. Was she saying what I thought she was saying?

Eliza put down her whisky glass, then took my hand. Before I knew what was happening, she dropped to one knee.

My breath caught in my throat.

This was actually happening.

Oh my fucking god.

"Poppy Frances Voss. You make me very happy, and I know now that you're my soulmate. We got here the long way, but we made it. I bought our cottage, and I want to live in it together. Which means it only seems right to ask: will you marry me?"

For a moment, the world went absolutely still. The fire held its breath, while outside, the moonlight froze. My heart thumped so hard I was certain it would wake the entire town, but somehow I managed to find my voice.

"Yes," I whispered. Then louder: "Yes, you brilliant, ridiculous woman. Of course, yes."

Eliza's face broke into the most radiant smile I'd ever seen as she stood.

"This was a spur of the moment thing, so I don't have a ring—"

I launched myself into her arms and stopped her words with a hot kiss. Our first as a newly engaged couple, but definitely not our last.

We held each other tight, swaying slightly as the fire crackled back to life, and I could feel her laughing against my neck. This woman who'd smoothed out the corners of my chaotic life, who'd shown me what home really meant, who'd just given me everything I never knew I wanted.

She pulled back and looked at me, shaking her head. "You are the biggest surprise of my life, you know that?"

"In a good way?" I asked, head tilted.

"In the best possible way."

THE END

Want more from me? Sign up to join my VIP Readers' Group and get a FREE lesbian romance, **It Had To Be You!** *Claim your free book here: www.clarelydon.co.uk/it-had-to-be-you*

Would You Leave Me A Review?

I hope you enjoyed this enemies-to-lovers romance that proves we all deserve a second chance at life and love! If the answer's yes, I wonder if you'd consider leaving me a review wherever you bought it. Just a line or two is fine, and could really make the difference for someone else when they're wondering whether or not to take a chance on me and my writing. If you enjoyed the book and tell them why, it's possible your words will make them click the buy button, too! Just hop on over to wherever you bought this book – Amazon, Apple Books, Kobo, Bella Books, Barnes & Noble or any of the other digital outlets – and say what's in your heart. I always appreciate honest reviews.

Thank you, you're the best.

Love,
Clare x

Also By Clare Lydon

Other Novels
A Taste Of Love
Before You Say I Do
Change Of Heart
Christmas In Mistletoe
Don't Marry Me At Christmas
Hotshot
It Started With A Kiss
Just Kiss Her
Nothing To Lose: A Lesbian Romance
Once Upon A Princess
One Golden Summer
The Christmas Catch
The Long Weekend
The Princess Match
Twice In A Lifetime
You're My Kind

London Romance Series
London Calling (Book One)
This London Love (Book Two)
A Girl Called London (Book Three)
The London Of Us (Book Four)
London, Actually (Book Five)
Made In London (Book Six)
Hot London Nights (Book Seven)
Big London Dreams (Book Eight)
London Ever After (Book Nine)

All I Want Series
Two novels and four novellas chart the course
of one relationship over two years.

Get great bundle deals and other offers when you
buy direct at clarelydon.shop!